Friend or Foe:

Brice Simpson Hood Mysteries

Friend or Foe:

Brice Simpson Hood Mysteries

Imani Black

www.urbanbooks.net

Urban Books, LLC
300 Farmingdale Road, NY-Route 109
Farmingdale, NY 11735

Friend or Foe: Brice Simpson Hood Mysteries

ISBN 13: 978-1-64556-051-7
ISBN 10: 1-64556-051-1

First Trade Paperback Printing June 2020
Printed in the United States of America

10 9 8 7 6 5 4 3 2

Distributed by Kensington Publishing Corp.
Submit Orders to:
Customer Service
400 Hahn Road
Westminster, MD 21157-4627
Phone: 1-800-733-3000
Fax: 1-800-659-2436

Friend or Foe:

Brice Simpson Hood Mysteries

Imani Black

Prologue

"Why did you have to always control everything? Get in the way all the fucking time?"

Desiree Turner blinked rapidly, her heart ramming into her chest like a wrecking ball taking down a skyscraper. She was too shocked to speak and couldn't help her knees from knocking against one another. The harsh question resonated through her brain like loud clanging.

"Huh? Answer me! You always have to act so perfect, right? You easily forgot where you came from!"

The booming, shrill voice made Desiree shiver. Her lips moved apart, but no sound came out. She would've answered the question, but given the circumstances, an answer would probably have made things worse. Was this what they meant when they said the cat got your tongue? Desiree's mind turned into mush. She saw the faces of her children flash by her. Something in her gut told her it might be the last time she saw those faces.

"Oh, you ain't got shit to say now, Ms. Goody Goody?"

Desiree flinched as her tormentor waved a gun around, haphazardly dangling it in front of her. This had to be a nightmare. There was no way she could be seeing this correctly. Desiree was too afraid to move her hands to even pinch herself to check. Any sudden movements could be deadly, she reasoned—if reasoning was a thing with the kind of fear she was experiencing at the moment.

"Please." Desiree finally managed a shaky whisper. Her lips trembled so fiercely she couldn't even pronounce the

L in *please.* "Can't we talk about this? I . . . I can . . ." she murmured, tears racing down her cheeks in fast streaks.

The shock of seeing the familiar face made the situation even worse for Desiree. She couldn't think back to what she'd done to deserve this. In fact, she had never harmed a hair on anyone's head or ever muttered a malicious word about another person. Desiree had practically given up her entire life for everyone around her. It was her nature to take care of others. All she could think of was, *why me?*

"No! Don't you understand there is nothing to discuss? This has to be done! Especially now! You think I'm that stupid now that you've seen my fuckin' face?"

The crazed but familiar eyes were scarier for Desiree than the fact that she was staring down the end of a wavering silver handgun. She'd seen guns before, but never had she had one pointed at her.

Desiree started to pray silently. She should've seen this coming. But how? Why? A million thoughts played in her head, rewinding, staticky like an old VHS movie. Desiree quickly scolded herself. She had ignored the writing on the wall, all the signs.

"After all I've—" she whispered, closing her eyes. Her words were cut short. Someone she knew all too well had just opened fire on her.

Chapter 1

Brice

Brice sat across from his sister Ciara and smiled as she picked up her glass of water and took a sip. He knew he was being goofy with her, but he'd rather that than everything they'd been through before. Smiling now was the best medicine for the tears he'd shed over her in the past.

"What?" Ciara asked, watching him over the rim of her glass. "It's just water."

"I know. I know," Brice said, putting his hands up for an immediate truce. "I'm just admiring you and everything about you, that's all. Still out here killing it, despite it all. I'd call that black girl magic." He made sure to keep his tone supportive.

Ciara's shoulders slumped with relief. Brice's did too. She was learning to trust her big brother again, and Brice was learning to let her.

They'd had a hard time getting their relationship back in order after everything that had happened when she was sixteen. It had been four years, and Ciara was an adult now, but Brice still couldn't shake the experience of almost losing her to the streets. He was Ciara's big brother, but he acted more in the capacity of her father. He had stepped in where his alcoholic stepfather had stepped out. *Overprotective big brother* had been an understatement back then, but Brice had quickly learned that if he sheltered her too much, she would never really learn the ways of the streets—or the world, for that matter. It was his sheltering in the past that had left Ciara naïve and open to the smooth talk of a sex trafficker. He still worried himself sick about her sometimes.

He picked up his own drink, a Heineken, and took it to the head for a swig.

"Ah!" He winced as the cold brew hit his throat. He was praying it would hit his brain as hard to ease his mind. Brice still struggled with PTSD and intrusive memories. They were sometimes better than others, but one thing remained the same—he couldn't control when and where they'd tramp into his mind.

"So, what's new?" Brice asked Ciara, putting his beer down noisily and looking at her across the table of a quaint restaurant in a newly gentrifying section of Brooklyn. A lot had changed, but at the same time, a lot had remained the same as it was back then. Brice had continued the same traditions he'd had with his sister—a monthly, or at least every six weeks, meetup to chat. After Brice left home and landed the promotion to detective, he didn't have as much time for Ciara as he had before he became (in his assessment) a hotshot at the NYPD. But, just like now, he'd carved out time for her as much as he could. Back then, Brice had looked forward to spending time with Ciara, even if it meant taking her on one of her expensive mini shopping sprees.

"Nothing new. Same old things. School, work, home. Boring, boring, boring," Ciara said, letting out an exasperated breath. She ran her pointer finger over the condensation on her glass and darted her eyes around the restaurant. Things felt awkward for them again. It never took long for it to get like this.

Brice shifted in his seat, immediately uncomfortable with her response. He looked up at her, and concern creased his brow. He lived on pins and needles when it came to Ciara and her safety. It was still hard for him to shake everything that had happened.

"But what's wrong with that?" he asked, which was different than what he'd done in the past. Just as the question left his mouth, his mind reeled backward to right before their lives had imploded. Brice forced a weak smile, but as usual, he couldn't keep that old memory from flooding back into his head. Another swig of beer didn't help either. With him, the memories did what they wanted, and so did his mind. Brice had grabbed Ciara from school and taken her to her favorite spot. It was their tradition. He asked her what was up with her, and things had gone left from there.

"Nothing is up," Ciara snapped. "Why you always asking me that question as soon as we alone?" Ciara continued in typical nasty-attitude teenager fashion, rolling her eyes and folding her arms across her chest.

"Ay, ay, what's that attitude all about?" Brice asked in return, looking at his baby sister in a new light. His eyebrows crinkled so far into the center of his face he felt like they'd stay that way permanently.

"I know Mommy told you," Ciara snapped, rolling her eyes and bouncing her legs under the table.

Brice couldn't lie even if he wanted to at that moment. She was only sixteen, but his sister knew him well enough to know that their mother had indeed told him that Ciara had not come home until 2 a.m. one night, and when confronted about her whereabouts, Ciara had shoved their mother and run to her room. This wasn't typical behavior for Ciara.

Although Brice wanted to shake the truth out of his sister, he tried to remain calm in his questioning. "Well,

I'm waiting for you to tell me your version," Brice replied, keeping his voice even. She was a teenager, and he tried to understand, but his patience had begun to grow thin.

"You're my brother, not my father. I don't have to tell you nothing," Ciara spat, pushing her chair back and standing up.

Her sudden movement surprised Brice, so much so that he jumped into action.

"Where do you think you're going? Sit down," Brice instructed in a harsh whisper, trying not to attract the attention of numerous customers eating at Dallas BBQ downtown.

"I don't want to have these meetings anymore. I'm not one of your suspects to be questioned all the time," Ciara replied acidly as she rudely got up from the table and stormed for the exit.

Brice's pride and feelings had been crushed like a bug on a windshield. His hands shook fiercely as he dug twenty dollars out of his pants pocket and threw the money on the table before he headed out after his sister.

He spilled out onto the street in front of the restaurant, his chest heaving. He spotted Ciara's bright coat weaving through the crowd on the sidewalk.

"Ciara! Ciara! Wait!" Brice called after her as he picked up his pace. She ignored him and picked up her speed. Brice's chest heaved harder, and his mind raced with questions and anger.

He'd never seen his little sister so uncharacteristically rude and disrespectful. They'd been best friends since she was born. Up until that point, Ciara usually told him everything. Brice even knew when she had her period before their mother. Ciara confided in him about her crushes and even her little spats at school. If something was bothering her, Brice assumed she would have told him about it.

Brice finally caught up with her. He'd grown winded and out of breath when he finally grabbed her arm roughly.

"What are you doing?" he wolfed, holding onto her with an iron grip.

"Get off of me!" Ciara screamed, wriggling to get free and managing to get some nasty glares from some of the patrons bustling up and down Fulton Street.

"Ciara, what is wrong with you? Why are you acting like this?" Brice gritted through his teeth, wringing her arm to bring her closer to him. "What the hell has gotten into you?"

"Ouch! Get off!" she screamed again. This time, people stopped and stared.

"Yo, man, the girl said get off her. You need to find one your own age," a tall guy with a do-rag and baggy jeans said, moving closer to Brice and Ciara.

"This is my fucking sister. Mind your fucking business," Brice spat, still holding on to Ciara's arm with a death grip. She wriggled and fought him like he was a total stranger trying to kidnap her. Brice experienced both shock and hurt all at once.

"Who the fuck you talking to?" the skinny stranger snarled. Suddenly, as if they grew out of the brick buildings, six other dudes surrounded Brice like a hungry pack of wolves circling their dinner.

"I'm a fucking cop, so back the fuck up!" Brice shouted, letting go of Ciara for a second to pull out his shield. When he let go of her arm, Ciara broke free and ran. Distracted by the group of thugs and worried for his safety, Brice couldn't run after her.

"Fuck!" he huffed, eyeing the group evilly.

"Yo, man, we were just trying to help the girl. You know what I mean," the main guy tried to explain with his hands raised in surrender, unwilling to challenge Brice's shield.

Brice spun around to display his badge, hoping to disperse the crowd that had gathered to watch. Out of his peripheral vision, he watched his sister's pink jacket disappear around the corner. Exasperated, Brice finally walked back to his car and promised that he would be giving his sister a serious talking-to when he caught up with her.

That day would forever be etched is Brice's mind, as it set off a series of life events he wouldn't ever forget.

"Nothing is wrong," Ciara answered, breaking up Brice's memory of the past. "I wish you and Mommy would stop asking me that constantly. I'm not a kid anymore," she said, slightly annoyed. She wanted to understand her big brother's concerns, but at the same time, she wanted to forget all that had happened to her. It had been a dark time in her life, but everyone around her acted like they were the victims and not her.

Brice drank the last of his beer. He lowered his eyes. "I know, baby sis. You're right, but I'm always super worried about you. I love you more than you know," he said softly. The even tone of voice and understanding way was a sign of Brice's growth. The old Brice, the one who'd been haunted by his past and had always been angry, would've taken offense and gotten defensive with his sister. Not the new Brice Simpson. He'd learned fast that being on the job had the potential to take you out if you let it. He'd found himself a good therapist and wasn't afraid to say it.

As a homicide detective, Brice saw some of the worst crimes against humanity. After all, his career as a detective had blossomed out of one of the most horrific cold cases in New York. Brice had been a young street thug turned police officer when he was promoted to detective.

That was kind of unheard of in the Department. Before gaining his gold shield, Brice was a New York City patrol cop for six years. He'd shot two fleeing armed robbery suspects who had turned their weapons on Brice's partner, wounding him in the stomach. Brice was lauded by the NYPD for his heroic and courageous actions and earned a promotion to detective as a result.

What the Department didn't know was that, yes, Brice had given chase and drawn his weapon, but the only reason he hadn't also been shot was that one of the robbers was Brice's childhood best friend, Earl. Brice and Earl Baker had been friends since before they were born. Their mothers met in the free prenatal clinic in downtown Brooklyn and realized they only lived a block from each other in the same projects. Brice and Earl were born two months apart and had literally grown up together. On their first birthdays, each was the first guest to arrive at the other's party. Before they started school, they had play dates when their mothers had face-to-face appointments at the welfare office, and when they started kindergarten at the same school, they held onto each other like Celie and Nettie from the *Color Purple* after the school tried to put them in separate classes.

Brice and Earl had always been inseparable in everything they did. For as long as each could remember, they had done everything together, including committing the heinous act of rape. When Earl first suggested that they rape one of their middle school classmates—a special education student who had a huge crush on Earl—Brice had told him no. But Earl always had a way of getting in Brice's head, calling him a faggot and sissy if he didn't give in to Earl's every whim. Brice would always remember that day so clearly—the girl's screams, her vacant eyes after the third boy climbed off her, and the fact that she never returned to school.

When Brice went to high school, he poured himself into his academics, and Earl became more immersed in street life. The day Brice received his diploma, Earl got sentenced to three years upstate for armed robbery. In the time that Earl had been locked up, Brice became a police officer. He thought that if he fought enough crime, he could erase his past. Brice had never shared his profession with his best friend or with any of his friends from the old neighborhood, until that fateful day when he came face to face with Earl on opposite sides.

Brice could still hear Earl's words every time he thought about it.

"Wait, nigga. Don't shoot. Wait the fuck a minute! B-boy? You a fuckin' cop?" Earl asked, calling Brice by his childhood tag name. Earl's wide-stretched eyes and hanging jaw said that he was clearly shocked to see his former best friend in the gravee blues. That was what they called the navy blue NYPD uniforms on the streets, making reference to how many black boys the NYPD had put in the grave.

Brice ignored Earl's question but kept his gun trained on his old friend. They locked eyes, their past indiscretions standing between them like a giant ogre, scary and threatening to eat them alive.

"Drop your weapon!" Brice screamed like Earl was any other criminal in the streets.

"A'ight, B-boy, I'ma drop my weapon," Earl said, calmly placing one hand up and preparing to bend down to drop his weapon.

"Fuck that!" Earl's accomplice screamed out, raising his gun.

With that distraction and without thinking first, Brice opened fire on both of them. He watched Earl fold to the ground like a deflated balloon.

"Damn, B-boy, you was my brother from another mother," Earl rasped before throngs of police officers descended upon the scene in response to the 10-13 that Brice had previously called over the radio.

Brice found out a few hours later that he had "heroically" taken the suspects down. He had not planned for Earl to find out his secret like that. Brice was determined to take his promotion to detective and fuck the wheels off of it to move up the ranks. The further removed he was from the streets, the easier it would be to live with the choice he'd made during the robbery.

So, Brice's first day as a detective was both sad and proud for him. He looked at his new gold badge again and again. He even breathed on it and rubbed it on his shirt to get it to shine. Brice was enamored with himself, and he liked the sound of his new title, Detective Brice Simpson.

That first day, he'd placed his belt badge back on his brand-new Armani suit pants, stretched his arms out, and looked around the bustling detective squad room of the Brooklyn North Task Force. He tapped his fingers on his new desk—an old, gray, rickety holdover from the 70s. He had finally made it. As a patrol cop, the only thing Brice had was a tiny steel locker sandwiched between slews of other lockers in his precinct, but street patrols and uniforms were a thing of the past. Brice was a detective, and he had a chip on his shoulder the size of the Rock of Gibraltar.

Brice looked around the room at the WANTED posters. Being only twenty-eight years old at the time and from Brooklyn himself, he recognized more than a few faces on the posters. He probably knew where to find the suspects, too.

"Hey, Simpson, you think the good commissioner promoted you to sit there and look at the manicure

Kim Ling gave you?" Detective Sergeant Carruthers yelled out as he walked toward Brice. His joke garnered snickers from the rest of the squad.

Brice felt his cheeks flame over. He opened his mouth to pipe up, but he didn't get the chance.

"Save it. Here you go, some work. I know you're not used to it, but up here, we work," Sergeant Carruthers said, slamming a stack of case files on Brice's desk.

"I ain't never scared," Brice came back jokingly, letting out a short, nervous chuckle.

Looking down at the files, he saw a big red sticker labeled: COLD CASE *files.*

"Aww, shit," he cursed, flipping through the stack. He looked up and saw that the other detectives were staring and laughing at him. Brice's insides churned.

"The new guy gets the dogs. You know, the shit no-body else wants. We don't care how much cops and robbers you played as a street cop. Solve those sons of bitches and you really earn this promotion," Sergeant Carruthers said, popping his suspenders that looked stretched to the limit over his huge gut.

Brice reluctantly flipped through several of the cold case files. Many of the cases were related to indigent people found dead under bridges and in abandoned buildings. Some were of known gang members found dead in project elevators and stairwells, and others of dead crackheads. But one case stood out from all the rest. A fourteen-year-old girl had been found bludgeoned to death in a dumpster behind a Brooklyn bodega.

Brice opened the folder, and on the inside cover were several crime scene photographs. Brice winced and almost gagged, thinking of the pain the girl must have endured. He could hardly make out the girl's face in the pictures. Her head, from the neck up, resembled a blob—a red clump of flesh with no definition. Brice wasn't able to distinguish her eyes or nose. Her hair was matted with blood. Whoever had murdered her left her butt naked. She'd been beaten all over her body and then dumped atop bags of trash, an indistinguishable mass of flesh and blood. Bugs had already started eating away at the flesh by the time the pictures were taken.

Brice shuffled the photos and looked at the girl after she had been cleaned up by the medical examiner. Although her face was completely disfigured, Brice was able to tell that she was just a baby, her breasts barely developed, her fingers small and slender like delicate straws. The medical examiner had ruled the cause of death as a brain hemorrhage.

Who would beat such a young girl so unmercifully? *he thought with his fingers closing tightly around the file.*

He meticulously reviewed each piece of paper and flipped through all the notes. A handwritten Post-It note had been left in the file, where someone had scribbled: Runaway prostitute got herself killed. Case closed. *Brice squinted his eyes into little slits and feverishly turned the pages to find out which detective had been assigned the case.*

"D'Giulio," Brice mumbled under his breath. "It fucking figures. A white prick. If she was a white runaway, would he have come to the same conclusion?" Brice asked himself under his breath. It was apparent that the detective who had been assigned the case didn't bother to fully investigate before deeming it a cold case.

Eager to get his career off to a good start, Brice glanced at the address where the body had been found. He grabbed his gun out of his desk drawer and put it in his shoulder holster.

"I'll be back!" he yelled to no one in particular.

Little did Brice know back then that the cold case would be the real start of his career as a detective and

*also the beginning of a series of events that had changed
his and his sister's lives forever.*

"Well, let's change the subject," Brice said to his sister,
finally snapping out of his reverie. He'd let the long
stretches of memory interrupt their date long enough.
His therapist had tried to help him control the nightmares and flashbacks. It didn't always work out so well.
He'd been doing much better with it than in the past, but
he still wasn't free of what he believed was karma for
what he'd done as a kid.

"Yes, thank you," Ciara said, her words coming out on
a long sigh.

Brice opened his hands as if to say, *Well, talk.*

Ciara picked up her water again. "I'm dropping out of
college," she said as she put the glass down. She looked at
Brice and quickly averted her eyes.

Brice's nostrils flared, and he immediately knitted his
fingers together to keep them from curling into fists on
their own. It was a method his therapist had recommend-
ed.

"Say what?" They were the only words Brice could
muster at the moment.

"I'm leaving college because school is just not for me,
Brice. I'm twenty years old now. I have the right. I will
not have my feet held to the fire for the rest of my life for
something that happened when I was sixteen. It was a
childish mistake back then, and I've moved past it, even
if you and Mommy haven't," she said flatly but with
enough feeling that the words felt like ice cold water had
been thrown in Brice's face.

He balked a little, taken aback all over again. This
time, instead of getting angry right away, Brice cleared
his throat—another therapy-taught method to slow down

his racing brain and to keep him from saying something he'd later regret. Brice still couldn't help his rocking jaw, though.

"So, how will you take care of yourself in the future if you don't go to college?" he asked levelly. "You know the job situation all over the United States . . . no education, no life."

"Well, that's what I wanted to talk to you about," Ciara said tentatively, gnawing on her bottom lip like she always did when she knew she was about to piss her brother off.

Brice raised his eyebrows as if to ask, *Really?* He just knew his sister must be losing her damn mind if she thought he was going to take care of her financially as an adult. He'd done enough for her in the absence of what her own father could do.

Brice had grown up in the Kingsborough projects in Brooklyn. As a child, he had watched helplessly as his alcoholic stepfather beat his mother. Each time Brice had tried to help her, he'd end up beaten up so badly that he'd have to miss school the following day. Brice took to the streets and started acting out as a way to vent his frustration with his home life, but when Ciara was born, one look at her and Brice vowed to always take care of her. Up until this moment, Brice had lived up to his end of the promise, although his sister never made it easy.

"It's not what you think," Ciara clarified as she watched Brice's facial expressions display ten different emotions at once. "I not going to sit around doing nothing, Brice. I'm going to move to Vietnam and teach over there," she announced, smiling as if she'd just said something good. "It's such a good opportunity to give back and do some good for the world."

Brice felt like five bombs had gone off in his ears. He instinctively put his fingers to his temples and moved them in a circular motion. Speechlessness was something that didn't happen to Brice too often, but right then, Brice couldn't find one word. Ciara had put Brice and his mother through enough, but this would take the whole entire cake. He swallowed hard, still at a loss for words.

Just then, his work cell phone vibrated next to him on the table. It was his lieutenant.

"I have to take this," Brice huffed, shooting up from his chair, completely relieved for the distraction. Work had saved the day once again.

"Of course you do," Ciara mumbled, shaking her head. "Nothing has changed."

Chapter 2

Brice

Brice rushed to his black Suburban and sped down to Brooklyn Hospital. There would be no stopping for lights or stop signs that day. Not after the call he'd just received.

When Brice pulled up to the scene, his eyes grew wide. He didn't think so many vehicles could even fit on the already crammed Brooklyn block.

"Damn, this can't be a regular crime scene. What the hell is going on?" Brice asked himself out loud, his eyes wide with questions. The crime scene was lit up like Times Square. There was a festival of lights in front of him, no less than six regular patrol cars with blue-and-white wig-wags flashing, the Crime Scene Unit van, and the city medical examiner's vehicle were also parked in front of the hospital.

Brice wasn't new to anything he was seeing, but something felt different about the scene. He could tell by the number of cars that this crime scene had been pushed up to important.

"Hey, Simp. Female DOA, no valuables missing, except they took her identification out of the wallet. No witnesses. Scouring the area for surveillance footage . . . so far, nothing. Best guess is we will take a few pictures, show them around inside to ID her. We got uniforms fanned out all over the other floors and inside the hospital. Oh, and we got a full, perfectly intact shoe print in a small spot of oil on the parking lot floor. Crime Scene doing a cast of that," the patrol sergeant reported to Brice, who wrote feverishly on his little black notepad.

Brice took a deep breath, flexed his neck, and then walked over to the sheet that covered the body. The top half of the sheet was soaked through with dark red blood. He lifted the left corner and took a peek. He dropped the sheet back over the body.

"How soon are they going to be able to identify?" Brice asked stoically. He'd seen a lot of dead bodies, but this one was particularly sad. The woman looked like she could be someone's wife or mother, and Brice would bet his life that she was.

Brice and walked over to where Michelle Grafton and Lucille Teller were standing huddled together. Michelle acknowledged Brice first.

"Hey, Simpson. Pretty sad, wouldn't you say?" Michelle asked. "A beautiful woman. Not too old, either. Nothing really amiss. Weird."

Brice shook his head at her. They'd known one another for years now. She had been Brooklyn's chief medical examiner for nearly ten years. She had testified at several high-profile trials, and she was the best at determining causes of death. She had been a godsend to the homicide squad.

"Is it me, or does it seem personal?" Brice asked, rubbing his chin. "We got people fanned out in the hospital trying to make an ID. How long before you can make a positive one from the remains?" he continued, asking more questions before he got the answer to the first one.

"Probably going to be at least twenty-four hours, unless we come up with her actual ID and can ID her from there," Lucille interjected. Lucille wasn't a big fan of Brice. In fact, she and Brice had had their fair share of ups and downs. Lucille was, by all means, a forensic genius, but she didn't believe in letting detectives rush her or dictate how she conducted her examinations. Lucille also didn't believe in letting Michelle play boss to her either, although Michelle was technically her boss.

"I'll see how fast I can get something. Let's see what kind of missing persons come in within the next few hours. Judging from the rings and nice clothing, she had a few bucks. Whoever did this wasn't out to rob her. That rock alone would've made a thief very happy," Michelle told Brice. She was simply repeating the things Lucille had just told her, but Michelle knew that Lucille was going to keep the information to herself, so she took the liberty of sharing. Michelle saw Brice as a collegial friend, unlike Lucille, who viewed Brice as a big pain in her ass.

"But why take the time to take all of her identification?" Brice asked.

"That's a good question, Simpson. I guess you'll be the one figuring it all out," Lucille answered. "This one is all yours, right?"

Brice got the call a few hours after he left the crime scene. The woman had been identified as Desiree Turner, a nurse at Brooklyn Hospital. Brice turned to his computer and punched in the name. He squinted at the screen when the woman's list of known associates and family members popped up. Brice sighed and pushed back in his seat.

"Big K," he whispered. "Kevin fucking Turner. I remember you. How could I forget your reign over Brooklyn back then?" Brice mumbled.

He punched a few more keys and moved closer to the screen to make sure he was reading it correctly. "So, they let you out after all that time. I thought they gave your ass life," Brice grumbled.

Once again, his street ties related back to his work. It was inevitable for Brice, who thought of himself as a simple Brooklyn kid turned cop. Brice wasn't called the hood detective for nothing. He'd always kept one foot in the hood and one step ahead of criminals. He was known on the streets as Simp, and on any given day, a person wouldn't be able to decipher a difference between Brice the detective and the local corner boy. It always worked to his advantage. Brice had the swagger of a rapper and the smarts of a genius. He had always been into fashion, so to say he was a snazzy dresser like most Brooklyn dudes was an understatement. He definitely didn't subscribe to the NYPD detective–obligatory sand-colored trench coat, dress shirt, slacks, and a tie. Never. Not for Brice. He wore his name brand jeans, whichever sneaker was out, or Timbs in the winter. Brice wasn't about to give up his street cred for the job.

Brice reviewed some more information and found out that his victim was the wife of former drug kingpin Kevin "Big K" Turner, who had recently been released from prison after serving sixteen years. Brice rubbed his chin and squinted his eyes.

"So, she survived amongst his enemies the entire time he was locked up, and as soon as he gets home, she's shot dead with no apparent motive," he mumbled as he flipped to the next screen on his computer and compared the information to a file he'd pulled from the archives.

"Hey, Cuomo. Come with me somewhere," Brice yelled out to an older white detective that he sometimes took in the field with him to give him an edge in the hood. One thing about the bad guys in the hood—they never really fucked with white cops, especially the fat, balding, older ones.

Chapter 3

Cheyenne

When the landline phone in her apartment rang in the middle of the night, Cheyenne immediately knew something was wrong. Her mother was the only person who called her at the apartment she shared with a roommate in Austin, Texas. Anyone else contacted Cheyenne on her cell phone, which hardly rang during those days.

"Cheyenne," Amber, Cheyenne's roommate, called out in the darkness of her bedroom.

"Hmm," Cheyenne moaned, although she was awake from the phone ringing anyway. She was cranky because she had already been tossing and turning, feeling like something was off. She'd chalked it up to pre-test jitters. They had an early start the next day with their first round of exams upon them, so Cheyenne had written off the feeling that had kept her up tossing and turning most of the night. Neither she nor Amber wanted to be up that late.

"The phone is for you. It's your father," Amber grumbled, annoyed.

Cheyenne flung her blanket off, wishing that they had spent the few extra dollars on a cordless phone instead of the stupid landline that plugged into the wall.

"Thanks," she groaned out as she brushed past Amber, stomping her way to the living room. Cheyenne's heart-rate sped up. Her father never called her, much less this time of the night. Within a millisecond, no less than five hundred thoughts shot through her mind.

"Hello?" Cheyenne huffed into the receiver, squeezing it so tight her knuckles paled. It was her father, for sure. Her heart stopped beating for a few seconds, and her legs had suddenly gone weak. He was practically screaming into the phone, his words a garble of highs and lows.

"Daddy? I can't understand you. What are you saying?" Cheyenne asked urgently. She was definitely jolted into full wakefulness now. Something was wrong, that much she knew. Her father continued sobbing into the phone. Cheyenne's body went ice cold, and her teeth began to chatter. She had never heard her father cry in her life. Even when he'd been snatched away from their family and locked up like an animal, he hadn't shed a tear.

"What? What are you saying? Something happened to who?" Cheyenne asked, her voice going so high-pitched it hurt her own ears.

Amber was standing in front of Cheyenne now with wide eyes. She was moving her lips to silently ask Cheyenne if everything was okay. Cheyenne put her hand up in a halting motion to Amber.

"Okay, calm down," Cheyenne said, her voice cracking. She heard her father take a deep, shaky, wet breath. He started speaking again. She was finally able to understand what he was saying.

"Something bad happened to Mommy?" Cheyenne asked calmly at first, not really registering what he was saying. Her face crumpled in confusion. There was no way something bad could happen to her mother. She was the best person on earth. Nothing bad could happen to her. Then, suddenly what her father was telling her finally settled into Cheyenne's brain.

"Something bad like what?" she asked, her words coming out slowly. She held the phone tightly to her ear.

No!" she screamed so loudly Amber jumped and looked like she'd seen a ghost.

Her father had said, "Cheyenne, your mother is gone."

Cheyenne collapsed to the floor like someone had kicked her legs out from under her. There was no way she could live without her mother. She was and always had been Cheyenne's whole world.

Cheyenne still didn't know how she'd made it from Texas to Brooklyn in one piece. Amber had come along to make sure she got there safely. Amber was just a sweetheart like that. The entire trip home was a blur for Cheyenne. Bus, train, plane—all a blur. Amber and Cheyenne didn't talk much, but their unspoken body language let Cheyenne know that she wasn't imagining things. Her mother was dead. Murdered. She wasn't going to believe it until she saw it. Proof was what she needed, but definitely not what she wanted.

According to her father, no one knew anything about the circumstances surrounding her mother's death, except that she had been murdered. Shot to death. No robbery, no motive. Just cold-blooded murder.

Kelsi, Cheyenne's best friend from childhood, hadn't called Cheyenne after she spoke to her father. Cheyenne had checked her cell phone several times as she traveled, but she had never gotten a call from Kelsi. That was odd, but Cheyenne figured Kelsi was probably just as distraught as she was. After all, Kelsi had practically been raised in the Turner home. She was more like Cheyenne's sister than her friend.

When Cheyenne arrived at her building, there was a candlelight shrine outside dedicated to her mother. Her father met her outside. As soon as Cheyenne stepped out of the cab, she started screaming. It was real. Her mother, her best friend, her whole world was gone. Dead. Cheyenne's legs refused to work, and her mind refused to accept it.

"Hi, baby girl." Her father greeted her with a forced smile. His eyes were visibly swollen, and he trembled as he pulled her into him for an embrace.

Cheyenne looked around at all the people outside. All the candles. It was real. Her mother was dead.

Murdered. She couldn't stop repeating that in her head. *Murdered.* But why?

"Who would do this? She never hurt nobody! She never hurt nobody! Why?" Cheyenne screamed through tears. "Why? No!"

She caught a glimpse of a few people from the neighborhood crying and wiping their tears away. Everyone loved her mother. That was a fact.

Her father grabbed her and held her, but even he couldn't keep her from dropping down to the ground where people had placed candles and teddy bears in her mother's memory.

"No! No! God, no!" Cheyenne could not stop screaming. Her body shook all over, and her head pounded. Everything seemed to be moving in slow motion. Cheyenne just knew she would wake up from a nightmare any minute.

Cheyenne couldn't remember how and when they were able to get her upstairs, but she did remember walking into the apartment and collapsing again. There was no life without her mother. None at all. Her mother had been everything to everyone all of Cheyenne's life. When her father had been snatched from their family, it was her mother who'd kept them afloat. Cheyenne squeezed her eyes shut at the thought.

The hot summer day in August 1996, when the police took her father away, they'd also taken the Turner family's house. They trashed it before they took it. Cheyenne remembered her mother explaining to her that what the police had done was called "asset forfeiture." Her mother said it wasn't the regular police; instead, it was the Feds that executed a search and seizure warrant on their place that day. They had destroyed Cheyenne's room and almost every room in the house. They took all the family's jewelry, clothes, fur coats, artwork, couches, and beds. They'd dumped out their cabinets, closets, and garage. They had pulled up the floorboards and the carpets. Cheyenne never understood what they were looking for when they had taken sledgehammers to the walls.

Who hides things inside of walls? she remembered thinking when she saw the huge holes.

At nine years old, her family and her life had been devastated. There was no fixing it. Without her father, the Turners had nothing but the few clothes her mother managed to gather before it had all been destroyed or seized.

Her mother had a small stash of cash that the police hadn't gotten to, and someone from across town brought her some money they'd owed to Cheyenne's father. None of that lasted long. Desiree Turner and her two children ended up moving to the sixth floor in the same building Cheyenne's best friend Kelsi lived in, in the Carey Gardens projects.

"Back to the projects from where we came," her mother said sadly the day they moved back. She told Cheyenne it was the apartment her father had grown up in when he was a little boy. He'd kept it after his mother died.

Cheyenne had assumed they'd always lived the lavish life she'd been accustomed to down in the gated community called Sea Gate. She didn't know her mother and father had ever lived in the projects when she was a baby.

At first, it was exciting living in the same building as Kelsi. It was easy for Kelsi to just come upstairs to the Turner house to play, eat, and do all the things they liked to do. After a while, Cheyenne realized that living in the building where her father used to work was terrible. She had never seen a roach in her life until they moved there. There were so many roaches that her little brother, Lil Kev, refused to walk on the floors in their apartment. He would scream until their mother or Cheyenne picked him up and carried him everywhere. The constant noises in the hallway all night kept Cheyenne up, since she had been used to living on a quiet, tree-lined block in Sea Gate. Kelsi told Cheyenne she would get used to the noises, but Cheyenne never really did. Instead, she just grew accustomed to not getting much sleep.

By the time 1998 rolled around, Cheyenne was eleven, and Lil Kev was four. Like a faucet turned off, just like that, their mother had finally stopped all her crying over their father's absence and their living situation.

"Look! Look at what I did for us!" her mother exclaimed one day, throwing a stack of papers onto their small kitchenette table.

Cheyenne looked at her mother with her head tilted and brows crumpled, then picked up the stack of papers. She crinkled her forehead more and looked at her mother strangely.

"It's college! I got accepted to college. I'm going to school for nursing," her mother said excitedly.

Cheyenne's eyebrows flew up into arches on her face. "Wow, Mommy! That's great!" she said enthusiastically. In Cheyenne's mind, she selfishly wondered what was going to happen to her and Lil Kev while their mother went to school.

"I have to make things better for us while your father is gone. I wasn't on the system all this time, and I'm not going on it now," her mother said that day. Then, as if she could read Cheyenne's mind, she broke the news to her and Lil Kev that they would have to stay with fat Ms. Lula at night while she went to work and school.

Cheyenne groaned. She knew that Ms. Lula and her house stank like corn chips and ass. She hated every time they had to go there. But her mother was too determined to let Cheyenne and Lil Kev's complaints deter her. As much as they cried, their mother held her head up high, left them, and pursued a nursing career.

When her mother had a break from school, she would pack them all up—Cheyenne, Kelsi, and Lil Kev—and they would take the same long van ride upstate to see her father. Her mother would sacrifice everything to make sure she visited her father. If it was visit day for her father, her mother didn't care if she missed school, work, or they missed school. There was nothing more important to Desiree Turner than going to see her husband. She was as loyal as they came. When most women would've moved on with their lives as soon as they heard his sentence being read in court, her mother stood steady, stuck out her chest, and made a promise to hold her father down no matter how long it took.

Cheyenne couldn't ever forget the first time they visited her father. He had only been gone for a month, and she'd been missing him like crazy. Her mother dressed them all in their best clothes. She herself wore a pretty yellow-and-orange sundress that brought out her complexion. She had accessorized the dress with gold bangles and a pair of tan espadrilles. Kelsi and Cheyenne were dressed alike in bright sundresses—Kelsi's aqua green and Cheyenne's fuchsia.

Her father was still on Riker's Island at that time. Cheyenne remembered that the guards at the jail treated them like animals. They were searched like thieves. Lil

Kev's milk had to be poured out of his bottle, and her mother's pocketbook was dumped out.

"This is just stupid! We not in jail here, you know!" Kelsi sassed to the guards.

That was the one thing Cheyenne loved about her best friend. She never backed down from a fight or confrontation, even with adults.

When the guards brought her father out to see them that day, he had chains on his hands and feet. He sat on the opposite side of a broken-down table, and after one hug for each of them, they weren't able to touch him again. In one month, her father had changed drastically to Cheyenne. He just didn't look healthy. His skin had gone dry, his hair had grown out into a small afro, and he looked way older than he had the day he was arrested.

Cheyenne thought to herself that her father was dying inside that place, that he would never make it out of there alive. She cried for almost the entire visit. She hated seeing her father in that stupid orange jumpsuit when she was used to seeing him in nice, crisp, name brand clothes.

Kelsi, on the other hand, was overjoyed to see him. She even tried to hog Cheyenne's father's conversation from her mother.

Lil Kev refused to even look at their father that day. If he tried to touch Lil Kev, he would scream at the top of his lungs. Finally, her father relented and never tried to touch her baby brother again.

"What's up with my baby boy? He forgot his old man already?" her father asked, his voice cracking like he was about to cry.

As young as he was, Lil Kev sensed that it would just be best to cut his ties with their father right away. Not Cheyenne. She'd held onto the hopes that her father, Kevin "Big K" Turner, was going to win his appeals and be home with them in no time. At least, that was what her father had told her he was "working on" every time they visited him after that.

It wasn't until 2003, when Cheyenne was sixteen years old, that she finally stopped believing in her father's appeals story. Seven years of the same old story had turned her into a cynical, bitter teenager who didn't believe in shit. Her father had been transferred from Rikers Island to Upstate New York, which signaled to Cheyenne that he was going away for longer than they'd all expected. She was old enough by then to figure out that her mother had no more money to pay lawyers and that her father's street influence and connections had dried up, so none of his former employees came up off any money to foot his appeals bill.

When Cheyenne did her own silly form of research, she found out that her father had been sentenced under New York's Rockefeller drug laws, and no amount of appeals could reverse the draconian sentencing guidelines that came with those laws. It was a lifetime behind bars unless a miracle happened and something changed about the system.

Kelsi was the only one who faithfully accompanied Cheyenne's mother to visit her father. Her mother didn't take Lil Kev anymore because he never spoke to his father, and it made the visits harder on everyone. Cheyenne stopped going as well. It had become too painful for her to see her father aging ten times faster than if he'd been home. Seeing him in shackles and handcuffs, helpless, useless, had also taken its toll on her emotionally. She suddenly found herself really angry with her father. Cheyenne guessed years of watching her mother bust her ass to become a nurse, all while keeping food on the table and clothes on their backs, made her resent him for leaving them.

Her mother would act like she didn't get the memo that Cheyenne wasn't visiting her father anymore. The night before each visit, her mother would still try to get Cheyenne to change her mind.

"Y'all need to go to bed so we can get up and get to the vans early. I like to find seats in the front so I can be first on that line when we get up there," her mother said one evening as she stood in Cheyenne's doorway, a warm smile spread on her beautiful but tired face.

Cheyenne hated seeing her mother so tired all the time. She worked twelve-hour shifts four days a week as a nurse at Brooklyn Hospital. Then, her mother would use her days off to either shop for things for her father or visit her father. Cheyenne didn't know how her mother did it—stay loyal like that. To Cheyenne, there was loyalty, and then there was stupidity. In her eyes, after so many years of getting nothing in return, her mother was bordering on stupidity.

"I'm not going. But you already knew this, since I didn't go the last three times y'all went," Cheyenne told her mother flatly that evening.

Her mother let out a long sigh, and her face went dark. "Cheyenne, I know it hasn't been easy, but he is still your father. You know that he would've never left if he had his choice. He is powerless right now, but it is not his fault. Kevin would've given his life to be here for us," her mother replied, her tone stern but soft.

She had been telling Cheyenne and Lil Kev the same thing for years at that point. Cheyenne had grown tired of her mother making excuses for her father. Cheyenne could not understand the kind of love her mother had for her father, and she could only hope to have anything close to it when she grew up. Even though her mother had worked herself to the bone and had to live in the filthy projects, she never showed one ounce of resentment toward her father. Not even one ounce. That night, Cheyenne turned her back and pulled her blanket up to her neck. She was done discussing the issue with her mother. If she ever laid eyes on her father again, it surely wouldn't be while he was behind prison walls. That was Cheyenne's final proclamation on the topic.

"Have it your way, Cheyenne, but he loves you more than he loves his own life," her mother said with feeling.

Cheyenne sucked her teeth, wishing her mother would just turn off her light and get out of her damn doorway.

"Well, Kelsi, if you're going with me, be up," she heard her mother say, her voice filled with defeat.

The door clicked closed. Cheyenne finally relaxed. Then she heard Kelsi rustling with her blanket on the other bed in the small bedroom. Kelsi was rocking. Cheyenne could tell from the sound the mattress made. Kelsi rocked when she was mad.

"You know what, Cheyenne? I wasn't going to say nothing to you, but you are a fucking spoiled brat," Kelsi gritted.

Cheyenne could tell that Kelsi's teeth were clenched as she spoke. Cheyenne knew Kelsi so well. Cheyenne popped her eyes open in response to her friend's words.

"No, correction. I *was* a spoiled brat. Now I live in the projects with the roaches and rats and crackheads just like everybody else," Cheyenne snapped back. She hadn't meant for it to come out like that, but it was too late. The words had already left her lips.

Kelsi jumped up and turned on the light. Her eyes were hooded over, and her face had folded into a snarl. Cheyenne saw the hurt etched on Kelsi's forehead like a mask. Kelsi moved on her legs like a boxer ready to pounce.

"What the fuck is that supposed to mean? Like everybody else like who? Like me? Oh, you won't go visit

your father because he got arrested, and *you*, Princess
Cheyenne, was reduced to living the projects like Kelsi,
the poor bitch, daughter of a crackhead who lives with
roaches and rats? You are fucking disgusting, Cheyenne!
Your father was so good to you when he was out on
these fucking streets! You lived in a *real* house and now
you have to live in the projects? So what? You don't
have enough clothes to throw away or give to the poor,
destitute daughter of a crackhead? Oh, woe is fucking
me, Cheyenne! Why don't you remember all the things
he *did* do for you while he was here? How he loved you
like no man ever will! How he gave you everything and
risked his freedom to do that! How he loved your mother
and showed you how a real man is supposed to love you!
Why don't you fucking love him and appreciate him like
I do and thank God he is your father, instead of wishing
everyday he was your father like I do? You fucking
disgust me! I'm going home!" Kelsi ranted and pointed in
Cheyenne's face with every word like she wanted to slap
the shit out of her.

Cheyenne's eyes stretched as wide as dinner plates,
and her mouth hung open. She couldn't even respond to
what Kelsi had said.

Kelsi slammed the bedroom door and left. Cheyenne's
shoulders slumped, and her chest felt like a two-ton
elephant was sitting on it. The tears came hot and fast.
Cheyenne couldn't have stopped them even if she wanted
to.

That night was the first time Kelsi and Cheyenne had
had a real disagreement in all the years they'd been
friends. That night was also the first time Cheyenne
realized how much Kelsi really loved her father.

It was over three hours after Cheyenne returned home
from medical school to deal with her mother's murder

when Kelsi finally showed up. Cheyenne was lying on the couch with a cold compress over her eyes when Kelsi came in. Kelsi rushed over to Cheyenne.

"Oh, Chey . . . I'm so sorry," Kelsi cried out, bending down and hugging Cheyenne. "I'm so, so sorry," Kelsi repeated.

Cheyenne's floodgate of tears started up again. "Why? Why? She didn't deserve this! She was a good person," Cheyenne sobbed. "She would never hurt anyone. Everyone loved her! I loved her!"

"I know. I know. She didn't deserve it. I'm so sorry. I'm so, so sorry," Kelsi cried as she held onto her best friend. "She didn't deserve it at all."

The day after Cheyenne arrived in Brooklyn, the detectives showed up at the house. There were two of them—one white and one black. Cheyenne didn't really trust the police; she didn't care if they were white, black, blue, or green. In her assessment, the police were responsible for every single negative thing she'd ever gone through in her life.

Detective Brice Simpson introduced himself first, leaving the fat, white detective behind him like an assistant. Detective Simpson was the detective who stood out to Cheyenne as soon as he introduced himself. Oddly enough, and for a fleeting moment, Cheyenne thought the detective was strikingly handsome with a well-groomed mustache and goatee. His hair was cut low with waves that were perfect. He seemed like any other guy from her neighborhood. He even wore jeans with a nice V-neck sweater instead of a suit and trench coat like most detectives she knew about.

Detective Simpson walked into the apartment with a commanding presence, but Cheyenne still sensed his sympathy for her family's loss. He did all the talking. After the introductions, the white detective with Detective Simpson mostly took notes.

"Let me first say again, I'm deeply sorry for your loss," Detective Simpson said, looking from Cheyenne to her father to Kelsi and back to Cheyenne.

He spoke with a sincerity Cheyenne didn't expect. "Cops are dicks" had been her philosophy so long she didn't know how to think now in the presence of one so relatable.

"Your mother was shot in cold blood. There was nothing taken from her. We found all her jewelry, wallet, everything intact, except her ID was missing. When we see things like this, we think it's personal," Detective Simpson said, staring directly at Cheyenne, who quickly darted her eyes over to her father.

A sob bubbled up from Cheyenne's throat, and she threw her hand over her mouth. Her father shifted on the couch, where they all sat huddled together. Detective Simpson gave Cheyenne a minute before he continued. She dug the balls of her hands into her eyes to clear away the tears and focused on his face again. She was shaking visibly. Her head pounded.

"Is there anyone you could think of that would have something personal against your mother . . . your wife?" Detective Simpson asked, looking from Cheyenne to her father and back again. He spoke like he knew more than he was letting on in Cheyenne's opinion.

Cheyenne wasted no time. She shook her head vigorously back and forth as the tears started up again. She felt like someone had a hand around her throat. She couldn't speak, but her body language said enough.

"Man, my wife was as gentle as they came. Nobody would want to hurt her," her father answered on their family's behalf. "This is a shock to us all."

Detective Simpson gave her father a look. The detective shook his head like he wanted to understand the man sitting in front of him, who wasn't shedding a tear although his wife had just been brutally murdered and his daughter was sobbing into his chest.

"What's been going on at home? Any drama? Any conflicts?" Detective Simpson asked, lacing his fingers together in front of him.

"Nah, man. Everything here was peachy. We are a close family, and my wife was everything to me. To all of us," Big K quickly answered.

Kelsi stood up and moved to the love seat directly across from Detective Simpson. He looked over at her. She lowered her eyes and started swinging her legs in and out. Cheyenne noticed. She knew her friend so well.

"Well, my fath—he, um, just recently came home from being in prison," Cheyenne piped up.

Detective Simpson turned his attention away from Kelsi and back to Cheyenne.

"Things haven't been so peachy," Cheyenne blurted honestly. She shook her head and wrung her hands together. "My brother is on the street selling drugs. Working for a dude that is my father's known enemy. Kelsi basically has lived with us since we were kids because her mother is on crack and used to really abuse her, which she still struggles with. I just left for college, and there was a bunch of craziness going on right before I left. I just don't know if any of it is related to something like—to . . . this," Cheyenne rattled off, letting out all of their family secrets. She didn't care whose feelings got hurt or who was offended. She would say anything that might help the detectives find out who killed her mother.

Kelsi sucked her teeth, and her nostrils flared, but she didn't say a word to Cheyenne about the description of her life.

Detective Simpson sat quiet for a few minutes. His eyes had questions, so Cheyenne knew more were coming.

"So, you've been gone to medical school in Texas? Your brother is gone from home? Who was here? Just your parents?" he asked, his forehead creased.

"And her," Cheyenne said, tilting her head toward Kelsi. "My best friend who, like I said, has been basically living with my family since we were kids," Cheyenne said, looking over at Kelsi now.

Kelsi stopped swinging her legs in and out. She'd had enough of Cheyenne speaking about her like she wasn't even in the room.

"Excuse me. I need to use the bathroom," Kelsi said as she jumped up from the love seat like she had springs on her butt. She rushed to the back of the apartment and slammed the bathroom door.

"I guess she's emotional, huh?" Detective Simpson asked. "Pretty hard losing someone close to you, blood related or not."

Cheyenne shook her head in the affirmative. "To give you some clarification on the type of person my mother was—she took care of Kelsi like she was her own child. How many women can you say would do that? There is no one I could think of, for any reason in the world, that would just shoot my mother down like a hunted animal," she told him. "There is not one soul I could think of that would ever hurt my mother. When you get to know her, you'll see what I mean, detective," Cheyenne said through sobs. She laid her head back on her father's shoulder.

Detective Simpson took a deep breath and bit down into his jaw. He looked at the other detective, who stopped writing at that point and looked up and around like he'd been lost in his notepad.

"Cheyenne, I usually don't make promises when it comes to my cases, but I'm making the exception for you.

I promise you I will find your mother's killer, and when I do, I will make sure that person never sees the light of day again," Detective Simpson told Cheyenne with feeling. "Oh, and I'll start with speaking to each family member separately. Including Kelsi," Detective Simpson said, shooting her father a squinty-eyed look.

Then the detective stood up. "I'll be at the station tomorrow. Why don't you all come down and we can get started?"

"Thank you. I really appreciate it. Everybody will speak to you willingly," Cheyenne replied, looking at her father for confirmation. He opened his hands and nodded slightly.

"Trust me, my mother didn't deserve to die like that," Cheyenne continued through tears. She stood up and shook Detective Simpson's hand. She looked in his eyes, and she saw a sincerity she had never seen from anyone other than her mother. Cheyenne knew then that he was going to solve the case.

Chapter 4

Cheyenne

Being home from medical school sent Cheyenne into a deep depression. She'd barely eaten, and talking was out of the question. Lil Kev had come home only twice since she'd been back in Brooklyn, a fact that disturbed Cheyenne. He hadn't said much to anyone, and she hadn't seen him shed a tear for their mother. Cheyenne knew her brother had grown more selfish as he got older, but she never expected it to be like this. He had to be the angriest young person she knew on the planet.

On the first full day at home, Cheyenne forced herself to get out of bed after a sleepless night. She padded into the kitchen. Everything there reminded her of her mother. The cow-spot patterned dish towels and potholders hanging neatly from little pegs above the sink had been her mother's quirky joke one time after they drove cross country on college tours for Cheyenne. The gleaming silver dish rack had been her mother's prized kitchen accessory, because when her mother was growing up, all her family could afford were the cheap, plastic ones that quickly grew mold. Everything in the house had a lighthearted explanation for being there. That was how fun her mother was.

Cheyenne swallowed hard and stood in front of the refrigerator. She yanked open the freezer to get ice for her glass, and there it was. Cheyenne sucked in her breath.

The glass slid from her hand and shattered into pieces as it hit the tile floor. Cheyenne reached out and touched the frozen cake top, and as if she had been teleported to that place and time, her mind reeled back.

"Surprise!"

Cheyenne almost jumped out of her skin when she walked into the Carey Gardens community center. Her cheeks flamed over, and her heart thundered with excitement. She clutched her chest to make sure her heart didn't jump loose. There were so many people huddled together. Cheyenne didn't even know what to say or do. She stood frozen, her mouth and eyes wide.

"Aha! We got you!" Kelsi yelled as she ran straight into Cheyenne with a big bear hug, breaking up the awkward moment.

"Surprise, baby girl!" her mother yelled and then grabbed her and kissed her on the cheek.

Everyone in the room laughed, talked, and cheered Cheyenne on.

"Oh my God! I can't believe y'all got me so good. I really thought I was coming here for Tanya's baby shower," Cheyenne replied, red-faced. The crowd laughed. Cell phones popped out from everywhere to snap pictures and videos of her.

"Yo! You are so hard to surprise. You are mad nosey! All day you kept asking me where I was going, what I was doing, why I'm not coming with you to get your hair done, then caught an attitude because I wouldn't tell you! Damn! You are one nosey-ass chick!" Kelsi complained jokingly.

She was right. Cheyenne had copped a salty attitude when she thought Kelsi was brushing her off all day so she could be with her lowlife boyfriend.

"Yes, lawd! Hiding stuff from you is almost impossible. I had to keep everything for the party hidden in the nurses' lounge at the hospital," her mother followed up with the biggest grin she could muster on her face.

Cheyenne reached out and gave her mother another big hug. She could never know how much Cheyenne appreciated her.

"Well, y'all both know I am an investigator on the low. Neither one of y'all can do anything without me, so this was totally a surprise. Y'all did real good hiding this one from me," Cheyenne joked. She felt over the moon happy. At that moment, she loved her mother and Kelsi so much.

It definitely turned into a party. The entire neighborhood had come out. Even Ms. Lula, who'd gotten so fat over the years it was hard for her to get out of her apartment, was there, shaking her cane to the music. Some of Cheyenne's high school and college friends were there too. She couldn't believe her mother and Kelsi had pulled it off without her even having an inkling something had been going on.

"What up, sis? Congrats on graduating and happy birthday," Lil Kev said dryly as he bopped in and gave Cheyenne a quick tap-hug. She noticed that her brother acted like he was embarrassed to hug his own sister. Cheyenne also noticed the six seedy-looking street dudes he'd brought with him. She shrugged, thinking maybe they were supposed to be Lil Kev's thug entourage. Yeah, right. He was still her baby brother. Period.

"Thanks, baby bro. But you know we need to talk, right?" Cheyenne said to Lil Kev, her tone serious.

Cheyenne hadn't forgotten that he had not been home in three days. He had not been listening to their mother at all, and they'd all been worried sick over him. Cheyenne was glad to see him there safe and sound, but she still intended to give him more than just a piece of her mind when they were alone.

"Nah, we ain't gotta talk. I'm a man. I'm a'ight. Enjoy your party . . . nerd," Lil Kev said, trying to make light of the situation.

Cheyenne immediately noticed the strain on her mother's face as she watched their interaction. For her mother's sake, Cheyenne dropped the subject. For the time being.

Cheyenne went back to the party, intent on enjoying herself so that her mother's hard work wouldn't be in vain. The music pumped. Her mother had gone all out on the food. All of Cheyenne's favorites—fried shrimp, fried lobster tails, collard greens, candied yams—were there in abundance. The decorations were beautiful. Everything, including the beautiful sequinned drapes that had transformed the community center into a high-class venue, was gold and purple. Her mother had always said those two colors together reminded her of royalty. Cheyenne agreed that everything there was fit for a queen.

Cheyenne had been making her rounds, saying hello to all her friends when the music suddenly stopped. They all turned to see what happened. Cheyenne knew from experience that stopping the music at a hood party was like keeping the earth from rotating. She saw her mother standing next to the DJ setup.

"Hello! Hello! Can I have everyone's attention, please," her mother said into the DJ's microphone.

Everyone there turned to face her. The room got quiet. Cheyenne looked at her mother. She was absolutely beautiful; she still had it. All the years of hard work and sleepless nights had done little damage to her mother's flawless face. Of course, she had gained a few pounds—women did as they aged—but she still had a nice stomach, legs, and round hips.

"Today is a very special day for me, my family, and especially for my daughter. I don't think God could have blessed me with a better daughter. Cheyenne, you are kind, smart, beautiful, and all a mother could ask for in a daughter and best friend. I am very proud of you. We have been though a lot as a family, but you never left my side." Her mother choked out her words.

Cheyenne had already started crying just watching the beautiful soul that she was proud to call her mother. Kelsi swiped at her face, trying to make sure no one saw her tears. Lil Kev rolled his eyes and put his head down, trying to hide his emotions, too.

"I wanted to give you this party as your coming out. You are a woman now. There are things you will learn as you get older. I will be here for you through it all. So, with that said, I wanted your twenty-first birthday to be more memorable than you could've ever imagined. I have one more surprise for you," her mother said behind the bright smile that always danced on her face.

Hushed murmurs immediately spread over the crowd like a wave. Cheyenne heard some of her party guests whispering, *"She's gonna get a car,"* and *"Maybe it's the keys to a new condo."*

Cheyenne's eyebrows rose into arches. Her mother had done enough for her. She'd paid for Cheyenne's entire college education, books, food, clothes, and everything. She had told Cheyenne she did not have to work while she went to school. Cheyenne knew that had taken a financial toll on her mother. She'd watched her mother work overtime shifts, come home, get five hours of sleep, and head right back to work, all for her and Lil Kev. Cheyenne just couldn't imagine her mother giving her much more.

"Cheyenne, for years I have wanted to give you this gift. I prayed and I prayed about it. Well, today, I can

*finally give it to you. Come on in!" her mother yelled into
the microphone excitedly.*

Cheyenne's face crumpled in confusion. Everyone
watched as the door beside the DJ setup opened slowly.
The room went pin-drop quiet. Then, loud cheers, yells,
ohs and ahs erupted in the room.

Cheyenne's eyes flew open as wide they could go. She
felt hot all over her body. Her stomach curled into a
knot. Tears sprang to her eyes.

"Oh my God! It's Big K! Big K!" Kelsi was the first one
to acknowledge him verbally. She dashed for him and
ran into him for a hug. He smiled and returned her
embrace, but he never took his eyes off of Cheyenne.

Cheyenne couldn't move. Her feet had become rooted
to the floor. Her mouth had suddenly gone cotton-ball
dry. She hadn't laid eyes on her father in the six years
since she'd stopped going to the visits. He was the same,
but different. Cheyenne tried to remember the last time
she'd seen him, but her mind drew a blank. She blinked
rapidly, but she could tell she was crying because her
father's silhouette became blurry as the tears obscured
her vision.

Cheyenne put her hand over her chest. Her heart
raced painfully against her ribcage. She choked on her
own breath now.

Daddy? Is that really you? My daddy? *Cheyenne said
in her head, but the words wouldn't come.*

"Congratulations, baby girl," her father said, his voice
as deep and soothing as Cheyenne remembered it. He
grabbed her and pulled her into him.

Cheyenne had finally taken enough air into her lungs
to keep herself from passing out. She swallowed the
tennis ball–sized lump that had lodged in her throat.
She didn't know what to say to him or how to react
toward him.

"Daddy," Cheyenne finally croaked out breathlessly.

Her father kissed the top of her head and squeezed her hard with his huge, muscular arms. He had gotten bigger than Cheyenne ever remembered him being. He'd also grown a full beard. Cheyenne could feel the beard hairs on her head.

"Yes, baby girl, it's your daddy. I'm home. I'm finally home," her father said.

Cheyenne could tell he was crying too.

"I've missed you so much. You're so beautiful. I'm so proud of you," her father spoke into her ear.

Cheyenne inhaled her father's scent and silently thanked God he was back.

When he finally let her go, he wiped away his tears and hers. He held Cheyenne out in front of him and took a good look at her.

"Wow! What a lucky man I am to have such a beautiful baby girl," her father huffed like his breath had been taken away.

Cheyenne smiled. Her father still had some of the qualities she remembered.

"Where's my little man at?" her father asked Cheyenne, scanning around for Lil Kev.

The crowd opened up so her father could go embrace his son. Lil Kev had been standing with his little crew, talking like nothing special had happened. He acted like his father being home hadn't fazed him one bit. Lil Kev's face went stony when he saw his father moving toward him.

Cheyenne's heartbeat sped up again.

"What's up, Junior?" her father said proudly, stretching his arms out to embrace his son, her brother.

Lil Kev side-stepped, and his eyes went into slits, his lips pursed. He looked his father up and down like he was a stranger in the street.

"Yo, nigga. My name is Kev. I ain't none of your Junior," Lil Kev spat, scowling and poking his chest out toward his father.

The entire room watched the exchange, including a shocked Cheyenne. Her mother stepped over.

"Kevin! Don't you dare be disrespectful! No matter what has happened, he is still your father," her mother interjected angrily.

Cheyenne could see the hurt on her father's face, yet he still smiled. He'd never taken his eyes off Lil Kev.

"Nah, it's all right, Desi. I understand. I got penance to pay to my li'l man. I got years to make up. I'm willing to put in the work," her father said, a fake smile painting his face.

"Nah, nigga. You don't owe me shit. The streets is my daddy now. I don't need no just-free nigga trying to tell me how this is done," Lil Kev growled, brushing past his father and mother.

His crew of cronies gave his father dirty looks as they followed Lil Kev out.

Cheyenne was heady and hot with embarrassment for her father. She knew her father wasn't used to that kind of rejection, especially publicly. When her father left Coney Island, he had been a man who commanded respect from everyone, family or not.

"Kevin! You come back here. Kevin!" her mother screamed at her brother's back. Tears were running from her mother's eyes.

Cheyenne imagined that her mother must've felt the same shame and embarrassment that Cheyenne felt on behalf of her father. Cheyenne wasn't even a man and she felt emasculated at that moment for her father. She reasoned that it must've been something for her father to take the high road in front of all of those people.

"Let him go. Things will get better with time. I'm no stranger to challenges," her father said as he shoved his hands deep into the pockets of his jeans. "This celebration is about my baby girl anyway, right? So, let's party. There's a lot of things to be happy about today!" he cheered. The crowd agreed, and the party started back up.

Cheyenne watched her father closely after his fake pep talk. She could see her father's jaw going square. His homecoming wasn't going to be as happy as he thought.

"Chey? You all right? What happened?" Her father rushed to her side now, snapping Cheyenne out of her memory. "Your foot, it's bleeding," he said, frantically moving around to grab a towel.

Cheyenne didn't realize when the glass dropped, the shattering shards had pricked the skin on the top of her foot. "I'm . . . I'm fine," she stammered, putting herself back in the present, which meant realizing again that her mother was gone. Forever.

"Come sit down," her father said, grabbing her elbow and escorting her over to a chair. "I heard the crash and didn't know what was going on."

"I don't know what happened, Daddy," Cheyenne said, her voice quivering. "Who on earth would do this to her? There is no one I can think of. Can you?" Cheyenne asked, the tears coming back again.

Her father sat her in the chair and then plopped into his own chair. He sighed loudly and put his head in his left hand. He paused awkwardly, and without looking up at Cheyenne, he said, "I don't have an answer, baby girl. I'm lost too. I don't know who would hurt her."

Cheyenne looked at him through her tears, but he never looked at her.

The first night her father was home, Cheyenne thought their apartment seemed much smaller than it had in years. Her father's presence took up more space than any of them was used to. With the exception of Lil Kev, they all sat around talking the night after the surprise party. Cheyenne had stared at her father and thought to herself that he'd aged a lot in twelve years. His newly grown beard was sprinkled with gray, and he was starting to lose the hair in the middle of his head. Although he was still strikingly handsome, a few lines had begun to branch out from the sides of his eyes. His teeth were not the bright white Cheyenne remembered them always being when she was a kid. He'd gained a lot of weight, but it was all solid muscle. Everything about him seemed foreign to Cheyenne. His voice was louder, and his body was bigger than when he'd left.

The only thing that didn't seem to change was his expectations. Her father thought things with all of them were the same as they had been in 1996 when he'd been taken from the family. Cheyenne could tell right away he was going to have a hard time learning that he was no longer the center of everyone's world.

Her father's was the first voice she heard when she awoke the day after he came home. It felt strange since she wasn't used to hearing a man's voice in their house in years. Cheyenne listened that morning and could tell that her father wasn't alone. She was correct. When she padded into the kitchen in her robe and slippers, she saw that her father and Kelsi were up together. They were so engrossed in their laughter and conversation they hadn't even heard Cheyenne approach.

As she walked closer, she could see the side of Kelsi's face. Kelsi seemed to glow like a teenager meeting her first love as she spoke to Big K. Cheyenne raised her eyebrows at the sight of them.

"Y'all up early," Cheyenne said, her voice still filled with remnants of sleep.

Kelsi's face was turned away from where Cheyenne stood, but when she heard Cheyenne's voice, she jumped like Cheyenne was a ghost she wasn't expecting to see. Cheyenne had thought Kelsi's reaction strange, but she put it out of her mind. Her father smiled, but he seemed a bit jumpy and jittery too.

"Hey. Baby girl," her father sang, quickly pushing away from the table. He went over to Cheyenne and kissed her on the cheek. "I hope we didn't wake you up. Kelsi was just telling me all of the Peaches stories I've missed. Boy, I tell you. Gone for twelve years and some things ain't change one bit. That Peaches is something else. Always has been," her father rambled, but something was funny about his voice. Nervousness, mixed with trepidation, was the best Cheyenne could describe it.

At the time, any suspicions Cheyenne held left her mind as fast as they had come. Why would she suspect her best friend, who was like her sister, and her father? That was crazy!

They sure didn't seem like they were talking about Peaches. All that laughing. Ain't shit funny about how Peaches is whoring herself out and smoking all of the crack she can find, *Cheyenne said in her head as her father and Kelsi broke up their little pow-wow.*

Kelsi had never joked with Cheyenne about Peaches. Mostly she avoided speaking about Peaches at all. Cheyenne knew Kelsi hated her mother with a passion. Cheyenne shook off any ill thoughts she'd had.

"Where's Mommy?" Cheyenne asked her father and looked around. She wanted her tone to show that she didn't appreciate all of her father and Kelsi's laughing and reminiscing without her mother there. Especially since Cheyenne hadn't gotten a chance to have any alone time with her father yet herself. She also thought reminiscing, laughing, and sharing light moments should be for her mother to be doing on her husband's first full day home from a twelve-year bid.

"That crazy lady went to work. Can you believe her?" Kelsi answered Cheyenne's question right away.

A flash of heat spread through Cheyenne's body. She shot Kelsi a look. Kelsi acted like she hadn't seen Cheyenne's dirty look.

"Hmph, her husband just came home after all this time, and she agreed to work someone's shift for them instead of staying home. Not me. I would be locked in a room somewhere, laid up with my man for days. Even my kids wouldn't be able to get in or interrupt our flow," Kelsi continued, trying to sound like she was joking.

Cheyenne thought she heard a hint of disgust underlying some of Kelsi's words when she spoke about her mother leaving to go to work. Cheyenne tilted her head to the side, squinted a little bit, and gave Kelsi the side eye. She didn't like anyone talking about her mother. Kelsi of all people knew that about her.

"Um, she is not crazy. She has a job. Which is more than I can say about a lot of people. Plus, I'm sure she had a good reason to go in today. I guess she figured he's home now and he ain't going nowhere with nobody else, so why not make the money? It's probably just for a few hours anyway," Cheyenne grumbled defensively.

Cheyenne's message to them both was clear. Kelsi got quiet. Her father had a big, dumb grin on his face.

Cheyenne grabbed a breakfast shake out of the refrigerator and started back toward her room.

"How about we go down to the rides today?" her father yelled out as she walked away. She didn't know if he was trying to make light of the tension-filled exchange that had taken place or if he was serious. She paused for a few minutes.

He can't be serious. How old does he think I am? *Cheyenne thought and rolled her eyes without letting him see.*

Kelsi hadn't said a word. Cheyenne figured Kelsi was thinking the same thing she was thinking: He has clearly been gone too damn long.

"Um, yeah. You've been gone way too long. The rides are no place to go nowadays. Half of them are gone or broken down. Nobody dares eat at that Nathan's anymore. Trust me, nothing around here, including the rides, is like it was in 1996," Cheyenne lectured, trying to keep the obvious disappointment out of her voice. She immediately felt sorry for her father. The transition home wasn't going to be easy if he continued to live in the past.

"Did you still love her?" Cheyenne asked her father after snapping out of her memory of the past.

Her father looked at her strangely and jumped to his feet. "I do love her. I will always love her," he said emphatically. "You don't ever have to ask me a question like that again," he said, storming out of the kitchen, leaving Cheyenne alone.

Chapter 5

Brice

Brice didn't know what else to say to his mother. Once again, just like before, her nerves were harried over his sister. Brice pinched the bridge of his nose and wished he had an entire bottle of headache pills to choke down. He had watched his mother go through so much over the years. She'd been a victim of domestic violence, she'd been discriminated against in the workplace, and she'd lived through close calls with almost losing both of her children to the streets. Brice wished he could save her from any more heartache.

He stood in front of his mother, helpless and speechless. He'd expected her to call him once she found out Ciara's plan to run off to Vietnam with no friends or family there and no knowledge of any other part of the world but Brooklyn, New York. Brice knew his mother would be devastated, and he was right.

"I don't know where I went wrong," his mother said, wrapping her arms around her herself tightly. She moved aimlessly on her feet. "She will kill me of a heart attack, you know. That must be what she's trying to do. But why? What have I done? What haven't I done? I've dedicated my whole life to you both. What did I do wrong?" she said, flopping down onto her couch, too exhausted to keep moving.

"C'mon, Ma. You know you've done your best. Of course it wasn't anything you did or didn't do," Brice said, walking over to his mother. "And no one is going to die of anything, heart attack included," he said in his stern way of comforting her.

Brice was frustrated with everything his sister was doing, but he couldn't show it. Once again, Ciara had them living under stress, day and night. It hadn't taken that long to end up back here. Brice and his mother had been in this place before—scared, unsure, and lost for a solution when it came to her.

Brice sat down next to his mother and put his arm around her shoulders. He wanted her to know they were a united front, in it together.

They sat in silence for a few minutes. Silence wasn't Brice's best friend when he was under any kind of stress. And, just like all of the other intrusive thoughts he struggled to get rid of, Brice was triggered. He closed his eyes and tried to shake it off, but again, his memory betrayed him.

Brice paced in circles on the same floor in his mother's house. Beads of sweat lined up on his hairline like ready soldiers.

"Sit down for a minute," his mother said as she fanned herself. Brice made her nervous. On top of her sixteen-year-old daughter being missing, his mother didn't need his attitude and tension as another stressor.

"Why didn't you call me on Friday? I'm a cop for goodness sake. You know how it looks for me to report my sister missing after she's been gone three days?" Brice reprimanded her.

He immediately regretted his tone. Brice hadn't meant to be so hard on his mother, but he'd gotten emotional because she'd waited so long when Ciara might've been in danger.

His mother began crying.

Brice shook his head and breathed out loudly. "Ma, I didn't mean it. I'm just upset and nervous," he apologized and put his arm around her shoulders.

When his mother called, Brice had been buried in evidence and paperwork regarding his case. The dead girl, Arianna Coleman, already had him on edge. Brice immediately sent three squad cars out to scour the streets of Brooklyn, looking for his little sister. His commanding officer had asked him to stay behind with his mother. They said Brice was too emotionally wired to be actively involved in the search for his own sister.

At that time, it was not like Ciara to run away. She was sixteen years old and had never stayed out overnight without permission to be at a friend's house. And even that was rare.

Although he was looking for his own sister, Brice wasn't able to stop thinking about what the mother of the victim in his case had said. Her daughter was a good student and wouldn't have run away. But the mother had also noticed changes in her daughter's behavior—coming home late from school, angry all the time—changes that were eerily similar to his sister's. The entire situation made Brice's stomach muscles clench. He wiped his hands down his face and held his head in his hands, trying to be patient while waiting for the search results.

Brice felt torn up inside, like he'd failed his sister and his mother. Things like this weren't supposed to happen to his family. He had worked hard to get his mother out of the projects and into a nice brownstone in Bed-Stuy. He'd joined the police department to help victims and their families, not to become a victim's family.

Finally, there was a knock on the door. Two familiar NYPD patrol officers stood there.

"What's up, Simp?" one of the officers said, his tone sorrowful.

Brice stepped out onto the stoop to speak to them. He didn't want to upset his mother any further, especially if it was bad news.

"What did they find out?" Brice asked, cutting to the chase.

"Man, her trail ran cold. She hasn't been to school in a couple of days. Some girl at the school said a guy in a big fancy car came to pick her up on a few occasions, but she couldn't remember the type of car or any other pertinent details," the cop explained to Brice.

Brice reacted like a bomb had exploded in his head. He swayed on his feet and didn't even realize it. He suddenly felt a rush of heat and got lightheaded. This was all his fault. He had become so consumed with his career that he hadn't even realized his sister was in trouble.

"So y'all going to keep searching, right?" Brice asked, blinking rapidly to clear the black spots from his vision.

"Well, we will turn it over to midnights," the other cop replied. "But we already searched the places you said she might be."

"I want the whole fucking city combed! I don't care if it's street by fucking street. This is my sister. She didn't run away!" Brice exploded and pushed one of the officers in the chest. The veins in Brice's neck throbbed.

"Whoa, man. I will pass on the message," the lead cop said with finality and then turned to leave.

Brice punched at the air. His head pounded. He needed more information. The mystery of it all had been driving him crazy.

What happened to make my sister change so suddenly? What is she trying to hide?

Brice tried to compose himself before he went back inside the house to speak with his mother. He knew she would have a million questions, and he needed to find the answers fast.

He stormed back into the house, rushing past his mother. He'd decided against milling around, talking to her any longer. Before his mother even had a chance to fire a single question, he stormed straight for Ciara's bedroom.

Banging open the door, Brice pillaged through his sister's personal effects like a man possessed. He opened dresser drawers and threw clothes left and right. He went into the closet and pulled clothes off hangers and dumped the neat stack of sneaker boxes, looking for hidden clues. He even got on his knees and looked under her bed. When his efforts turned up empty, he pulled the comforter and sheets from the mattress and even examined the mattress itself to see if anything had been stashed inside or underneath.

He began to tremble all over. His anxiety caused him to start coming apart mentally. But that didn't stop him from continuing his search.

Brice walked to Ciara's desk and emptied out the drawers one by one. Papers sprinkled over his feet like large snowflakes. Brice pulled the last drawer out and spotted Ciara's diary. He bent down and picked it up and noticed that it was locked.

"Fuck this," Brice grumbled, picking the lock with his pocket knife. With the sharp metal edge, he cut the small piece of leather that connected the lock with the book pages. He flipped through the pages of the diary and fi-

nally found a page that piqued his interest. Brice's heart sank when he read the lines: He said he loved me. He said he is going to make me a star.

Brice felt like someone had kicked him in the heart. He dropped the book and raced out of the room, straight past his mother.

"Brice? Brice! What is it?" *his mother called out behind him.*

Brice's heart pounded almost out of his chest. He used the back of his arm to wipe sweat out of his eyes. He was a man possessed.

Once Brice found out about the history of the man his sister had been seeing, he took to the media and the streets. He didn't wait around for the NYPD missing person's squad to do shit for him. Brice knew how they operated, especially when they figured a girl was just a sixteen-year-old runaway.

"She's my fucking sister!" *Brice screamed, banging the desk in front of his former sergeant.*

"I don't give a fuck! You don't go to the media unless you have clearance from the Department!" *Sergeant Carruthers barked, his pale face turning hot pink.*

"Sarg, I have investigated these fucking runaway cases for years, and I never went to the media. I mean, what makes this case so special? I understand she's a cop's sister, but they run away too," *another detective named D'Giulio interjected.*

Brice hated the guy and didn't know why he'd even been included in the meeting about his sister.

"What, motherfucker? She is not a fucking runaway! She is a missing fucking person! Somebody took her off the street!" *Brice screamed. The vein in his neck pulsed fiercely up against his skin.*

"Simpson, there are ways to handle this. It's a conflict for you to be involved. You are too emotional. Missing persons is handling it," Sergeant Carruthers said.

Brice bit down into his jaw. "Do you have an answer for me to give my mother? Huh? She wants to know why her fucking son is a hero cop but can't find his own goddamn sister!" Brice exploded, rocking on his feet.

Sergeant Carruthers did not have an answer. He exhaled.

"I want the fucking commissioner himself to tell me I can't help with the search for my sister. I want you bastards to put yourself in my shoes. If it was one of your precious daughters that were missing," Brice barked, pointing an accusing finger in Sergeant Carruthers' face. Brice didn't plan on backing down.

"I had enough of this sideshow bullshit. A runaway is a fucking runaway any way you slice it," D'Giulio said with a slick smile on his face.

Suddenly, Brice felt like the walls had closed in on him. The corners of his eyes went black, and he couldn't see anything out of his peripheral vision. Without another word, Brice whirled around and punched D'Giulio in his nose. Blood spurted onto Brice's clothes.

"Ahhh!" D'Giulio screamed and fell to the floor.

Brice jumped on top of him and hammered him in the head and face with his balled fists. Sergeant Carruthers scrambled from behind his desk and grabbed the back of Brice's jacket in an attempt to pull Brice off of D'Giulio.

Sergeant Carruthers was no match for Brice's brute strength. Brice bucked like the Incredible Hulk, sending Sergeant Carruthers stumbling backward.

"Help in here!" Sergeant Carruthers screamed out. The door to the sergeant's office suddenly burst open, *and several detectives swarmed in and descended on the heap of tangled arms and legs.*

They finally pulled Brice upright, but by then, D'Giulio was unconscious. Brice's chest heaved in and out with fury. His knuckles were a scraped, bloody mess. His clothes were splashed with blood, and the back of his jacketwas ripped. With wild, wide eyes, Brice looked around at all of the faces staring back at him like he was a madman.

"Get a bus right now!" Finally, one of the detectives got over his shock long enough to order an ambulance for D'Giulio.

"Detective Simpson, you are suspended indefinitely. Hand over your gun and shield and get the fuck out of my precinct!" Sergeant Carruthers barked.

"Brice? Brice? Did you hear what I said?" his mother called out to him, breaking his trance.

"Oh, um, yeah . . . um, no," Brice stammered, shivering a tiny bit. "Wha . . . what's the matter?" He shook his head to make sure he was present mentally to hear what his mother was saying.

"We can't let her run off to another country. You know she doesn't make the best decisions. I'd be sick every day and night," his mother told him. "Halfway across the world, you can't get to her, no street smarts. It just won't work."

"I'll try my best to convince her again not to go, but she's an adult. We are going to have to face it. Ciara is not a teenager anymore. She will do what she wants, no matter what we say. We may be out of luck this time," Brice said ruefully.

"She's still my baby. Please, Brice. I know you get busy at work, but I need you to make sure she doesn't run off. Please," his mother pleaded. "You remember how it was back then. The hospital. The memory loss. The nightmares. The close call with her life," his mother recounted.

Brice did remember. He pictured himself back when he'd almost singlehandedly saved Ciara. He'd been a suspended cop totally unhinged by the need to rescue her.

Brice paced and ran his fingers over the cold steel of the shiny silver .45 caliber Desert Eagle special. Pop had come through big time and gotten it for him. The gun made Brice feel powerful.

The girl who helped him told Brice that chances were his sister's captor was still right there in New York, hiding in plain sight with Ciara. She let Brice know that the bastard's first method of making money was putting young girls on the streets. Next, the porn industry. Brice cringed, thinking about his sister doing either. He vowed to kill that son of a bitch with his own hands when he found him.

Brice hadn't gotten much sleep, nor had he eaten a decent meal during that time. He had lost everything that meant something to him—his job, his sister.

Brice let the girl helping him take him to the place his sister was being held.

"You get me inside, and then you get the fuck out of dodge. You hear me?" Brice whispered to the girl who'd told him where to find his sister.

"It's me, Dave. Casey," the girl called into the intercom system to the guy who held down the place Ciara had been held captive.

Brice stood off to the side. His police training told him that he was being stupid. He had walked into possible danger like a fool with no kind of backup—a one-man army, which could be deadly for everyone. It was too late once he thought rationally.

When the guy pulled back the doors, the girl smiled and stepped aside. Brice rounded the corner and pounced on the man so fast there was no turning back.

"Where the fuck is he?" Brice growled, his hot breath blowing on the guy's face.

"H—who ya looking for?" the surprised man croaked out.

"Jordan, motherfucker. You know who!" Brice said in a low, harsh whisper, his gun at the man's chin.

"You have to ask Mikey. I don't know," the guy said weakly.

Brice released him with a shove and stepped over him. He stormed down a long hallway toward the sounds at the back of the suite.

Brice used his raid boots to kick the door open and was startled by a high-pitched scream of a woman. Then he spotted a fat white man, hovering over a bed with a camera. The man's eyes stretched so wide he looked almost like a cartoon.

"Where the fuck is that coward, Jordan Bleu?" Brice yelled out, rushing toward the director.

"He left, man. I swear. He ain't here. Said something about leaving town. That he was going to see the man he gets the girls from. The one that's a cop. I don't know, man," Mikey stuttered. He had already dropped the camera and put his hands up in front of him as if they could shield him from the big-ass gun Brice had aimed at his fat titties.

"What? A cop?" Brice asked.

"Yeah, man. Jordan got girls on the street, and he gets girls for underground movies from this white guy. I think he said the guy is a cop," Mikey blabbed, his words rolling off his tongue so fast he couldn't even get them out right.

"Where does he go to get the girls from? This white guy. Where is he?" Brice asked as his chest swelled.

"Man, I don't know. I swear," Mikey pleaded.

Brice walked over to him and hit him on the back of the neck with the butt of the gun.

"Agh!" Mikey screamed out.

"Now. Where does he go to get the girls?" Brice asked again.

"All I got is the cell phone number. I swear, man. That's all I got," Mikey moaned, his fat girth spilling over the floor like a beached whale.

He directed Brice to his desk. There was a piece of paper there with a number and no name. "Jordan had written that down and forgot it there. That's the new number the man gave him," Mikey explained, almost crying.

Brice folded the paper into his pocket. He looked around. Three girls sat naked, cowering in a corner. "How old are these fucking girls?" Brice asked, going back to stand over Mikey with the gun aimed at Mikey's head.

"They told me they were eighteen," Mikey whined, sounding like a straight bitch.

"Everybody get dressed and get out of here!" Brice yelled to the girls. Their faces were filled with horror. At his command, they scrambled around like hens running from the slaughterhouse.

"If you contact Jordan and tell him I was here, I will kill you myself," Brice threatened.

Brice's hands trembled as he dialed another detective's number. He exhaled all of the air in his lungs when Page finally picked up.

"I need you to do a reverse phone lookup on a number," Brice huffed into the phone, his voice shaky. His counterpart agreed and told Brice he would call him back.

It didn't take him long to get back to Brice. When the phone rang, Brice fumbled with it, his nerves on edge.

"Yeah," Brice answered. "Fuck!!" he screamed in response to what the detective told him. The number had returned no information on the public internet. Brice had to call in a favor to the Feds.

In a panic, Brice scrolled through his cell phone contact list. He would need a favor from an old friend, an FBI agent he had met while standing patrol on a dignitary homicide. Special Agent Lisa Striker had taken a liking to Brice. They'd dated, but it didn't work out. Brice hadn't heard from her after the breakup, until Agent Striker called when she heard about his sister. Agent Striker told Brice she would love to get in on the search for Ciara, but the Bureau had prevented her from getting involved because Ciara had been classified as a runaway by the NYPD.

When Agent Striker picked up the line, Brice didn't waste his time with pleasantries and fake inquiries about her well-being. He got right to the point of his call and gave her the phone number in question. She told him she would go into the Bureau's databases and get right back to him.

"I hope you're sitting down," she told Brice when she called back. "The name associated with this number

is listed as unknown, but the billing address came up. When I ran the billing address, it came back to Anthony and Carmelita D'Giulio. When I ran Anthony D'Giulio to match the address, he came up as an NYPD detective!" Agent Striker announced.

Brice thought his heart would thunder out of his chest. "Motherfucker!" Brice screamed so loud his throat itched.

"Brice, what is it?" Agent Striker asked, shocked by his outburst.

"I want you to meet me. I may have stumbled onto a human trafficking ring, and they have my sister," Brice announced. Renegade, suspended cop, or not, he knew he was going into danger.

Brice's feet were moving the speed of light, and then the shots vibrated in his ears. He stood in shock, his hands shaking uncontrollably and sweat dripping from every pore on his body.

Brice watched as Detective D'Giulio's body lurched forward, falling just inches from Ciara. He wasn't sure where the shots had come from at first, but his sister was his first priority.

"Ah!" Ciara cried out, covering her face

"Be careful. The other one has a gun too!" Special Agent Striker screamed out, her gun still smoking at the tip. She came through for Brice and Ciara that day.

"Stay there, Ciara! Drop your fucking weapon!" Brice screamed as his sister's captor leveled a weapon at him. They both pointed at each other, looking like two cowboys at a showdown.

"I'm not going out like this, son. Not over no bitch," the captor said, holding his position.

Brice heard his own breath in his ears.

"We just both going to have to die." The captor continued talking shit.

"Well, let's get ready to die then, cowboy," Brice said calmly.

"Fuck you!" the man screamed out, cocking his gun to the side.

Bang! Brice seized his moment. The captor fell backward, his gun flying from his hand.

"Ahh!" he screamed out. Brice had gotten him right in the shoulder of his shooting hand. Brice hadn't wanted him dead. Not yet.

Before Brice could reach him, he heard the thunder of feet. When Brice turned around, there was a swarm of law enforcement, some NYPD and some FBI.

Agent Striker had Ciara, trying to console her.

"Simp, you all right?" a fellow detective asked, racing over to Brice while the backup stormed the man who'd held Brice's sister captive like he had a bomb strapped to him.

"I'm fine," Brice replied, dropping his illegal gun on the floor. He knew it would disappear. He ran over to his sister and hugged her so tight he thought she would stop breathing.

"I'm sorry I failed you," Brice cried into her hair.

"We got an ambulance waiting for her," another detective said.

Brice sat vigil at his sister's hospital bedside, not even leaving to change his clothes. The hospital kept her for observation and to run a battery of tests. Ciara couldn't remember much of what had been done to her, for which Brice was grateful. He was also grateful as he watched his mother lay next to his baby sister, rubbing her hair and acting as if she never wanted to let her child go.

***

"I remember even when I don't want to. I'll try my best to convince her not to do this, but I can't promise anything," Brice replied in a low whisper. "But I will damn sure try."

Brice left his mother's house with what felt like the weight of the world on his shoulders. Reliving his sister's close call was harrowing enough, but also thinking back on his suspension and the fight he'd endured to get his job reinstated was not something Brice liked to have on his mind. He also hated to remember Ciara in the hospital, suffering through the healing from her experience. Brice had hurried to find a therapist after coming close to losing everything back then.

Back at his desk, Brice was back into the murder of Desiree Turner. He pinched the bridge of his nose and sighed loudly as he pored over Kevin "Big K" Turner's criminal record one more time. He wanted to know everything about Big K, other than his street legend, before he brought him in for questioning. Brice had spoken to Big K briefly in the days since his wife had been found shot to death in the parking lot at her job, but he felt Big K wasn't telling it all. Brice thought he could see the deception in his eyes, but he couldn't place it. Would he murder her, or did he know why she'd gotten murdered? Big K hadn't admitted to trying to get back into the drug game, but Brice knew his type. They didn't see their life worth anything if they couldn't reclaim what had been theirs when they'd been taken off the streets.

Brice flipped through more of the old reports on Big K. Although he was a mere kid back then, he knew that Big K had been the man on the street in Coney Island back in the day. According to the reports, Big K had been taken down after an informant blew the lid on his well-run operation. His kids were young when he got pinched, and now his son tried to fill his illegal business shoes.

"If he was as big in the streets as I remember and as these reports say he was, I know a few street dudes that can tell me some more about him," Brice mumbled to himself. "Yup, I know just the person to see," Brice said, pushing up from his desk chair and grabbing his gun and badge in a flurry. He had to do what was familiar to him—hit the streets.

Brice sat nursing a drink inside the crowded restaurant/club Sugar Hill on Dekalb Avenue, waiting for his old friend to show up again. It was their spot every time Brice needed to put his cop side on the back burner and step into his street side. Back when his sister's life was in danger, this was where he'd come to get what he needed to save her. Brice had sat in the same spot back then, looking at naked photos that a sex trafficker had taken of his sister. Back then, and even now, the thought of Ciara being touched by a man made Brice deaf, dumb, and blind with rage. As he waited, he remembered how he'd studied the address where his sister was held. He had mapped out a few routes in and out—side streets, determined whether there was high traffic, what the nightlife was like. Brice even played out the scenarios of when he met his sister's captor face to face back then. Brice saw himself adding one more bullet to the bastard's dome.

Before his work in therapy, Brice had always wanted his revenge to be served ice cold.

He had tried to be patient with the search for his sister, but the legal way hadn't been fast enough. He'd taken things into his own hands, and to this day, Brice believed if he hadn't saved Ciara, he might have never seen her again. They NYPD surely hadn't been doing a good job on her case.

"If it ain't the hood's detective. I'll be damned."

Brice heard the familiar voice from behind and felt a pat on his shoulder. He turned around slowly, smiling at the new moniker he'd earned in the streets.

"My nigga, you ain't never fail me yet. What's good, man?" Brice said, standing up and exchanging a hand slap and shoulder bump with his long-time friend. Avery "Pop" Michaels was one of the street dudes Brice and Earl had grown up with. While Pop and Brice were not as close as he and Earl were, Pop was around enough when they were younger to get into several mischievous capers with them. Unlike Earl, Pop was always a smooth dude. Even as a kid, he did his dirt on the low, making all the parents in the neighborhood refer to him as the "good one." Pop wasn't into the fifteen minutes of fame thing. He didn't commit blatant and brash crimes like Earl did. Pop was more of a behind-the-scenes, kingpin type of dude.

Pop had made his living on the streets but had turned his dirty money into legitimate investments, and he had dudes all over Brooklyn working for him. As smooth as he was, people knew not to sleep on Pop. He was still a well-known, notorious force to be reckoned with.

Pop also hadn't found out until Earl's funeral that his old friend Brice was a cop. Although he knew the story surrounding Earl's death, the way it was spun was like Earl had tried to mirk Brice, and Brice had no choice but to shoot him. Pop knew that Earl could be a wild boy, so although he had been skeptical of all cops back then, he didn't hold it against Brice. Pop figured one day he'd have to call in a favor. But years ago, it was Brice who'd called in the favor when he'd come to the same place and asked

Pop for a gun and a bulletproof vest. Brice had lost his gun, badge, and everything else to suspension back then.

"I'm maintaining. When I saw that case on the front page of the *Daily News*, I figured you'd be calling sooner or later," Pop said, shaking his head. "Damn shame. And here I was thinking Brooklyn was changing for the better. They shot her down like a dog. Real fucked up."

Brice rubbed his full beard, deep in thought. "Yeah, fucked up is an understatement. I heard you know her son, and I know damn well you know who her old man is." Brice got right to the point. With him and Pop, there was no need to bullshit and play hide the ball. They were both there for a reason.

Pop chuckled. "You just getting right down to it, huh?" he said to Brice. "That's what's up. I guess you got a job to do."

"So, let's talk," Brice said, not giving in to any joking. He'd promised Cheyenne Turner he would find out what happened to her mother, and that's what he intended to do.

Pop took his seat, and the club staff flitted around him like he was the king of New York. Brice was always amused by how commanding Pop's presence was in the place.

"I mean, what you want to know? You the cop, right?" Pop asked. "I'm just the nigga that you accusing of knowing some shit that I might not even know," Pop commented slickly.

Brice raised his eyebrow at his unlikely friend. They sat in silence for a few seconds before Brice spoke up.

"The kid, Lil Kev. Tell me what you know about him," Brice asked flat out. "He's been avoiding me, and I heard he's had some strain with his family about his line of work." Brice continued, tilting his head knowingly. There was no need to be overly specific in a public place. Brice understood that Pop was a smart man, and Pop understood the same about Brice.

"Yeah, I heard of the kid. Works for one of my under-lings, Scorpio. I mean, the kid is a wannabe, you feel me? He wants to be like his father was back in the day, but he ain't cut out for that," Pop told Brice.

Brice nodded his understanding. "So, he thinks he's tough, but not really," Brice said, making more of a summary statement than asking a real question.

"Right," Pop agreed. "From my understanding, the kid hates Big K. I mean, I can't blame him. The nigga was gone all of the kid's life, came back trying to be father of the year. You and I both know shit like that don't work. To be perfectly honest, I don't have no love for Big K. Back then, when I was on my come up, even locked up that nigga tried to step on my neck. I wouldn't say he was my worst enemy, but he ain't no friend," Pop said honestly.

He would only ever talk like this to Brice. Pop had some leverage—a certain gun that was used in an attempted murder of his sister's captor—over Brice, and knew he could never bring him down, or else.

"You ever meet his wife back then?" Brice asked.

Pop contemplated his answer. "Nah. I mean, back in the day, everybody in the street life knew of her. She was one of the baddest chicks in Brooklyn. I was way too young to have a woman like that. Niggas was loyal to Big K for a while and helped her along, but that dried up. Niggas also tried sleeping with her as soon as he was locked up. I don't think that worked out for most," Pop relayed.

"Any contact with Big K after he got home?" Brice asked straight out.

"Not with me. That nigga knows better than to approach me," Pop replied. "He hates me, and I hate him. Simple and plain."

Brice's shoulders slumped with disappointment, but Pop kept talking.

"But he did roll up on Scorpio to confront him about his son," Pop continued.

Brice perked up. "And? What did you hear about that?"

Pop chuckled sarcastically. "Shit, what you think I heard? Scorpio is already a loose cannon. Can you imagine some old motherfucker, long-time-ago gangster, broken-down older dude rolling up on these young cats, talking about leave my kid alone?" Pop asked rhetorically. "That shit ain't go well. Scorpio put a gun in that dude's mouth, sent him to his knees, and made his own son threaten him in front of mad dudes. So basically, Big K got humiliated by his own kid. Needless to say, that part ain't work out.

"I did hear the nigga turned to some of his son's own enemies to get back in the game. Even got some work from them and then owed them mad money when he couldn't move the product because he ain't got no workers. All of those niggas that worked for him back in the day have long faded away . . . dead, locked up, or gone legit as fuck and turned into preachers and shit."

"Damn," Brice huffed, absorbing all the information he was receiving. He knew writing it down wasn't an option with Pop. Brice always had to keep his street interactions like casual catching up and conversation. Anything resembling an official police questioning would get him zero cooperation, even from the street dudes he still considered to be his friends.

"A kid that will turn on his own father doesn't give me the warm and fuzzies at all," he commented.

"For real. I heard the kid was mad at the mother, too. You might not want to rule that nigga out as a suspect. For one, she had gone legit. She had benefits and shit, and I'm sure her kids knew that. Lil Kev had got caught up in some shit and owed Scorpio a lot of money. You might want to check into him a little further, but bringing him down to the station ain't gonna be the way. You know the code of the streets—ain't nobody but my dumb ass talking to no five-o," Pop said, sipping his drink.

"Where does he hang out?" Brice asked.

"Come on, B-boy." Pop sighed, calling Brice by his old nickname. "You know if a nigga tell you that, I'm hotting up spots and fucking with my own money. I think you should stick to going by the house, talking to his people, and go from there," Pop said honestly. He wasn't about to go that far with Brice. Friend or foe, Pop wasn't a snitch.

"No worries. I appreciate everything you gave me so far," Brice said. He finished up his drink, stood up, and gave Pop a pound with his fist. "Good looking out."

"It's nothing," Pop replied. "I hope you find out who did that shit. Honestly, that shit broke my heart."

"I'll find out," Brice said. "Her death won't go unsolved on my watch."

Chapter 6

Brice

"Thanks for coming down to talk to me, Kelsi," Brice said, parting a smile. He knew how girls like Kelsi and Cheyenne felt about the police. Brice wasn't so far removed from the streets that he couldn't say he didn't completely understand.

Kelsi shook her head slowly. Brice could see her hands shaking. When she noticed that he'd noticed, she quickly put them under her thighs.

"Am I under arrest or something?" Kelsi asked, her words shaky.

"No, no. We're hoping you can shed some light on things so we can figure out who would want to hurt Desiree Turner . . . or, um, what did you call her?" Brice said, putting down a stack of files and a CD in front of Kelsi. It was a tactic detectives used to make a person think they knew more than they actually did.

"Ms. Desi," Kelsi mumbled. "I called her Ms. Desi."

"You called her Ms. Desi? Okay. I've heard she was almost like a mother to you. Is that right?" Brice replied, using his most sympathetic voice.

Kelsi shook her head in agreement but didn't look at Brice or even in his direction.

"You want to talk to me about that?" Brice asked, fighting to make eye contact with Kelsi. He was sure to keep his voice level and soothing. From the time he'd met the whole family and Cheyenne Turner had introduced Kelsi as someone as close as family, Brice had been intrigued. He'd seen a lot of things, and he was always interested when he saw certain reactions. Kelsi had been there the first day he went by, but she seemed to have made herself scarce after that. Brice wanted to talk to her, maybe get an idea of her relationships with everyone in the house, and maybe get a better picture of the family dynamic.

Kelsi lowered her eyes to her lap. Brice could see tears falling straight down onto her clothes. She shook her head in agreement. "I'm sorry for crying," she managed.

"I understand," Brice replied.

"Ms. Desi, she . . . she was like a mother to me in the beginning . . . when I was little and growing up," Kelsi murmured.

"Tell me how she became almost like a mother to you, Kelsi," Brice said, pushing a small pack of facial tissues across the table toward her.

Kelsi blew out a windstorm of breath and shook her head side to side slightly. Her shoulders slumped, and she huffed out another long breath.

"I guess I need to start with how my mother *wasn't* a good mother to me." Kelsi sniffled. "You would have to know the whole story to really understand it all," she said. "It's a lot. I've been through a lot. All of my life, I've been going through shit."

"I know it's a lot, but I am here to listen. I have nothing but time," Brice said. "I'm trying to get to know everyone. I'm trying to understand who Ms. Desi was so I can help figure this out," he said, using Kelsi's name for Desiree Turner on purpose.

Kelsi seemed to contemplate what she was going to say. She lifted her eyes for a quick moment and then lowered them to her now fiddling fingers in front of her. Her lips were moving, but no sound was coming out, almost like she was rehearsing what she was going to say before she said it.

"I think you need to look into someone at Ms. Desi's job that drives a BMW," Kelsi blurted, her legs swinging in and out under the metal table. She'd totally deflected his question about her own relationship with Desiree.

Brice tilted his head and crumpled his brows. Kelsi's statement was abrupt, out of place. It seemed to come out of nowhere. But he listened.

"Ms. Desi... she... um, I think she was seeing someone else. Maybe the person got jealous," she said, twiddling her fingers even faster now.

"What makes you say this, Kelsi?" Brice asked, confused. None of the other family members had mentioned Desiree seeing anyone other than her husband, who'd just gotten released from prison. Even he hadn't let on that his wife might've been having an affair.

"I heard them. They argued about it a couple of weeks ago," Kelsi continued. She saw the vacant look in Brice's eyes. "Big K and Ms. Desi, they argued about it. About her getting rides in a BMW. It was loud and angry, but it was clear what the issue was, and that was it."

"What happened?" Brice asked, picking up his pen.

"I heard Big K's deep voice first that night. I've been around long enough to know that the way he was yelling meant he was at the end of his rope. He was hurt or angry or both. I heard him yelling, and he said to Ms. Desi, 'You think you the man around here, Desiree! You dish me a little allowance like I'm a fucking kid. You take me shopping like I'm a fucking woman. I can't put food on the table, and you fucking let me know it every single day! I can't even get niggas in the street to throw me a fucking bone in this game, even though I was the one who fed their asses back in the 90s! Do you know what that's like for me, Desi? Do you?'

"His yelling had woken me up, and I knew Cheyenne was up too," Kelsi said, her legs swinging harder under the table.

Brice listened intently. He also watched her body language closely. Brice was a master at interpreting body language.

"Me and Cheyenne both opened our eyes. I noticed that the sun wasn't even up yet. *What they arguing about now?* I thought, even though my mind was still all fuzzy with sleep. I listened closely but didn't really have to because they were so loud.

"Big K wasn't the only one yelling. Ms. Desi did too. 'Kevin, you need to forget being in the streets! You are forty years old, not twenty something. If you feel inferior because I work every day, pay the bills, and do what needs to be done around here and for you . . . go find a real job! I've done nothing but try to make you feel at home since you've been here. Yes, I leave money for you just so you don't have to feel like you don't have. Of course I bought you clothes. What else would you have worn? All of your outdated clothes from the 90s? I'm the breadwinner. So fucking what? Get over it! Kevin, I'm not going to stop doing what I have become accustomed to doing out here without you,' Ms. Desi had screamed at Big K. She was never really the type to raise her voice, so I knew that she had to be pretty upset.

"That didn't stop Big K. He seemed to get even more offended, which made him get louder and louder. 'Doing without me? Without me seems to be a fucking theme around here! Yeah, seems like you became accustomed to doing a lot without me. A whole lot without me. You think I don't see? Who is the motherfucker in the beamer who picks you up every day? Huh? Who the fuck is that? I bet you he made it all good around here without me!' Big K had barked at her," Kelsi went on, recounting the argument with angst playing on her features like a movie.

Brice stopped writing and looked up Kelsi. "Wait," he said. "Go back. Was he accusing her of something, or was he just mad and mentioning the car or the person with the car was his way?" Brice asked for clarification. A husband enraged at the thought of his wife having a possible affair might change things with the murder investigation. This was the first inkling he'd gotten of any familial trouble.

"Well, to me, it seemed like Big K was saying Ms. Desi was doing something wrong." Kelsi shrugged innocently.

Brice squinted at her and ran his hand over his beard, deep in thought.

"I can't say for sure, but I saw Cheyenne turn over in her bed when she heard the yelling, too. I knew she was thinking the same thing I was thinking. We were both confused. Neither one of us had never heard of someone with a BMW picking Ms. Desi up for work.

"But once Big K said it, Ms. Desi got furious. 'Oh, please, Kevin. That is a doctor from my job, who happens to be kind enough to come to this fucking hellhole to pick me up and take me to work. I don't see you volunteering to get me there. You've been home two months. Not once did you even ask me about my work. Not once did you ever ask me how hard it was for me to become a nurse. A head nurse at that!' she had screamed loudly, and he responded back just as loud.

" 'Nah, I haven't asked you because you're too busy being gone all the time. When you are here, you want to sleep or do whatever it is you like to do. I can barely get time to fuck my own wife. You know what that's like? Huh? Nah, you don't, Desi. I've been gone twelve fucking years. Twelve years I spent yanking my dick, dreaming about the day I could touch you again. Hold you in my arms like I used to do! And in the two months I've been home, you've barely kissed me, much less fuck me! You

know what that does to a man?' Big K had yelled. It was
the most emotional I'd ever heard him get in the time I
knew him, which was most of my life. To me, he sounded
like he was going to cry. That really broke my heart. I
hated to hear it. They had always been my favorite couple.
My favorite people, period," Kelsi lamented, shaking her
head somberly. "I wanted to see them together forever."

"What happened after that? Did the argument die
down?" Brice pressed.

"From what I remember, Ms. Desi told Big K he was
being ridiculous. I remember her clearly saying to him,
'What you're accusing me of is unfair. Just like you've
been gone twelve years, I've been alone for twelve years. I
haven't had a man in my bed. I haven't looked at another
man. I haven't been intimate with anyone—except you,
during those cold, horrible conjugal visits. So, I'm sorry if
I've gotten accustomed to going without sex, love, intima-
cy, but that's what I had to do to survive the soul-stirring
loneliness I've suffered for twelve years!

'You've changed too, Kevin. Your touch is not the same.
You are not the same loving, tender, caring man that left
me in ninety-six. Kevin, you may not want to hear it, but
everything for us has just changed.' And she was crying
by then. No, it was more like she was sobbing. And Big
K slammed the door and left. I remember jumping when
he left the apartment because he had slammed the door
so hard the whole apartment shook," Kelsi went on. She
wiped tears from her cheeks.

"I got up and walked over and got into the bed with
Cheyenne. I hugged her tight from behind. I could tell
she was crying, and I told her not to cry. That it was going
to be all right. I told her that married people fight, but
after a little while, things would fit together for both of
them. I comforted my best friend even if I didn't believe
it myself. I told her that her parents would be happy just

like back in the day when we used to go to the rides with her father. When Big K would kiss up and love up on Ms. Desi every minute they were together."

Kelsi parted a halfhearted smile and shifted in her seat like the memory of good times had lit up in and faded out of her head as fast as a camera's flash. She breathed out loudly.

"I didn't know if I believed it, but I said it. I wanted my best friend to stop crying. Cheyenne didn't say anything more that night, but I could tell she was happy I was there for her, like she had done for me so many times over the years."

"So, no one ever knew if Ms. Desi actually had an affair or was seeing another man?" Brice asked. He didn't want to seem like he was being insensitive to the victim's reputation, but every fact had to be examined in a murder investigation.

"No one knew anything. It could've been true. If you ask me, Ms. Desi acted differently towards Big K than we were all used to. I know Big K felt kind of less than a man with the way things were going around the house, with everyone really, except me. I had the same respect for him that I'd always had since I was a kid.

"I was always thinking about the point he was making after I heard that argument. I never knew Ms. Desi got a ride to work from a man. I could see how Big K could take that the wrong way. After all, we did live in the projects. Doctors coming to the projects in nice whips were taking a risk. A man who took a risk like that on a woman wasn't just trying to be helpful, if you ask me.

"You have to understand. Big K was a man with a lot of pride. He was used to being treated like a king, but when he came home . . . that didn't happen with anyone except me," Kelsi said.

"A doctor, you say? A doctor with a BMW?" Brice repeated, scribbling wildly on his pad.

"Yeah, maybe that's who you should be looking for—someone at the hospital that drives a BMW," Kelsi said, flattening her hands on the table. "So, can I go now?" she asked.

"Not just yet. I want to circle back to Ms. Desi being like a mother to you. I want to go over how you got so close with the family and what that was like," Brice said, not letting her off the hook so easily.

Kelsi sighed loudly. "Can I use the bathroom first? I need a little break," she said.

"Sure. I could use one too. Let's take ten minutes and pick this back up," Brice said, smiling. Right then, he knew Kelsi might know more than she was letting on.

Chapter 7

Kelsi

Kelsi rushed into the precinct bathroom, busted into a stall, and vomited violently. She just made it to the toilet and avoided throwing up all over the floor and her shoes. When she was done, she leaned her back against the cold steel wall of the bathroom stall, letting her chest rise and fall until she was calmer. Kelsi had to pull herself together. This was a lot on her. She knew what she had to do for her own sake and the sake of the baby she was carrying that no one else knew about.

The ten minutes were almost up. On shaky legs, Kelsi walked out of the stall and over to the bay of sinks. She splashed cold water on her face and looked up into the mirror.

"Fuck, you look a mess," she grumbled to herself. She'd practiced and practiced, but nothing could prepare her for speaking with Detective Simpson. Telling him the whole story was out of the question, and Kelsi knew that.

She inhaled deeply and exhaled loudly, wondering how she'd gotten herself to this place. Years and years of shit she'd endured, and now this.

Kelsi met the female police officer who'd escorted her to the bathroom right outside of the door. They didn't say a word to one another as they walked through the

precinct to get back to the room she'd been in with
Detective Simpson.

He was standing outside of the room, smiling when
Kelsi returned. Again, her stomach swirled with nausea,
and she wanted to throw up.

Back inside, Kelsi took the same hard metal seat. She
noticed the soda and half a hero sandwich on the table.
Now, her stomach growled. Kelsi couldn't chance it.
Someone had warned her about the cops being overly
nice, feeding you, or giving you a cigarette when they
wanted to trap you into saying something that might
get you hemmed up. She wasn't falling for it. Besides,
if she took one bite of that sandwich, with the morning
sickness, she might throw up on the table.

"I got you something to eat," Detective Simpson said,
nodding toward the sandwich and soda. "I am starving.
I hope you don't mind if I have mine while we continue
talking," he said.

Kelsi shook her head. "I'm good. Not hungry. And be
my guest," she replied.

Detective Simpson pushed his food to the side. Kelsi
noticed, but neither one of them commented.

"Okay, so, getting back into this, Kelsi. We spoke about
the argument between Big K and Ms. Desi," Detective
Simpson said, using the names Kelsi called them. "But
earlier, we also talked about how you got so close to the
family. We kind of moved on from that, but I want to get
back to it," he continued.

Kelsi swallowed hard. She knew he was going to ask
that again. Hashing up the past wasn't something she
wanted to do, but what choice did she have? In order to
get this detective off her back, she had to get it all out.
That much she knew.

"I guess the best way to start this is from the beginning of my fucked-up life," Kelsi said.

Detective Simpson's eyebrows went up and came back down quickly. Kelsi noticed.

"I never knew my father, and I never really had a mother, if that's even possible. A kid with no father or mother. That was me. As the story goes, the day I was born, my mother, Carlene Jones, who was fifteen years old at the time, was in the mirror, shaking her pregnant ass to Eric B. and Rakim's 'Paid In Full,' doing the whop when the labor pains hit her like a thunderbolt. I was making my entrance into the world, whether she liked it or not. After spending seventeen hours giving birth to me, Carlene never held me. She never looked at me. She refused to acknowledge that I was her child. My Nana said Carlene didn't name me either. Carlene referred to me as *it*. 'You take it and feed it. You hold it,' Carlene had told my Nana.

"Nana said the white nurses at the hospital helped her come up with the name Kelsi. Nana didn't want me to be one of the Shenquauqas of the world. '*Kelsi is a universal name*,' Nana always preached. 'You can go anywhere with that name, and people won't judge you before they meet you.' Nana always had high hopes for me from day one," Kelsi relayed. She reached across the table and took Detective Simpson up on his earlier offer of tissue.

Detective Simpson stared at her, hanging on her every word. He already felt sorry for her, Kelsi could tell, as he looked at her with sympathy. She picked up on it.

"But don't feel sorry for me. I had my Nana for a while," Kelsi said this sentence, and the thought made her smile more than she had since sitting down in front of the detective.

Detective Simpson nodded, agreeing not to feel sorry for her.

"My Nana said I was the prettiest baby she had ever seen. 'Girl, you ain't have one piece of birth trauma, unh-uh. No egg-shaped head, no swollen eyes, no pale skin . . . nothing. You came out just as pretty as you wanted to be. Smooth skin, eyes perfect, and a head full of pretty hair,' Nana told me when I was five. Nana said she stayed at the hospital, held me, fed me, and changed my diapers, which continued after we went home.

"By the time I was two years old, I thought Nana was my mother, and Carlene—well, I didn't think about her at all. I hardly ever saw her. She was like a distant cousin or a relative who popped in after a long car ride to New York from down south. Most of the time, when she came to the house, she slept the entire time and ate ravenously when she woke up. Carlene ran the streets, partying and having a ball.

"Nana says Carlene was always a hottie. She got her cherry popped at ten, and it was downhill from there. From what I remember, at that time, Carlene was a shade lighter than the blacktop of the street. She had thick, dark brown hair that was cut in a Salt-n-Pepa hi-low with the back shaved, and she always wore the biggest gold doorknocker earrings. She also wore rings on all of her brightly painted fingers like that man Mr. T from the *A-Team*. Carlene had a regular face, nothing exceptionally beautiful about it. Nana says Carlene's voluptuous body was what got her all of the attention. Those double-D cup breasts, that reindeer ass, and her ability to use them to get what she wanted.

"I was the complete opposite of Carlene. My skin was what Nana's old lady friends called *creamy caramel, almost yella*, My hair was spongy, thick but soft, and would curl nicely with just a little bit of water and grease.

It wasn't real long, but it was a good grade, according to Nana. My eyes, Nana said, '... is the only thing you got from that damn Carlene.' Our eyes are beady and kind of close together, the one thing that linked me to Carlene, and also the one thing about my face I always hated.

"The trouble started on my eighth birthday. I had been flitting around the apartment Nana and I shared, waiting for my party guests to arrive. I had peeked at my Cinderella cake four times already. 'Kelsi, by the time the people get here, that cake is gonna be poked full of holes,' Nana had laughed. I still don't know how Nana always knew everything. Maybe parents do have eyes in the back of their heads. Real parents anyway, not the kind like Carlene.

"Everyone began arriving at the party around three o'clock. Why I remember that time, I don't know. I got so many compliments on the pink lace dress Nana had gotten me. I whirled around and around like I was Cinderella.

"Nana announced it was time to sing happy birthday about two hours into the party. Everyone crowded around as I kneeled on one of the kitchen chairs with the cake in front of me. Nana shuffled toward her bedroom to get the matches she always hid from me. 'Just for your safety,' she used to explain.

"As Nana looked for the matches, there was a loud knock on the door. Nana's friend Ms. Bessie answered it. When she pulled back the door, Carlene waltzed into our apartment like it was her birthright to be there. I remember it as clear as today how she came in like a gust of cold air. The kind that took your breath away in the winter and made tears drain from the corners of your eyes.

"Carlene's clear plastic platform heels clicked against the ceramic floor tiles like firecrackers popping. I can remember it like it was yesterday. Her skin gleamed with Vaseline, shining like thick, freshly poured molasses, and her newly pressed hair was pulled into a greasy ponytail with baby hair lying flat with small dips in it around the sides of her head. I was in awe of her because I didn't know her. To me, Carlene was always like a purple, sparkly unicorn or like a rainbow with gold at the end of it. Magical, yet unreal.

"I eyed her that day in amazement. I wished I had a sparkly, tight red dress like hers. I remember running my hands down my flat chest, wishing I had a set of knockers sitting up under my chin like Carlene did. To me, she looked like a movie star. The skimpy dress showed off much more than it covered, barely coming fully under her ample behind.

"I smiled at her. I wanted her to smile back at me. She never did. Carlene's eyes were dull. All of that sparkle in her clothes, but none showed in her eyes. I had not seen her in a year and was kind of glad she had come to my birthday party.

"Nana, on the other hand, wasn't as happy to see Carlene. At some point, Nana had emerged from the back of the apartment with the matches. Nana's face had folded in on itself, and her eyes hooded over. Nana's dislike of Carlene could not be contained. Her feelings of disdain were like those trick cans filled with rubber snakes. No matter how many times you closed the lid, it popped right open, letting the snakes jump out at you.

"I remember feeling strangled by the thick rope of tension that lassoed around all of us as soon as Nana realized Carlene was there. 'Why you coming up in here looking like a whore?' Nana had whispered harshly in Carlene's ear, trying to keep the partygoers from overhearing. 'You ain't got no better clothes than street walker clothes?'

Carlene had sucked her teeth and smirked evilly. 'No matter what you say, you can't blow my high t'day. It's my child's birthday, and I came to celebrate,' Carlene had trumpeted, then took a long drag on her Newport. Carlene walked over to the table, flicked her lighter, and lit all eight of my candles. It was the first time I felt caught between the two of them, but it wouldn't be the last," Kelsi said, rolling the wadded tissue around the palm of her hand.

Detective Simpson put his hand up and said he didn't want to interrupt her but wanted to make sure the story would be leading to how she met the Turners. Kelsi had relaxed, talking to him a bit more than she'd expected.

"You need some water? A snack?" Detective Simpson asked Kelsi. "Something other than the sandwich or soda?"

"No, thank you. I just want to get through this," she said, her words coming out more like a croak than full words.

"Okay, finish," Detective Simpson said, leaning back in his chair.

"The day of my eighth birthday party, after Carlene showed up, I was the only one who could see worry and fear creasing Nana's face. Nana stood off in the background, scowling, her jaw rocking feverishly. I stood in front of my cake and with my eyes shut real tight, and I made the same wish I had made year after year since I could understand what wishes were. I would come to understand the meaning of one of Nana's favorite sayings: *Be careful what you wish for. God don't answer wishes, and fairies who answer wishes are the devil in disguise.*

"That night, when everyone left, I wondered why Carlene was still there, and so did Nana. Nana and Carlene weren't like the mothers and daughters you saw on TV. There would be no long talks, laughter, and trips to the mall together.

"I could tell Nana was agitated. She'd smoked a half a pack of Pall Malls in a matter of a few hours. I just sat in silence, playing with my new birthday gifts and stealing glances at my biological mother, who I didn't even really know. Carlene tried to make small talk with Nana, but it didn't work. Nana treated Carlene worse than she treated Ms. Ollie Mae, a nosey, gossipy lady at our church. Now, that was bad, because Nana couldn't stand Ms. Ollie Mae.

"Finally, Carlene had given up trying to make small talk with her mother. It got quiet for a little while—too quiet, if you ask me. Then, Carlene let out a long sigh, like air escaping a hole in a tire. She stood up and smoothed her dress down over her big butt. She interrupted the eerie silence by dropping a bomb on us. Carlene could've blown up a whole city with her announcement.

"Smacking her shiny, glossy lips, Carlene used her inch-long red painted thumbnail to flick something from under her equally long pointer nail and calmly said, 'I wanted y'all to know that I'm gettin' married, and I'm coming to get Kelsi when I do. We gon' start living like a family. She gon' have what I didn't have . . . a mother *and* a father.'

"As young as I was, I remember feeling like bombs had exploded around me. My ears rang, and my stomach knotted up immediately. I clenched my butt cheeks together to keep from shitting on myself. The floor even started shaking underneath me.

"Nana jumped up to her feet, ready for battle. Nana's face had crumpled like one of those devil masks you see in the costume store at Halloween time. She moved in on Carlene like a lion about to take down a fine, sleek gazelle.

"Nana jutted a finger toward Carlene's face. 'You ain't takin' this child nowhere! This here is my baby! You don't even have a damn place to live. Look at you! All shiny and bright to cover up the dirt and filth that lives in your soul. You ain't interested in being no mother to nobody. Pushing one out don't automatically make you the mama. You ain't interested in being a mother or decent woman period!' Nana had accused cruelly, her pecan face turning dark as it filled with blood.

"I kind of felt bad for Carlene. She looked like Nana has slapped her in the face and kicked her in the gut with those words. I could see Carlene's neck moving as she swallowed a few times. She inhaled until her chest swelled. Then, Carlene bounced back quick, like she was used to Nana saying stuff like that to her. She raised one side of her mouth into an evil smirk. Her eyes went into slits, and she started circling Nana as if to say she wasn't backing down.

"Carlene's heels clacked against the floor each time she said a word. 'Let. Me. Tell. You. Something.' *Clack*. 'Your insults don't work on me no more.' *Click*. 'I ain't a young, dumb kid that cares about what you think of me no more.' *Clack*. 'Let's not talk about who ain't fit to be a mother!' *Click*.

"Carlene stopped moving. I guess she was going in for the kill and wanted to stand her ground. 'You always trying to put me down in front of my child! I got a place to live, I'm getting married, and I'm taking my child with me. Ain't no courts ever gave you that baby. She's mine, and you ain't using her to get no second chances in life. You had your chance to be a mother, and you failed! You a failure, just like the failure you raised!' Carlene had spat, rushing over and getting close up in Nana's face.

"Both of them seemed to be on the brink of hysterics. They stood toe to toe, eye to eye. I was hoping no one threw a punch. The tension swirling around the apartment was so thick I could've sworn I saw it circling red over the entire place. I continued to twirl the Cinderella figurine from my cake, my little fingers shaking as I tried to act like nothing was happening. But my thundering heart and flaring nostrils probably gave me away.

"My birthday dress suddenly felt scratchy and too tight against my skin. That was the first time I remember feeling afraid. Not scary movie afraid, but deathly afraid, like something real bad was going to happen. The kind of fear that knots up your insides so bad you feel like pissing, shitting, and vomiting all at once.

"There was no more discussion about it that night. Nana and I thought nothing of it after Carlene left. Thought nothing of it until the day Carlene came back to get me." Kelsi blew out a long, exasperated breath, like telling her story was exhausting her, draining all of her energy. She took a long pause and reared her head back so she could stare up at the ceiling as if that would help her with the pain of the memories.

"Take your time," Detective Simpson said, seemingly locked in to her pain.

"'No! I don't want to go! Please!' I had screamed through tears, holding onto my Nana's waist as tight as my little arms could grasp. I had even locked my fingers behind Nana's back to make my grip even better. The spot where I buried my face was wet with my tears and snot.

"'You are my child, and you are going where I go!' Carlene had screamed, grabbing me roughly around my ribcage, tugging me towards her. I felt like my shoulders would pop out of the sockets from me holding on so tight.

"'Please, Carlene! I'll do anything. Just let her stay. Ain't no reason for you to take her now. She being raised right here with me. Don't be hateful. Please leave this baby be, Carlene. Just leave her be,' my Nana had sobbed, holding onto me equally as tight. She wasn't going to let Carlene take me. I was sure of that, but I still held on as tight as I could," Kelsi relayed through tears. Her legs bounced so hard under the table they made a sound.

Detective Simpson looked powerless at the moment. He appeared as if he would feel every single ounce of her pain from back then. "Let me know if you need another break," he said during one of Kelsi's long pauses.

"We held onto each other, me and my Nana, but that didn't help," Kelsi continued.

" 'Don't make me call the police on you, lady! I did it once, and I'll do it again!' Carlene warned Nana, her voice a high-pitched screech that made the insides of my ears itch. 'You making this harder than it gotta be. A child needs to be with the mother who gave birth to them, not a pretender looking for second chances because they couldn't do it right with their own child they gave birth to. I'm telling you. I'm gonna call the damn cops!' Carlene had screamed at Nana.

"But Nana wasn't backing down. 'You gon' have to call them cops tonight or kill me, 'cause you ain't takin' this child from here unless it's over my dead body!' Nana had announced firmly. She wasn't letting go, and neither was I.

"I just knew that would do it. Carlene didn't look like the type that was into having contact with the cops. She wasn't going to call no cops.

"But Carlene tugged on my waist again, and I felt like I was losing grip. The bones in my fingers started cracking as I tried in vain to keep them locked together. 'Please! Nana, don't let them take me!' I cried and screamed. I felt my throat burning as I screamed as loud as I could. The salt from my tears was bitter on my tongue.

"'Come on! Let go! She ain't none of your momma! I pushed you out into this world, and if I want you with me, then you gon' be with me!' Carlene had growled, tugging on me.

"I buried my face deeper into Nana's stomach. I held my breath. I would have rather died from not breathing than to go with Carlene.

'Miss, we gotta go. Why don't you just let Peaches take her child?' Carlene's new husband had said calmly. He scared the living shit out of me, and that made me bury my face even deeper into Nana's soft stomach. I had forgotten his scary ass had come there with Carlene.

" 'Fuck you and your Peaches! I raised this child. The momma didn't want her! Did your new wife tell you that? Did she tell you she ain't interested in being nobody's mama? Did she tell you she ain't nothing but a two-bit whore?' Nana had screamed through tears.

"I couldn't ever remember seeing Nana cry before that day. I was still holding on so tight I could hear Nana's heart racing in my ear.

"'Two-bit whore? Two-bit whore? If I'm a two-bit whore, I was taught by the best!' Carlene had hissed at Nana.

"I didn't give a shit about their rivalry. I was watching my life literally flash before my eyes. So, I was spurned into action myself. 'Please, Carlene, let me stay. I'll call you Mommy from now on when you come. Just please let me stay with my Nana,' I had cried out, hoping she would just have a little bit of sympathy for me. The kind of pain I was experiencing felt like someone was dying in my arms. Every muscle in my body ached, and my head pounded. Just the thought of leaving Nana had me gagging on my tears and snot," Kelsi recalled, her shoulders shaking with sobs now.

Detective Simpson looked on pitifully. He wrote a few things down, but for the most part, he listened to Kelsi.

She couldn't lie to herself. This being the first time she'd ever recounted her life like this was kind of freeing. Over the years, many people had suggested therapy to her, but where she was from, therapy was for weak people and crazy people, and that was it.

"Carlene seemed hurt when I begged to stay with my Nana. 'You ain't gotta call me Mommy when I come because you coming with me now!' Carlene had screamed at me, sounding a little like she wanted to cry. I could tell she was hurt, maybe even a little embarrassed. Now that I think about it, maybe she felt betrayed by me, her only child, who was acting like she was the grim reaper coming to take me to hell," Kelsi said, shaking her head like if she could tell her mother sorry right then, she would have.

"But that still didn't change shit. Carlene was taking me. Her husband stepped to Nana and said, 'I believe the child's mother said to let her go, old lady.'

"The next thing I heard after that was a click. When I looked up to Nana's face, I saw the end of a black gun resting on Nana's forehead. I squeezed my eyes shut and buried my face deeper into Nana's stomach. I inhaled her scent. Maybe something in my little mind back then told me this was final. I remember saying a quick, silent prayer.

"It wasn't enough. The man lifted his gun and brought it down on Nana's head. I heard something crack. Then

I felt something dripping on the top of my head," Kelsi cried. Both of her hands had curled into fists on their own.

She looked up at Detective Simpson with fire in her eyes as she recounted one of the worst days of her life and the event that ultimately set her life on a crash course with disaster.

"He gun-butted your grandmother?" Detective Simpson asked, seemingly shocked.

Kelsi's jaw rocked, and her nostrils flared. "Fuck yeah. He hit Nana with that gun. 'God forgive them,' Nana had whispered as her body hit the floor. She involuntarily released her grip on me as she went limp.

"'Nana, wake up! You can't let them take me!' I had yelled. I still held on to Nana as tight as I could, but I was no match for his huge wrestler's arms.

"He swept me off my feet in one swift motion and carried me kicking and screaming to his rusty old white ragtop Cadillac Sedan Deville. He threw me into the backseat roughly and slammed the door. Then, he walked calmly to the driver's seat and cranked the car up. I remember the pungent smell of gasoline that engulfed the car and made me dizzy.

"By the time I scrambled up from the seat, I saw Nana stumbling out of the building. She was going to fight for me. No gun butt was going to keep my Nana from fighting for me. I looked out of the dirty car window at my Nana, who was running beside the car with blood leaking from her head as the bastard pulled away from the curb. Nana's face was covered with blood as she cried and screamed my name." Kelsi hiccupped several sobs, and her chest trembled.

"My Nana had screamed, and I screamed right back. 'Nana! Nana! Don't let them take me!' I remember putting my hands up against the glass and feeling as if I was being sucked into a dark hole, an alternate universe. Nana couldn't keep up. At first, I watched Nana from the window, but eventually, I had to get on my knees to see her. The further we drove, the smaller Nana got until I could hardly see her anymore. Suddenly, Nana's silhouette just disappeared into the distance.

"I never saw my Nana alive again. I had lost the only person who'd ever really loved me," Kelsi said.

"Wow, Kelsi. I can't imagine your pain and sorrow over that," Detective Simpson said. "So, it was that event that led you to meet the Turners?" he asked.

"Yes, it was the very first thing that led to me eventually becoming part of the Turner family, but it wasn't the last," Kelsi replied, prepared to tell it all.

Chapter 8

Kelsi

Kelsi was exhausted when she walked back into the apartment. There was a crowd of people there, rallying around Cheyenne in the wake of Desiree's death. Kelsi tried to slip in and go into the back room, but Cheyenne noticed her and called out to her. Kelsi froze, spun around, and plastered on a fake smile.

"Hey, Chey," she sang. "You all right?"

Cheyenne called her over, but there were too many people.

"I'm exhausted. Let's talk tonight," Kelsi replied, darting her eyes around, a signal only her best friend would understand. It meant Kelsi needed alone time, which sometimes she did. Cheyenne got the picture, finally. Kelsi darted to the back.

Once she was in Cheyenne's bedroom, she closed the door, leaned her back against it, and let out the breath she had been holding. Her tears came fast and furious. Her entire body shook violently. Kelsi was inconsolable. Speaking to Detective Simpson had dredged up parts of her life she'd tried to forget. She'd tried to drink it away, drug it away, sex it away, and nothing had worked. She slid down to the floor, her legs too weak to maintain her weight any longer. Kelsi folded herself into a ball and covered her ears with her hands. She rocked back and forth as she was thrust back into a time and place she wished she could erase.

Kelsi had never been out of the Bronx in her life before Carlene and Took snatched her. She cried for the entire ride. Sitting on the hot, busted-up leather of Took's car, Kelsi could hardly breathe from the wind blowing in her face. Tears and snot were everywhere. She had white, dried, and crusted streaks extending from the corners of her eyes like war paint and running down her cheeks like the makeup on a sad clown. Kelsi continued to cry out of control. She didn't care. She wanted her Nana.

A few times during the eternity-long ride, Took turned his pale face around toward Kelsi and screamed, "Shut the fuck up, kid!"

Kelsi had never seen anyone who looked like Took. His skin was so white it was almost transparent. His hair was thick and nappy, but it was a golden, brassy blonde like it belonged on the head of a white person. Took's eyeballs were red with a black center. Kelsi pondered his features as she cried. She'd grown up to believe only white people had blonde hair and pinky-whitish skin.

At first, Kelsi thought Took was white, but his huge flat nose and nappy-ass hair quickly changed her mind. Anyone with red eyeballs had to be the devil, she surmised, but as she got older, she learned he was albino.

Kelsi could smell the difference in the air between the Bronx and Brooklyn as soon as they crossed the bridge. She put her arm over her nose. The funny smell made her want to throw up. It was like the ocean mixed with garbage—yeah, that was the best she could describe it.

Kelsi was still crying as they pulled up on the strange block. Her head pounded, and she had to pee badly. She peered out the window at an orange-and-blue sign

posted in a small patch of grass that read: WELCOME TO
CAREY GARDENS, N.Y.C.H.A. *The building was very tall, not
like the four-story walk-up where she had lived with
Nana in the Bronx. There were so many people outside,
kids and adults. Kelsi heard music blasting from a large
boom box sitting on a bench.*

*"Here comes the brand new flava in ya ear! Time
for new flava in ya ear!" The Craig Mack lyrics had
everyone outside jumping.*

*"Ow!" Carlene shouted, raising her hands over her
head and clapping. "That's my shit. This remix be
having me going." She rocked her head up and down.*

*As young as she was, Kelsi just wanted to tell her
mother to shut the fuck up. It wasn't nothing to fucking
celebrate about. But her Nana would not have approved
of Kelsi thinking about curses in her head.*

*"The block is hot! That means green for you, baby."
Carlene giggled, leaning in to kiss Took's ugly cheek. She
became a different person all of a sudden.*

*Took was preparing to park the car so they could get
out, but before he could bring it to a complete stop, three
scary-looking people—two skinny women and a very
sweaty man—rushed toward Took's window.*

*The first skinny woman began stretching her balled
fist toward Took. "Yo, Took, man, where you been? I
need a nick—" She was quickly cut off.*

*"Bitch, can't you see I just pulled up? I got my kid in
the car and shit. Have some fuckin' respect, you fiend!
Get the fuck outta here until I park my whip!" Took
screamed at the lady.*

*The skeletal lady and her counterparts jumped back
as Took purposely swerved the car like he was going to
hit them.*

I ain't his kid, *Kelsi thought.* I'll never be the kid of no
red-eyed devil. *However, since she never knew who her*

father was, it did feel kind of good to have a man claim her like that.

"Y'all gotta get out. I gotta go see Big K. I need to re-up. I ain't got no more shit, and as you can see, these fiends don't never rest," Took said to Carlene with an urgency in his voice.

Carlene leaned over and kissed him again. Kelsi gagged.

"Go get that work, daddy. I'll be waiting for you when you get back, so don't take too long," Carlene cooed in a husky, trying-to-be-sexy voice that made Kelsi's skin crawl.

Then she turned toward Kelsi. Her face changed. It was suddenly crumpled like she was smelling something real stink. "C'mon, get out! And wipe them damn crusty boogers off your face!" she yelled at Kelsi.

Kelsi's insides boiled. She rolled her eyes and made a feeble attempt to wipe the crusted snot and tears from her face. Wide-eyed, she exited the car, wondering what kind of life she was about live.

It was like a different world in front of that building. There were at least sixty things going on at once: people dancing, people arguing, people drinking, people smoking, kids playing, kids fighting, babies crying, babies sleeping. It was like all the people who lived inside that tall building with all those windows were outside, engaged in some activity, and they all stared at Carlene and Kelsi as they walked up.

Suddenly, Kelsi felt the heat of embarrassment flame over her face. She was ashamed of how she looked, who she was with . . . all of it. All eyes were on her. She had nothing but the clothes on her back. When Carlene and Took had snatched her from Nana, Kelsi was in what Nana referred to as "play clothes," so she wasn't in one of her best outfits. The jeans she wore were a little too high, and the T-shirt a little too tight. They were last year's clothes that Nana made her wear around the house when they weren't going anywhere special. Kelsi had plenty of nice clothes at Nana's house, but Carlene hadn't taken the time to bring Kelsi's clothes or toys, and Nana was too preoccupied with trying to keep her there to pack a bag.

As Kelsi walked toward the front of 2949 West 23rd Street—her new, strange home—she looked around at all the people as they looked at her. One set of kids caught her full attention. There was a group of girls playing double Dutch.

"Ten, ten, ten, twenty, thirty, forty, fifty, sixty, seventy, eighty, ninety, one up, two, three, four, five, six, seven eight, nine, two up!" They all sang in unison as one girl jumped in the middle of their rope.

One girl in particular caught Kelsi's attention. The girl was turning on one end of the rope, and as Kelsi stared at her, the girl smiled. Kelsi thought the girl was very pretty. Her hair was long and neatly done in a lot of ponytails. She wore yellow from head to toe, and it seemed to bring out her Crayola-crayon brown skin.

The girl kept her eye on Kelsi while she turned the rope made from telephone wire. Kelsi waved real quick and kept walking. She immediately wanted to get to know that little girl with the kind smile and kind eyes.

"Hey, Peaches, who you got there?" yelled an old, overweight woman wearing a housecoat. The woman's body spilled left and right on the bench she occupied to the left of the building's entrance. She was talking to Carlene, so it quickly became obvious to Kelsi that Carlene's nickname was Peaches. Kelsi had thought it was just something Took called her. To Kelsi, Carlene looked far from a peach.

"*This my daughter, Kelsi. I told you I had a daughter. What? You ain't believe me?*" *Carlene snapped back at the woman but continued switching her ass into the building.*

"*She's a pretty little thing. Sure don't look nothing like you!*" *the lady replied, cackling and coughing at the same time.*

Carlene kept moving full speed ahead like she didn't want the lady to look at Kelsi too long. "Lula is so got-damn nosey. Always try'na make somebody out to be a fucking liar," Carlene whispered to herself as she and Kelsi stood waiting for the elevator.

Carlene jammed her finger at the elevator button over and over like she didn't believe it would ever come. For the first time since they'd left Nana's, Kelsi could tell Carlene was just as nervous about this new living arrangement as she was. Carlene wouldn't look at Kelsi, but she could see Carlene's bottom lip quivering a bit.

Maybe she wants me to like her, *Kelsi thought.*

Carlene and Kelsi didn't speak a word during the elevator ride. Exiting the elevator, Carlene led the way. She rushed down the long, dimly lit hallway, and Kelsi followed. The stale air assaulted the insides of Kelsi's nostrils with a million different odors at once. She could smell the aroma of fried chicken, pee, fish, and garbage all rolled into one big whiff. As they passed one apartment, Kelsi could hear music blasting so loud the little knocker on the door vibrated. Another apartment had its front door wide open. The occupants inside moved around like they didn't even notice the door was open. Another apartment had huge dents in the door and bright yellow tape that said CRIME SCENE: DO NOT CROSS in the form of an X across it.

The projects were much noisier and busier than Kelsi was used to. What really got her was all the garbage on the floor in front of the incinerator.

They gotta live here. How come they couldn't just pull the handle and put the garbage in? *she thought, even as young as she was.*

Apartment 4G—that was what the black lettering on the door Carlene stopped at read. Carlene fished her keys from her pocketbook and opened the blue steel door.

"Home sweet, fucking home!" she exclaimed and then stepped inside like she was introducing Kelsi to a palace.

Standing at the threshold, Kelsi raised her eyebrows and covered her mouth. She felt a hard ball in her throat, and something funny was going on in her stomach. Tears sprang up at the edges of her eyes. The house stank like garbage and dirty feet. Beer cans, soda bottles, clothes, Chinese food boxes, and any other item of garbage you could think of covered the floor. Kelsi used the back of her hand to wipe her tears and cover her nose at the same time.

"You better stop acting like you too good and brang yo' ass on in here. This where we stay, so this is where you stay. Get all that other shit out of your mind. I'm ya mother," Carlene said, yanking Kelsi further into the hellhole.

Kelsi's sneakers made low, crackling sounds as the soles stuck to the sticky, dirty tiles on the floor. The floor was a sickening shade of gray, but Kelsi somehow knew the tiles were supposed to be off-white. She examined her new surroundings as she dodged the roaches scurrying back to their hiding places. There were so many of them that they couldn't find places to hide.

"Eeeelll!" Kelsi screamed as one fell from some place high and landed on her arm. She started jumping and moving and swiping at her arms to make sure it was off her.

"Bitch, you ain't ever seen a roach before?" Carlene hissed.

"Not this many, and not on me," Kelsi commented, disgusted.

"Too bad! You better get used to living here, because you sure won't be going back to live with that lady," Carlene snapped in response.

"And my name is Kelsi," she mumbled sassily. Carlene had taken to calling her the B-word, and she was getting tired of it.

"I call you what I want to call you . . . Bitch," Carlene retorted, getting so close to Kelsi's face that Kelsi could smell the Royal Crown grease in her scalp.

Kelsi finally moved far enough into the apartment to really assess everything she was going to have to contend with. She tried to find at least one thing she might've been able to live with there, but it wasn't easy. The apartment had no furniture in the so-called living room. Sheets covered the windows, instead of the nice lace curtains Kelsi was used to at Nana's house.

A small, raggedy plastic folding table with one chair and one milk crate that served as a chair sat to the side of the small kitchen. The kitchen sink had dishes piled in it and to both sides of it. The dishes had food on them so old that black, green, blue, and gray mold grew in tall piles on some of the plates. The stove was caked with old brown and yellow grease. So was the wall behind it. Kelsi was scared to open the refrigerator because there were so many roaches around it.

The kitchen had two ways to get in and out, so Kelsi exited on the side closest to the apartment door. She thought about making a run for it, but where would she go? Being in Brooklyn was like being in a foreign country for her. She would've never figured out how to get back to the Bronx. Nana had kept her too sheltered for that.

As Kelsi stepped out of the kitchen, she had a clear view straight down a small hallway that led to the back of the apartment. She noticed that there was only one bedroom.

Where will I sleep? *she thought sadly. She usually slept with Nana every night.*

Carlene emerged from a darkened room at the back of the apartment. "You gonna sleep right here," *she huffed, dragging a dirty foam mattress into the empty living room.* "And listen, bitch. There are rules to staying here," *Carlene continued as she lit the end of a cigarette.*

Kelsi's jaw rocked as she bit down so hard her temples throbbed.

I told you my name is Kelsi! *she screamed in her head.*

"First, don't touch the refrigerator and nothing in it unless you ask me or Took. You don't buy shit, so you don't eat shit unless we tell you to. Especially if you see a Pepsi in there. Don't you ever, ever touch my Pepsi. Drink water! Kids drink water. If I decide to give you something else to drink, you will. If not, drink fucking water. Period. Don't touch the TV or stereo in my room. Matter-a-fact, don't touch shit in my room or go in there unless I send you in there or call you in there. Don't leave out this house without my permission, or if me or Took take you out. You can't go outside unless I say you can go. There will be no fucking company in my house. These fucking kids around here are no good, and I don't want them in my fucking crib. You got chores around here, so you ain't gonna be bored at all. You gotta do the dishes and clean the bathroom, kitchen, and where you sleep at. Last of all, I see you growing up now, getting a little bit of buds for tits and rounding out to get a li'l bit of ass, so don't even think about looking cross-eyed at my man. That will get your ass thrown right outta here! Too many of y'all young bitches fuckin' people*

*old man and then yelling 'bout somebody touched y'all
or molested y'all. That shit don't fly around here, so
you better keep that li'l body to yaself," Carlene shot
off, contaminating Kelsi's breathing air with a cloud of
smoke as she finished up.*

*Kelsi bit into the side of her jaw until she tasted the
salty, metallic flavor of her own blood. Her hands were
locked into fists, and her vision clouded over in shades
of burgundy and red. Even as young as she was, what
the hell made Carlene think anyone wanted her albino
man? Kelsi wasn't even old enough to think about boys
her own age, much less a nasty-looking man like Took.*

*Her first night there, Kelsi tossed and turned. She
had never slept alone. She missed the scent of Nana's
butterscotch that comforted her every night because she
and Nana shared a pillow. Carlene hadn't even given
Kelsi a blanket, much less a pillow.*

*She slapped at her legs a hundred times through the
night. She felt needle-like pricks over and over again.
Scratching them seemed to make it worse. Kelsi finally
realized that bugs were biting her on the dirty mattress.
She got up and sat in the lone chair outside of the
kitchen. She used the milk crate to prop her feet up and
told herself she would sleep sitting up.*

*It seemed like as soon as she finally fell into a fitful
sleep, slouched to the side in the chair with her head on
the dirty plastic table, Carlene was standing over her.*

*"Get up, bitch! We got a appointment today!" Carlene
screamed, shaking Kelsi hard.*

*Dazed, Kelsi looked up. The smell hit her first. It was
like the nastiest underarm funk she had ever smelled in
her life. She blinked her eyes a few times to get them to
focus. They went wide. Carlene was damn near butt-ass
naked, wearing just a small camisole. Kelsi crinkled her
face and wanted to hide her eyes. Nana had never, ever*

let Kelsi see her naked. That was the first time Kelsi had ever seen a hairy pussy. She immediately closed her eyes.

"Bitch, I said get up! Now! I ain't gonna tell you again! I gotta be at a face to face in a few minutes, and you gotta be there too!" Carlene rasped, sounding like a monster.

Kelsi had no idea what Carlene was talking about. Nonetheless, she dragged herself up out of the chair. Her neck ached, and she could hardly turn it left or right. Kelsi had slept in her clothes because, of course, Carlene hadn't bothered to give her a pair of pajamas.

"I need a wash rag and towel," Kelsi mumbled to Carlene.

"Just wash your face with the one that's hanging in there. I gotta do laundry when we come back—if you hurry the fuck up and these people give me my check," Carlene grumbled in response.

The bathroom was worse than the rest of the house. Kelsi lifted her shirt over her nose as she surveyed how she would maneuver in that nasty-ass bathroom. The toilet seat was supposed to be light blue, but it was stained with yellow specks and brown streaks at the back. Behind the seat, on the white part, was hair, dirt, piss, and doo-doo stains.

Kelsi pulled her pants down and squatted over the toilet, trying to be careful not to have her skin come into contact with the toilet. She already knew from the day before that she wasn't so great at it. Again, some of the pee drizzled down her right leg and onto the back of her panties. To make matters worse, there was no toilet tissue. Carlene and Took had obviously been using newspaper and brown paper bags to wipe their asses. Kelsi wasn't doing that. She bounced a few times, hoping she could drip dry. She felt disgusting and wanted

*to take a shower badly. Nana had just let her start tak-
ing showers instead of sit-down baths when she turned
seven.*

*That idea quickly faded when Kelsi looked over at
the bathtub. "Yuck!" she whispered, frowning until her
cheeks hurt. The tub was black in the bottom, with rings
and rings of body dirt. It looked like it had not been
washed in years. The edges had old, caked-up soap
stains that would probably need a metal scraper to
remove. The wall tiles were black in between, and the
faucets were caked with green and gray stuff.*

*Kelsi turned back toward the sink and looked in the
stained mirror. Her hair was a mess, and her face had
red splotches on it. Bed bug bites. Her eyes were crusty
from the tears she had cried in her sleep.*

*She reached up for the lone face rag that hung stiffly
on the silver pole over the tub. She couldn't reach it,
so she had to step onto the tub for a boost. When she
snatched the rag down from the pole, she could tell if
it was dirty. It was so stiff it stayed bent in half like it
was still hanging on the pole even after she had it in her
hand. She swallowed hard, on the verge of hysterical
tears. She turned on the hot water and stuck the rag
under the stream. The water even seemed to repel from
that face rag.*

*Finally, she got it soft enough to wring it out. Kelsi
reluctantly put it up against her face to wipe away
the crust and sleep. She gagged. That rag stank like
somebody's ass. She threw it into the sink like it was a
poisonous snake.*

*Kelsi cupped her hands and splashed some water on
her face. She looked around and realized she had no
toothbrush. There was no toothpaste in sight, but a box
of baking soda on the back of the sink. Kelsi remembered
that sometimes she would watch Nana brush her teeth
with baking soda after using toothpaste.*

"That makes your teeth whiter," Nana told her once.

Kelsi decided to use the baking soda and her finger to brush her teeth. She pulled back the top on the baking soda.

"Ah!" she jumped and dropped the entire box on the floor. It was filled with so many roaches there was hardly any baking soda left. Tears immediately sprang to her eyes.

She jumped at the sound of Carlene banging on the door. Her heart thundered.

"C'mon, bitch! This ain't no fucking beauty pageant. Wash your face and let's go! If I miss this appointment, I gotta wait another four weeks for one," Carlene screamed from the other side of the door.

Kelsi felt hot all over. She cupped her hand again and got a little bit of water in her mouth. She swished it around and spit it out. She took some of Carlene's Royal Crown hair grease that sat on the back of the toilet and spread it on her face. That worked to get rid of the crusty streaks.

Kelsi came out of the bathroom, and Carlene was dressed and ready to go. She didn't even wash up.

Nasty, stink ass, *Kelsi said to herself. She would soon learn that Carlene was dirty in more ways than one.*

Kelsi and Carlene took two trains to get to Carlene's appointment. Kelsi fell asleep since she hadn't slept the night before. It was crazy how soothing the train was to Kelsi, even with all the strangers on it. The noise, the slight swaying motion, was comforting. Kelsi would take to the trains for comfort as she got older, too.

Kelsi was so hungry by the time they got to Carlene's appointment that she had a pounding headache. Her mouth had gone desert-sand dry, and her lips were cracked.

Carlene was bouncy and jittery like she had eaten a bag of sugar. "When we get inside, don't ask me for shit out that vending machine or nothing like that. Don't speak to nobody unless I tell you to, and I'll answer all the questions. You understand me, bitch?" Carlene told her, pointing a jittery finger in Kelsi's face like she had done something wrong.

Kelsi rolled her eyes. She'd become so ugly to Kelsi.

AID FOR DEPENDENT CHILDREN

Kelsi read the sign in her head. That was the line she and Carlene got on. They were far back on the line, too. There were so many people there. Kelsi counted at least eighteen pregnant ladies, and all of them had more kids with them, aside from the ones in their bellies. Some of them had little babies and were pregnant again, too. The line moved really slow as one name at a time was called.

Kelsi's legs and the bottom of her feet throbbed, on top of the drumbeat of pain pounding between her ears. She was dying to go sit on one of the dirty orange, yellow, or light blue chairs that were situated around the walls. There were no empty ones anyway.

It seemed like a lifetime before Carlene got to the lady behind the scratched-up Plexi-glass window.

"Yes, I have a face to face with my worker, Ms. Shelton, today. She needed to see my child in person to give me the food stamp and check increase," Carlene said, using the most proper English Kelsi had ever heard her speak in the few times she had gotten to see her in her life. "Jones is my name. Carlene. And this is my child, Kelsi."

The lady swirled her chair around, checked something, and turned back to the window. "Have a seat. Shelton got six before you. Your appointment was for nine o'clock. You late, you go to the bottom," the lady snarled like she had said the same line one hundred times that day.

Carlene let out a windstorm of breath. "Fuck!" Carlene grabbed Kelsi's arm roughly and pulled her into a corner. She flung Kelsi into the wall and turned into her. She was covering Kelsi from the crowd so no one could see the fear dancing in her widened eyes.

Kelsi couldn't understand what she had done wrong.

"Bitch, you see what the fuck you did taking all long? Now we gotta wait in here all fucking day. I was gonna buy you something to eat. Now you ain't gettin' shit," Carlene hissed, her breath smelling like a swirl of shit and cigarettes.

That was the first time Kelsi felt a ball of fire in her chest get a little bigger. She would come to learn as she got older that it was anger inside of her that was growing like a well-watered plant. With hunger pangs tearing her insides up and that fire in her chest, Kelsi pictured a thousand ways she could kill Carlene that day. She was eight at that time, but those thousand ways would multiply into millions as the years went by.

Now, Kelsi was pulled out of her miserable memories by someone pushing on the bedroom door. The door hit up against her back and snapped her back to reality. She slowly pulled herself up from the floor, her face covered in tears and her temples throbbing.

She stepped back from the door and stood in the middle of Cheyenne's bedroom helplessly. Big K rushed in and closed the door behind him. He rushed into her, grabbed her into his arms, and squeezed her tight.

"I've been wanting to give you a hug for days," he whispered directly into her ear. "I hate that I couldn't."

Kelsi stood stock still, her arms down at her side. She was mentally and physically exhausted by everything.

She could not respond to him. She couldn't think straight, her mind stuck in the past on things she'd tried to forget.

"What did the detective ask you?" Big K asked, finally pulling away from her so he could look into her eyes.

"About myself. About how I got caught up here," Kelsi droned, void of emotion, although she'd clearly been crying.

"And?" Big K pressed, his voice getting a bit stern.

"And all of this thinking back got me tired. I think you should get out of here before one of them comes back here," Kelsi said with a bit of authority in her tone.

"I'm here for you always. Remember that. We are here for each other," Big K said before he turned and left the room.

"Maybe that's the problem," Kelsi whispered after he was gone.

She walked over and fell onto the bed. Big K was the whole problem. She squeezed her eyes shut. The first time Kelsi had fallen in love, she was eight years old, and it was with him. It was love. Real love. The only thing Kelsi could equate with man-and-woman love. It was different than the love she had felt for Nana. That's how she knew that although she was a little kid, she was in man-and-woman love with her best friend's father. Kelsi knew it because when he was around her back then, her palms would sweat, her heart would race, and she could always feel her cheeks flaming over. By the time Kelsi was nine, she could even feel something tingling between her legs around him. It was not the kind of tingling that hurt like when someone who wasn't supposed to touch you there touched you.

Of course, he didn't know she was in love with him. She'd never told him. To him, she was just a kid. A kid who had become his daughter's best friend. A kid who he knew came from a fucked-up home and needed love and protection like a charity case.

Kevin "Big K" Turner had saved Kelsi's life and was the first man to ever give a fuck about her. So, she secretly loved him in return. She loved his coffee-bean brown skin, low-cut hair, deep-set shiny eyes, and the way he dressed and walked. He was the man in the neighborhood. Back then, Big K had been the only person Kelsi ever associated with real love, aside from Nana.

Kelsi cried into the material of her pillow. It was all she could do to keep herself from losing her mind.

Chapter 9

Brice

"I got her legs. You hold her arms," Earl instructed as their classmate fought under his strength.

"C'mon, sissy-ass nigga. Get ya dick out and fuck this bitch!" Earl screamed.

Brice stood stock still. The three other boys were screaming at him to hurry up. He fumbled with his zipper, his hands shaking. Brice gulped the golf ball–sized lump at the back of his throat and moved toward the girl. She was flailing futilely, no match for their strength.

"Fuck her, fuck her, fuck her!" the others chanted. It was like something out of a movie.

Brice could hear Earl's Eddie Murphy–sounding laugh. It made Brice's ears ring. He climbed up on the bed, the girl's legs already forcefully spread, waiting for him. He prepared to enter her against her will.

"Brice?"

The girl's strangled voice sent chills down his back. It was a voice he recognized very well.

"Brice? Brice? Brice?"

Brice jumped up from his sleep in a huff. His chest rose and fell like someone was pumping it up and down. His head pounded, as usual. The same recurring nightmare he'd been battling for years now was back for some reason. Brice was still convinced that all his work as a homicide detective was somehow the karmic consequences of the worst thing he'd ever done in his life—participating in the rape of one of his classmates back in the day.

Every case Brice had worked since, especially the Arianna Coleman case, had drawn out this nightmare. Now, with the cold-blooded murder of an innocent woman in his hands, Brice was right back where he'd started from. He still prayed that one day God would forgive him for what he'd done and free him of reliving it over and over again.

In the dark of his bedroom, Brice squinted and felt around on his nightstand for his cell phone to check the time—3 a.m. He rubbed his hands across his face and sighed. Brice had called his therapist the day before to make an emergency appointment. Noon couldn't come fast enough.

Brice hadn't brought himself to have the talk with Ciara yet. In fact, he'd been avoiding her, dreading the tension that had developed after she said she was moving to Vietnam. Brice's mother had been calling him non-stop about it. Maybe his worry was part of what had brought the nightmare back again.

Closing his eyes, he tried to go back to sleep. Who was he fooling? Brice knew he wasn't going back to sleep. He untangled himself from his bedsheets and sat up. He scrubbed his hands over his face again and picked up his phone, noticing a missed call from Cheyenne Turner's number.

"How did I miss this?" he grumbled, his own morning breath assailing his nostrils. He looked at the time again. There was no way he could return her call now. He'd have to wait for a decent hour.

The last time he'd spoke to Cheyenne, she said she was going to track down her brother and make him come in to speak with Brice. It hadn't happened. Everyone in the family needed to be questioned. Brice had made that clear the first time he'd spoken to them.

Brice was still a bit unsettled after speaking to Kelsi Jones. She'd painted the picture that there was definite trouble in paradise between Desiree and Kevin Turner. Kelsi had also told Brice that Lil Kev was in trouble with some dangerous people in the streets who might've exacted revenge on his mother while trying to send him a message.

Brice didn't know what to believe. So far, he had a dead mother and wife who lived her life right, a husband fresh out of prison, crazy with jealousy and accusing her of cheating with an unknown man who drove a BMW, a son in the drug game with enemies piling up, and a daughter who was too distraught to know anything except that her mother didn't deserve to be murdered.

Brice realized he hadn't had a chance to verify with Cheyenne anything that other family members had told him or do any more street reconnaissance. But not being able to sleep was a sure way to get some work done on the case.

Brice walked over to his desk and grabbed the case file folder. He flopped into his computer chair, clicked on the desk light, and read over the notes he'd taken during Kelsi's interview. Brice replayed some of the things she'd said and compared it to some of the things Cheyenne had told him. They'd both made statements that had raised the hairs on Brice's neck.

"Things with my parents changed after my father choked Lil Kev one day. With my brother gone from the house, probably for good, my mother and father argued incessantly. Kelsi and I had no choice but to listen," Cheyenne had said to Brice.

"I think you need to look into someone at her job that drove a BMW," Kelsi had told Brice. "I heard them. They argued about it a couple of weeks ago," Kelsi had continued. "Big K and Ms. Desi, they argued about it. About her getting rides in a BMW. It was loud and angry, but it was clear what the issue was—and that was it."

Now, Brice tapped his pen against the paper. Cheyenne had said that her father was different after he came home, but she hadn't gone into much detail. She'd also mentioned a few times that things with her brother had been very tense in the house.

Brice needed to know more about the Lil Kev angle of all of this. What if someone in the streets did shoot Desiree Turner down as a message to her son? Or what if he shot his own mother?

When Brice arrived at the Lafayette Gardens projects to check for Lil Kev, he already knew from speaking to Pop what to expect. This was Scorpio's stronghold, and he had the youngins out on the streets for him. Brice expected dirty looks and even some flex when he pulled up. Those young street hustlers didn't take kindly to strangers pulling up on them, especially in a darkly tinted SUV. Brice knew that could get him shot. Still, he felt for his weapon, blew out a breath, and got out of his truck.

Brice felt the heat of many eyes on him as he entered one of the buildings. He always had to steel himself when he went into the projects. For one, it took him back to a place in his childhood that he hated to think about. Second, Brice thought the inside of the buildings were worse than he'd ever remembered when he lived in the projects. It seemed like with each passing generation, the tenants cared less and less about the living conditions, and the city cared even less than the residents about keeping the buildings in livable condition.

Brice pushed through the bullet-hole-riddled front doors and stepped into the lobby. Several young dudes hanging around eyed him evilly. Brice was used to their type. He'd been working and living the streets of Brooklyn long enough to have seen all the wannabe gangsters he could take.

Brice nodded at the fake tough guys but didn't smile. His stoic face was the signal for *I'm cool, but I'll fuck you up if you try something.* Brice pressed for the elevator and looked around. Times had changed, and not for the better. The walls of the lobby were spray-painted with profanities, and all the mailboxes were missing their covers. Someone had taken a piss in the far left corner of the lobby. Brice shook his head in disgust. Even the working-class people that lived there had to suffer at the hands of the few that didn't care about their surroundings.

Brice had found out from Kelsi that her ex-boyfriend, Scorpio, kept an apartment in the building on the eighth floor for his crew of workers, one of whom was Kevin Turner, Jr. Kelsi had told Brice that more than likely he'd find Lil Kev at the apartment since he was on the hook to Scorpio.

Brice touched his gun to make sure it was there and was in the right proximity for a quick pull-out if he needed it. He took a deep breath and prepared for the unknown. He was wading in uncharted waters, which wasn't something that often ended up happening on his cases.

Arriving on the eighth floor, Brice used the door knocker for apartment 8G. He was out alone, no backup, no one alerted about his location. Risky, to say the least. Brice wasn't really on a police visit, per se, so he knocked like a regular person and not with authority like the police.

"Who the fuck is that?" a male voice boomed from the other side.

"Simp," Brice responded as if the person on the other side of the door knew him already.

"Who? Who the fuck—"

Brice heard bolts and locks clicking open. When the young guy pulled back the door, Brice came face to face with the long barrel of a big, silver handgun.

"Who the fuck is you? What the fuck you want?" he snarled.

"Whoa, whoa," Brice said, putting his hands up and noticing how hard his heart was ramming into his chest wall. Brice's eyes instinctively darted around, and his police brain started thinking about takedown methods and how fast he could get his gun before the guy would even be able to get a shot off.

"I said, who the fuck is you? And what the fuck you want? Hurry up, nigga, before you eat this lead," the young dude barked, his face scrunched tight.

"Put the gun down. I'm looking for Lil Kev," Brice said, keeping his voice level. "I don't care about nothing else y'all got going on in here."

"That nigga ain't here," the dude replied, lowering his gun slightly. "And who the fuck you think you are coming here like you five-o? *I'm looking for Lil Kev*," the young dude mocked.

"Look, my dude," Brice started.

"I ain't none of your fucking dude, nigga. Now, get the fuck from around here before I spill your brains out in this hallway," the young guy threatened.

"I'm a friend of his family. His mother just got killed, and I need to see him," Brice pressed on, unfazed by the fake tough guy in front of him.

They stared at each other for a few seconds. Brice looked over the guy's shoulder into the apartment. He saw a few underage girls drinking and partying, some weed on the table, a scale, and a few stacks of money. Brice shook his head, suddenly understanding why the kid might've been so on edge.

"Look, I'm here for Lil Kev, and Lil Kev alone. I don't give a fuck what y'all got going on inside there. I need to speak to him, and I'm not leaving until I do. Now, if you don't want all types of heat swarming this motherfucker in a minute, call Lil Kev or let me inside," Brice said, his tone stern and authoritative. He wasn't backing down. He was hoping he didn't have to pull out on this dude. Brice's new way of handling things was much different than the old Brice. Still, he started counting in his head—*ten, nine, eight, seven . . .*

"Look, I'll see what the fuck I can do. I ain't making no promises," the young dude said and then turned around. *Mistake number one: turning your back on somebody you don't know. Dumb ass*, Brice thought. If he was a robber, the young dude would've just gotten got.

"Yo, bitch, go call Lil Kev. Tell him he got a visitor and this pain-in-the-ass nigga ain't leaving," the dude called to one of the young girls inside.

Brice bit into his jaw. He immediately thought about his sister and what he would do to a young punk if he talked to Ciara that way.

The guy walked into the apartment and prepared to slam the door on Brice.

Brice stuck his foot in the way. "I'ma wait right here for Lil Kev," Brice said firmly. He and the young dude locked eyes and held the stare until the dude finally relented. "Don't be a tough guy. I already told you, I don't want nothing you got going on," Brice warned.

Brice heard some hard talking coming from inside the apartment, and the girl who'd been sent to get Lil Kev came running back to the front.

"That nigga is angry for no reason," she huffed, holding her head. "Nigga just going to slap me for no reason. I didn't want his ass no way," she complained.

"I fucking told y'all no fucking visitors. Don't call me out here for shit. Fuck don't y'all understand?" Lil Kev barked as he made his way toward the door. When he came upon Brice, he paused.

"Who the fuck are you?" Lil Kev asked, screwing up his face at Brice.

"Why don't you step outside and let me holla at you?" Brice replied, tilting his head knowingly. "This is about your mother."

Lil Kev sucked his teeth, but Brice saw something change in his eyes.

"My mother is dead, so ain't nothing you can tell me," Lil Kev snapped, but he still followed Brice into the hallway.

Brice looked him up and down for a second. He could tell Lil Kev wanted to be harder than he really was.

"I'm Detective Simpson, Kevin," Brice said, extending his hand.

Lil Kev ignored the gesture and sighed loudly. "I knew your ass was five-o. I told the cops before I don't know shit. You think if I knew who did that shit to my moms, I'd be still walking the streets? Nah, I would be locked up for killing a nigga," Lil Kev spat.

"I'm hearing you had a big blowup with your parents right before your mother's murder," Brice said, taking in another eyeful of the victim's son.

"You heard wrong, nigga," Lil Kev shot back. "I ain't even been around since my mother's husband been back. I don't fuck with that nigga. Period."

"I get that, but people are saying you made some enemies that might've wanted to get back at you, so they might've harmed your mother," Brice replied.

"Nah. The thing is, we don't extend to parents and children like that. A nigga got beef with me, he just going to take me down. Not my moms," Lil Kev said, boldly looking Brice right in the eye.

Brice felt more sincerity from Lil Kev than he had from any of the other family members except Kelsi. But he still wasn't going to rule him out. He made a mental note to himself to put a car on Lil Kev.

"I know how it is in the street, but not everybody plays by the rules," Brice reminded Lil Kev. Brice looked him up and down again, and something caught his eye.

"How'd you get that blood on your boot?" Brice asked, staring down at Lil Kev's Timberland boots.

"I had a nosebleed, nigga. What you trying to say? I would harm my own moms?" Lil Kev shot back. "A'ight, I'm done talking to you. You full of shit," Lil Kev said, starting for the apartment door.

Brice grabbed Lil Kev's arm and gripped it painfully tight. "I promised your sister I would find out who killed your mother, and that's what I intend to do. You can play hardball all you want, but if you know what happened or who did this to her and you don't say shit, you'll have to live with that the rest of your miserable fucking life. I grew up with dudes just like you—young, dumb, thought they were tough and badass, and you know where those niggas are? Huh? Pushing up fucking daisies or sitting behind bars, old and fucked up with nothing.

"Think about what I'm saying to you. Your mother would've died in vain if you don't stop acting tough and get your life together. You and your sister need to stick together more than ever now," Brice said through clenched teeth.

Lil Kev yanked his arm away and turned his back on Brice, but before he went into the apartment, and without turning back around, he said, "If you want to check out anybody, you need to look into her husband. He ain't none of my pops, but I don't trust that nigga. He been in the streets looking for a come-up. Tink about how much of a come-up he would get if my mother left him anything. Now, go investigate that shit," Lil Kev said. With that, he pushed into the apartment door so hard it banged open. He wasted no time slamming the door in Brice's face.

Brice rushed out of the elevator and back to his truck. He fumbled with his cell phone because his hands shook so badly.

"Michelle," Brice huffed when the medical examiner picked up the line.

"Detective Simpson, I left you a message days ago," she said, sounding annoyed.

"Sorry for the wait. Life and work collide sometimes," Brice responded.

"Well, we got back all the information. Like we suspected, your victim was in near perfect health. Death was caused by a bullet that pierced the heart. Lucille and the forensics folks have other news on the footprint," Michelle relayed, pausing.

"Yeah, and?" Brice asked, curling his toes up in his sneakers.

"Looks like it was about a size 9 men's Timberland boot," Michelle said in her official voice. "I have the pictures of the imprint and the scientific reports. As you know, that brand, although the bottoms look the same, they're not. There are unique characteristics to each boot's bottom pattern. So, now it's up to you to find the missing boot, because that's where you'll find your killer."

"Damn," Brice mumbled. His mind raced in a thousand directions. He'd just witnessed Lil Kev wearing Timberland boots and saw blood splatter on them. Brice knew getting his hands on the boots now would be impossible without some help.

Brice drove back to the squad like a madman. He needed to draft a search warrant for the apartment where Lil Kev was holed up. He needed to get his hands on those boots.

Brice's heart pumped so fast he could hardly contain his breathing. He rushed to his desk, dialed a number, and started whispering into the mouthpiece. He needed to call in a fast favor. Search warrants were a process, and they took time, something Brice felt like he didn't have at this point.

Brice sat at his desk, going over more things from the case. He'd reviewed the things found on Desiree Turner when she was murdered. He'd linked the BMW to a doctor at the hospital.

Brice felt a flash of heat in his chest when he researched Dr. Drew MacIntosh, a married surgeon with three children. Brice had spoken to a few staff members at the hospital, and they'd all admitted to suspecting that Dr. MacIntosh and Desiree had something going on. Brice marked his name as a potential person of interest, but he hadn't gotten to him yet.

As Brice jotted notes at his desk, he looked up to find another detective watching him. *Not again,* Brice said to himself. The last detective that had been overly concerned with his case and his work ended up being a co-conspirator on the huge sex trafficking ring that had captured Brice's sister.

Brice was about to question the other detective when his cell phone vibrated in his pocket.

"Hello?" Brice answered. "Wait, calm down! Ma, wait. . . . What ? I'm coming," Brice huffed, scrambling up from his desk. Between work and home, Brice felt like his head would explode.

Chapter 10

Brice

Brice was exhausted by the time he finished breaking up the fight between his mother and his sister. Things had gone far, and Brice had decided that Ciara needed to get out of his mother's house. Things had escalated, but Brice kept his cool when she ran off. He had no choice. She was an adult now. Brice stayed until his mother's valium set in and she fell off to sleep. He didn't know anymore how he was going to navigate being caught between his mother and his sister. It was getting to be a bit much.

Brice drove his truck to his house and pulled in front. The sky was dark, and he could barely see the front of his house.

"What the fuck happened to the light?" Brice grumbled as he moved the cone that he used to save his parking spot.

He climbed back into the SUV to park it in the spot. As Brice put the truck into park, he noticed a shadowy figure running away from his front door. Fear caused adrenaline to pump through his veins, despite all the training he'd received. He reached under his jacket for his weapon.

Brice frantically swung the SUV door open and exited, sliding on a slick spot of oil on the street. "Fuck," he huffed.

Getting his balance, Brice rushed toward his house, gun in hand, but it was too late. The dark figure disappeared down the street.

With his chest heaving in and out, Brice swallowed hard and slowly approached his gaping front door with caution.

What the fuck?

The only sound Brice could hear was his own heavy breathing. Moving methodically, Brice dipped his head in and out of the doorway as if he were bobbing for apples. He didn't see anyone inside.

With his gun out in front of him, he slowly moved inside. With his back against a wall, he dipped in one more time. He didn't see anyone. Brice cleared himself to enter, all the while maintaining a two-handed grip on his weapon.

Once he felt the immediate area was clear, he stuck his hand inside and clicked on the light in the foyer. Inching around inside the house, making sure to keep his back against the walls, Brice searched his entire house. Nothing. He exhaled a windstorm of breath and relaxed a little bit.

"The fuck?" Brice cursed aloud, confused about how someone would've gotten through the locks on his doors, and even more confused about who would want to break into his house.

He shoved his gun back into his holster and walked back toward the front door. Just as he rounded the corner from his living room, he bumped into someone.

"Whoa!" Brice yelped and jumped, reaching for his weapon and aiming.

The person he'd bumped into let out a small scream and put his hands up over his head.

"Mr. P, what the hell? You scared me. I could've shot you," Brice gasped, placing his gun back in the holster.

Although he would've clearly had the upper hand, Brice was completely unnerved by the entire encounter.

"I heard you yelling down the street, and I saw that person running from your house. They ran over my fence," Brice's neighbor said, his voice shaky.

"Did you see what he or she looked like?" Brice inquired. "Or when they got here? Were they alone? Man or woman?"

"I didn't see the face, but I believe it was a man," Mr. P informed. "Looked like a bad character with one of them hoodies on. You know the kind they use to commit crimes."

Brice turned his face so Mr. P couldn't see his expression. He thought his neighbor's comment about hoodies was a very white thing to say. For all Brice knew, Mr. P would've considered him a criminal if he hadn't found out Brice was a police detective.

"Thanks, Mr. P. If you see anything else, call 911. Just keep your doors locked," Brice said, slowly ushering his neighbor out the door.

Brice stood in his doorway and watched his old neighbor shuffle to his house and into his home. Brice let out a long, exasperated sigh.

With Mr. P safely inside his house, Brice walked back to his SUV. Bending into the passenger-side door, he retrieved all the Turner case files. As he lifted the stack of papers, a picture slipped out from one of the folders. A cold chill shot through Brice's body like someone had pumped ice water into his veins. Even in the dark, the person in the picture seemed eerily familiar. He picked up the picture and examined it closely. Brice shook his head from side to side and rushed inside the house.

Brice threw all the assignment information on his bed and spread it out. He started undressing, deciding that a hot shower and a drink was what he needed more than anything.

As Brice pulled his holster from his waist, his mind started putting a lot of things together.

"The killer has to be someone who knows me. They're following me," Brice whispered, grabbing the folders. Sitting down on his bed, he started going over what he'd learned from every single person interviewed about Desiree Turner's murder.

"I'm going to find you, and when I do, you're going to pay for what you did," Brice murmured. He had a brand-new fervor to catch the killer.

Chapter 11

Cheyenne

Cheyenne looked at herself in the long mirror behind her bedroom door. The black funeral dress she wore hung off of her. She'd lost at least ten pounds since her mother's murder. Cheyenne stared at her reflection, and the sadness in her eyes glared back at her. She shook her head as the tears started up again.

Her mind went to another place. Cheyenne had thought the saddest day of her life was the day she left for medical school in Texas, but here she was preparing to attend her mother's funeral.

Still, she remembered the sadness she'd felt. Cheyenne had decided to leave Brooklyn amid all the turmoil going on in her house at that time. She couldn't stand to see her parents at odds all the time. Her father had turned into an angry, bitter person, which was not how she wanted to remember him. Her mother had retreated into her work, and on the rare occasions that she was home, she didn't speak much. Lil Kev had completely moved out of the house. He would see them occasionally, but only when he knew their father wouldn't be around. Cheyenne couldn't stand knowing that the streets had taken hold of Lil Kev's life. Their mother had worked hard to make sure they'd turn out better than that.

Back then, Kelsi was in deep with her boyfriend, Scorpio, and on the low, she was still making sure her mother, no-good-ass Peaches, had food to survive.

Cheyenne felt she didn't have anywhere to fit in all that chaos. Most days, she felt lost, like she didn't belong anywhere. She would throw herself into her schoolwork, but since she had graduated from undergrad, she had even lost that. The decision to leave for medical school hadn't been that hard once she weighed her options—go away to med school or stay in the projects and deal with everyone else's drama.

"I'm going to miss you, Chey," Kelsi said, swiping at her tears angrily like she wanted to beat herself up for crying.

Cheyenne threw a folded pile of clothes into her big purple suitcase without looking at her.

"When you've been with someone every single day for years—which is most of our lives—you can't even imagine yourself one day without them," Kelsi continued.

Cheyenne stopped putting things in her suitcase and turned toward her best friend. "I love you so much, Kels. I'm going to make this doctor thing happen so our lives can be better. You will always be my sister. No amount of distance can ever change that," she said through tears.

Kelsi broke down. She flopped back on her bed and sobbed. Her shoulders quaked as she let the wracking sobs take over. Cheyenne sat next to her, pulled her up, slid her arm around Kelsi's shoulder, and cried right along with her.

Lil Kev didn't come to see Cheyenne off, but he sent one of his cronies with a package for her. She slid it into her oversized carry-on bag and decided she would open it when she got to the airport that day.

Her father didn't come to the airport either. Cheyenne was glad because the tension between her father and mother was enough to make Cheyenne want to throw up every time.

Kelsi decided to stay back as well. She told Cheyenne there was no way she could see her disappear into the airport and not lose it. They both joked that Kelsi would've screamed so loud the airport security would've hog-tied her and carried her away like a terrorist.

It was Cheyenne and her mother alone who made the trip to the airport that day. Her mother hired a cab service to take them to John F. Kennedy Airport. They left home two hours early so that her mother would have time to sit with her before she went through security. Once Cheyenne was checked in, she and her mother found a little restaurant that was right outside of security. Cheyenne didn't have much of an appetite.

Her mother's eyes were so sad. "I'm surely going to miss you. My baby's first time away from her mother in her life." She let out a windstorm of breath. "I can't believe you have grown up so fast," she said, dabbing at her tears with the cloth napkin from the table.

"Ma, I thought we wasn't going to do the sappy thing," Cheyenne complained. She had cried enough for one day.

Her mother put her hand up and smiled. She sniffled back her snot and wiped the last of her tears. "Okay, okay. I did promise. I'm just telling you how I feel, baby. One last thing—just know I am so proud of you that if I could afford to write it in the sky, I would. You are the strongest little girl on the planet, and I know you'll make me proud. There is nothing in this world that can match my love for you. I don't want you to think about anything going on at home. Just work hard and become the best doctor on the planet," her mother preached before the waitress interrupted them to ask for their orders.

Cheyenne didn't reply to her mother's touching speech because she didn't want to cry anymore.

***

Now, as she stared at herself in the mirror, Cheyenne felt a flash of anger in her chest. Why hadn't she replied? She should have thanked her mother for her kind words. She should have said something in response to how sweet her mother had been that day. Cheyenne bit down on her lip until she drew blood. She was angry at herself. She'd had no way of knowing that would be the last face-to-face conversation she would have with her mother. She thought about what she would've and should've told her mother:

"No, Ma, you are the strongest person I know on earth. You came from the bottom, and you made it all work for you. You are one of the most influential women in the world, and if I could, I would get on every media outlet in the world, on top of every mountain, and anywhere people could hear me and say my mother, Desiree A. Turner, is the most remarkable woman on the planet, and I love her more than life itself!"

That's what she would've said to her mother had she ever gotten the chance to see her beautiful face again. But instead, Cheyenne had been robbed of that opportunity.

Cheyenne jumped and whirled around in response to loud knocks on her bedroom door.

"Chey, baby girl, you ready?" her father called from the other side of the door.

Cheyenne breathed out loudly. She wanted to be alone; that's really what she wanted. She moved slowly to her door and pulled it open.

"You look good, baby girl," her father commented.

"You too," she said back, barely above a whisper. "Still no word from Lil Kev?" she asked.

"You know I wouldn't know that. You know how things are," her father replied, shoving his hands deep into his suit pockets like he didn't know what to do with them.

Cheyenne could hear the distress in his tone whenever he had to discuss Lil Kev. She shook her head.

It only took three weeks after her father came home for shit to hit the fan with her brother. Lil Kev came in the house with his key one night after being gone for more than a week. Their mother was in the kitchen. Kelsi and Cheyenne were in the bedroom, gossiping. Her mother's screams erupted loudly through the apartment, causing Cheyenne and Kelsi to run out to see what was going on.

"No! Kevin! Oh God! No!" her mother belted out.

Kelsi and Cheyenne scrambled to the front of the apartment.

"Let him go!" her mother screeched just as Kelsi and Cheyenne rounded the corner into the living room.

That's when Cheyenne saw it. Her father had Lil Kev down on the couch, choking him with one hand around his neck.

"Daddy! Daddy!" Cheyenne screamed, rushing over to the heap of bodies.

"You want to act tough? Huh, huh? I'm going to show you tough. I ain't these boys out in the street. I'm a man that just did twelve years with real motherfuckers that did real things on these streets. You ain't so fucking tough now, Junior," her father growled as he clamped down harder and harder on Lil Kev's neck.

Lil Kev was making a low hissing noise. Cheyenne could tell his oxygen was completely cut off. Kelsi tried pulling one of her father's arms, and Cheyenne tried to push his massive body.

Her mother was screaming, but Cheyenne couldn't understand what she was saying in the chaos. Lil Kev had turned a sickening shade of burgundy. Cheyenne knew her father was powerful enough to take the life right out of Lil Kev's scrawny body.

"Big K, please. Please let him go. I don't know if I could take you being gone again," Kelsi said soothingly.

Even amid the chaos, Cheyenne looked at Kelsi strangely. Something inside of Cheyenne felt weird. She couldn't place it. Besides, there was just so much going on, she just shook off the feeling.

Her father finally slowly released his grip on Lil Kev's neck. Lil Kev rolled onto the floor, holding his neck. He coughed and wheezed, trying to get his lungs to fill up with air.

Big K stood over her brother. Her father's chest rose and fell rapidly, and his fists were curled so tight his knuckles paled. "Now, li'l nigga, the next time I speak to you nicely, you speak to me nicely. I can't make up for the lost time, but that don't mean I'm going to be disrespected by my own youngin'," her father huffed, his nostrils flaring. He began walking to the back of the apartment.

Her mother rushed over to Lil Kev. "Kevin? Kevin? C'mon, baby, it's okay. It's okay," she comforted as she lifted Lil Kev's head and put him in a position she said would help oxygen go to his brain faster.

Cheyenne went completely silent. She was in shock. She had never seen her father get violent in her life. After he was locked up, Cheyenne had heard stories about how notorious her father was on the streets, but at home, he had been nothing like that. Cheyenne knew then that time and circumstances had changed everything. From that day forward, she realized that her father was definitely a changed man.

Chapter 12

Cheyenne

Cheyenne held onto her father's arm as they approached the front doors of the funeral home. She kept her head hung low to avoid all the flashing news cameras. She was already disgusted that the news media was still invading her family's private moments. They'd posted up outside of their building for the first couple of days after her mother's murder. Here it was, almost two weeks later, and they were still following the story. Cheyenne understood that her mother's murder was a big topic on the news—a well-loved nurse, mother, and wife gunned down right in the hospital's parking lot. The crime had shocked the city for a few weeks, but this was way over the top, in her opinion. The cameras and reporters wanted a story, making no exception for grieving relatives.

"Mr. Turner! Mr. Turner! Have they named any suspects yet?" a member of the news media yelled.

Cheyenne cringed as she dodged through the huddle of photographers.

"Cheyenne! Did the police look into your brother yet? Is it true he might be a suspect?" another shouted.

"Please," Cheyenne grumbled as she held her arm up to shield her face from the camera.

"Mr. Turner, was your wife having an affair? Did you know about a doctor she might've been dating? Were you two on good terms when she died?"

Cheyenne flinched at the questions being hurled at her father. She was clearly more uncomfortable with the experience than her father, who seemed unfazed by the disgusting accusations.

"Mr. Turner, most people would say the husband is the first suspect in cases like this. Would you agree?"

Finally, Cheyenne had had enough. She stopped walking and turned toward the harassing reporters, her face twisted into a scowl. "This is my mother's funeral! Have some decency and respect, for God's sake! This is not about a scandalous story for your ratings. Why don't you find someplace else to find gossip to hurl? Give us some peace. You people have no shame!" Cheyenne spat, scolding the story-hungry crowd of reporters crowding the doors right outside of the funeral home.

She regretted her decision to go through the front entrance of the funeral home. She should have known this would happen. She had decided at the last minute not to use the back entrance because she was hoping she'd see her brother out front. He had still been scarce around the house and hadn't checked up on her much.

"Chey, don't worry about what these people are saying. We know the truth," her father said, noticing the new tears that had sprung to her eyes and the distraught scowl on her face.

Cheyenne's legs felt like two lead poles as she pulled away from her father and slowly walked into the funeral home. The hairs at the back of her neck stood up, and the dress she wore suddenly felt itchy against her skin. The smell of embalming chemicals and flowers mixed with strong female perfumes made Cheyenne's stomach swirl with nausea. She quietly sucked in her breath as she moved farther into the large chapel room.

From the doorway, she could see the purple-and-gold casket in the center of the altar. One ray of light shone from the ceiling, illuminating the beautiful box so that it glowed angelically. The area around her mother's casket was surrounded by hundreds of flowers—roses, daisies, hydrangeas, and lilies.

Cheyenne's skin was riddled with goose bumps. She wrapped her arms around her chest and hugged herself for warmth. Losing her mother had to be the worst thing God could allow to happen to her. In Cheyenne's eyes, she didn't deserve that kind of punishment.

Her father had let her walk ahead of him. Cheyenne turned around and saw him standing at the back of the room with his hands shoved deep into his pants pockets. Cheyenne was kind of glad. She just wanted to go up to the casket alone. She didn't want to keep feeling responsible for everyone's emotions.

Cheyenne moved her head around and let her eyes scan the huge room for a few seconds. There had to be over one hundred people in attendance. She was looking for Kelsi, Lil Kev, or any other familiar face. She walked a little farther inside and spotted her roommate, Amber, sitting on the front pew, sandwiched between Ms. Lula and another one of their neighbors, Ms. Arlene. Cheyenne didn't see Lil Kev or Kelsi anywhere. She had expected both of them would be front and center.

"Hey," Cheyenne whispered, bending down to hug Amber. Both of the neighbors moved aside a few inches to give Cheyenne a little room to fit in.

"Hey, girl. You all right?" Amber replied.

"I'm just maintaining. Thank you for coming, Amber," Cheyenne answered. Her voice could barely be heard. It was raw and hoarse. Cheyenne had lost her voice from screaming, and it had never fully come back.

"I wouldn't miss it. You know that," Amber said softly.

Cheyenne lifted her sunglasses and dabbed at her eyes with a crumpled tissue. "It's just so unfair. She didn't deserve this. I will keep saying it. My brother is so angry with everyone, but we need to stick together right now. It's my fault, you know." Cheyenne began sobbing until her whole body rocked. "It's all my fault, Amber," she cried.

Amber couldn't hold her tears back either. The floodgates had been opened, and Amber and Cheyenne rode the waves together. Amber sniffled.

"It was not your fault. No one blames you, Cheyenne. There was no way you could've known or prevented this." Amber comforted her, rubbing Cheyenne's back soothingly.

Cheyenne leaned over and put her head on Amber's shoulder. They both sobbed together for a few minutes before her father interrupted. He still wore a stoic expression and squared jaw, which told everyone he was trying hard to contain his emotions.

"I'll sit here with her. I got her. She will be okay. . . . She has me," her father said, touching Cheyenne's shoulders and wedging his way between Cheyenne and Amber on the chapel bench. Amber moved her arm from Cheyenne's shoulder and backed off.

Something came over Cheyenne when her father did that. She seemed to grow angry and sick at the same time. He'd been hovering around her since she'd come home, but today, she craved her own space. She wanted time to grieve and think.

She bolted up from the bench and stumbled down the long aisle toward the exit. She shook her head. She didn't know what had overcome her. It was like her mother was there, touching her, telling her to get away from everyone. Cheyenne felt her mother's spirit in the room, and suddenly she couldn't stomach anyone else.

As she made her way to the exit, she was still scanning the room for Kelsi or Lil Kev. How could they not be the first people in the room after all her mother had done for them?

Suddenly, Cheyenne's eyes landed on a familiar face. A flash of panic and anger exploded in the center of her chest. Her eyes hooded over, and her jaw began to rock.

You finally show up here, and this is how you look? Fucking asshole little boy!

Cheyenne forged straight ahead in Lil Kev's direction. He tried to quickly avert his eyes, but it was too late. Cheyenne set her jaw and adjusted her dark shades. She turned her head to the left, pretending not to notice his little crew flanking him on both sides and coming her way.

"Sis!" Lil Kev called loudly, flashing a smile.

Cheyenne's eyebrows immediately lowered in scorn. She looked over her shoulder behind her and then back at her brother. Cheyenne couldn't believe Lil Kev was acting like shit was all good with them. She couldn't believe he didn't have on a black suit. She couldn't believe he had the audacity to crack a smile. Cheyenne's insides roiled with anger.

Is he really doing this like this? Is he crazy? Drunk? Stupid? Cheyenne stared at her brother like he had two heads. She walked up on him, her teeth clenched.

"Lil Kev, don't make a scene. Pay respects to Mommy, and don't start no shit," Cheyenne whispered harshly, close enough to his ear for him to hear it directly. With that, Cheyenne attempted to walk past her brother without causing too much of a scene. A funeral was not the time or the place to start a fight.

"Make a scene?" Lil Kev continued loudly, holding onto Cheyenne's arm, preventing her forward progress. His audacity knew no bounds. "Don't act like you better than me. I'll blow this whole scene the fuck up," he snarled.

Cheyenne could see in Lil Kev's eyes that something wasn't right. He could barely stand still. Maybe it was plain nervous energy, but Cheyenne suspected something else. The brother she knew would have never acted like this at his own mother's funeral.

"Let go of me and stop it," Cheyenne said through clenched teeth, wrestling her arm away from Lil Kev's grasp. She could feel several pairs of eyes on them now.

"Come on, bro. You need to be easy. Five-o up in here and mad news. We don't need the heat, bro. It ain't worth it." A young guy stepped out from behind Lil Kev and grabbed him, moving him back from Cheyenne's face.

Cheyenne shot the dude an evil glare. This was really not the time or place for this. Some people would never have class, regardless of how they were raised.

"What's going on over here?" her father said, stepping onto the scene.

"Nothing, Daddy. Keep calm," Cheyenne said, darting her eyes back toward Lil Kev. She shook her head in disgust. She didn't want anything to do with either of them.

"Just stay away from him and let things be. I'm going to lose it if Mommy's funeral is disrupted," Cheyenne whispered harshly before she stormed off.

Cheyenne's chest was heaving by the time she made it to the lobby.

How dare he act like this at a time like this? How dare he try to make a scene? And his little friends . . . those bastards. Cheyenne fumed. She paced the floor, stopping only to look at her watch. Her father had followed her to the lobby, standing nearby. She was so angry and worked up, she completely ignored his presence.

"Where the hell is Kelsi?" Cheyenne muttered under her breath. It wasn't like Kelsi to be this late, especially to something like this. Cheyenne dug around in her purse for her phone but was distracted by a few of Lil Kev's cronies coming out of the funeral chapel. They looked like they were up to no good. Cheyenne shook her head.

"Cheyenne," Detective Simpson called out from behind. She whirled around so fast she almost toppled over in her heels. The tension in her forehead eased, and she exhaled.

Thank God! A friendly face!

"Hello," Cheyenne said, smiling awkwardly. "I'm happy to see that you cared enough to come," Cheyenne huffed, extending her hand for a shake. She was clearly flustered and overly emotional, but equally as happy to see Detective Simpson. He'd been in contact a few times but hadn't given Cheyenne any updates on the case.

"I wouldn't miss it. Seeing people who show up and reactions is pretty important in any case," Detective Simpson said. "How are you holding up?" he asked, the same sincerity ringing through in his words.

"Honestly, I don't know up from down. I never thought in a million years I'd be doing this right now. I just can't—" Cheyenne cut her words short and shuddered. "It's just hard."

"I won't say I understand the gravity of the loss you feel, but I understand how hard it must be," Detective Simpson replied. He stepped closer to Cheyenne and whispered, "And I got some of the crime scene results back. Whoever was at the scene when your mother was murdered wore Timberland boots. I have to find the person who owns a certain pair of boots, and then I'll be closer to catching the killer."

"What? That could mean a whole city of people. This is Brooklyn. Everyone wears Timberland boots," Cheyenne huffed, her own voice just slightly above a whisper.

Detective Simpson shook his head. "You're not kidding. I have my work cut out for me. But I'm going to start with those closest to your mother." He gave Cheyenne a telling look.

"Everybody in my house has Timbs, including me and Kelsi. I'm sure it won't be a problem for us to produce them for comparisons. I can bring them all down to the precinct for you," Cheyenne said, still whispering and furtively darting her eyes toward her father.

"No, I don't want anyone to know until I can get the proper paperwork to examine the shoes. The only reason I'm sharing it with you is because you've been the most cooperative," Detective Simpson said, pushing his point home.

Cheyenne nodded her agreement.

"Everything just seems off," Cheyenne blurted, shaking her head for dramatic emphasis. "I feel like they've all been acting strange. No one is acting like themselves at all. It's weird, and I don't want to jump to conclusions, but if I didn't know any better and I were you, every single one of them would be a suspect in this," Cheyenne said honestly. She truly felt like that. Her father, her brother, and Kelsi were all acting weird and not in a normal grieving way.

"You let me handle it all," Detective Simpson replied. "You have much more to think about. Get past today and these next few days, and we will talk further."

"Thank you again. Not many cops care about people, even when the case is theirs. From day one, I always felt you truly wanted to find my mother's killer and that she wasn't just going to be another case file that you threw down on your desk. You're a good person, Detective Simpson, and I know you'll keep your promise to find the devil that took my mother's life for no reason," Cheyenne said with a deep sincerity of her own.

Detective Simpson smiled and nodded at Cheyenne. "This one definitely hit different for me. I'm working hard to figure it out, and I will keep my promise," he replied. "And you don't have to thank me. It's my job," he said.

With that, Cheyenne inhaled deeply and exhaled loudly. "And now I have to go do the hardest thing I've ever done in my entire life," she said, heading back toward the chapel doors.

Chapter 13

Kelsi

Kelsi had stood off to the side where no one could see her and watched as Cheyenne walked into the funeral chapel on Big K's arm like the perfect little family. Kelsi noticed Cheyenne's father's supportive hold on Cheyenne and the love and concern in his eyes. Rough waves of jealousy swirled inside of Kelsi like a high tide, making her feel like she was choking. Her eyes went dark, and her mouth flattened into a straight line. All the loyalty in the world couldn't buy her the love she'd been looking for, the kind Cheyenne seemed to have from Big K.

Kelsi hid behind her dark shades, furtively watching Cheyenne and her father. Kelsi's temples pounded, and her stomach curled into knots. She was supposed to have that. She was supposed to be happy after everything, after all these years. That's what Big K had promised her even as a little girl.

Kelsi didn't understand why God was always punishing her. She couldn't fathom why she seemed to be the only one unworthy of a perfect life. Big K had promised her a perfect life once. The exact words had come out of his mouth, but they were all lies.

Kelsi turned away. She couldn't stand to watch Cheyenne with her father's support and her arm looped through his. He showed up like the perfect parent now.

Kelsi chuckled to herself, but it wasn't funny. It was actually making her physically sick.

Kelsi shifted on her feet. Her insides ached with loneliness. It was the kind of loneliness that couldn't be assuaged even if she had walked into the funeral home amongst a room full of people. Kelsi knew deep down inside she couldn't even pay for the type of love and companionship she longed for. She had never had any love from her no-good-ass mother.

She knew that the love she had for Big K was unhealthy, but in her mind, it was the perfect love. It had always existed. Kelsi secretly wanted Big K to love her and only her.

Kelsi slipped into the back of the funeral chapel after she was sure Cheyenne and Big K were already seated up front. The pastor stepped up to the microphone and opened up the service.

"Tonight, we celebrate the life of Mrs. Desiree Turner, and I want to begin with the theme of tonight's memorial, and that is, God doesn't make any mistakes. Let me say that again. I said God doesn't make any mistakes."

"Amen," a few people in the crowd mumbled.

"We all need love. Do you agree?" the pastor asked.

Kelsi swallowed hard, her heart pounding and her hands growing sweaty. She didn't want to be alone, but she wasn't dressed for a funeral. She'd put on a hoodie and Timbs, a show of rebellion in her anger at Big K for abandoning her. But now, she needed to be near him, and even near Cheyenne. She got up and stumbled to the front pew. She wedged in next to Big K and grabbed his other hand. It was a bold move, but she wanted to let him know she needed him.

Kelsi could see Big K's perplexed reaction out of the corner of her eye, but she ignored it. She told herself that he would get it. That, in that moment, he would love her like she needed to be loved. She deserved as much, after all.

Kelsi curled her fingers around his the way she'd imagine a couple in love, like she'd seen Ms. Desi and Big K do it back in the day. Big K didn't return the affection; instead, he shifted and twitched in his seat like she was a disease that made his skin itch. Kelsi knew that they usually didn't do public affection because it was just weird. She was like his daughter in the eyes of everyone else, but she wasn't actually his daughter. This hand-holding now hadn't been discussed or planned or wanted by Big K. Kelsi felt her heart drop, but like usual, she put on a brave face. She had gotten used to playing the tough one out of everyone. She had also gotten used to years of rejection.

"We all need love, but you won't know love if you don't know God first," the pastor preached. "I'm telling you, God doesn't make any mistakes."

"Amen," Kelsi murmured. With that, she released her hold on Big K's hand and turned her body away from his.

After the service, Big K did his new usual—held onto his daughter like a precious gem. He made sure Cheyenne was okay, walked with her, comforted her, but he never even thought to come over and say anything to Kelsi. When she followed them out of the chapel behind the casket, he simply told her that he would see her later at the repast they were having for Ms. Desi back at the community center.

Kelsi wandered out of the funeral chapel alone, her mind spinning in a million directions, none of them good.

"Bastard," Kelsi grumbled under her breath. He wasn't getting rid of her that easily.

"Chey! Wait up!" Kelsi called out as she spotted Cheyenne about to get into the limousine. Kelsi bit into the inside of her cheek, inhaled deeply, and plastered on a fake smile as she half staggered, half sauntered over to her best friend.

"I can't believe y'all left me out," Kelsi said, slurring her words as she stepped to Cheyenne and Big K. Kelsi noticed Big K's body stiffen and his facial expression flatten.

"Leave you out? You were nowhere to be found. I waited for you as long as I could," Cheyenne said honestly. Cheyenne looked at Kelsi up and down and shook her head. "You're not even dressed for the funeral. And you smell like you've been drinking and smoking," Cheyenne snapped, disgust lacing her words. "I don't think you should come to the cemetery like this. Go home. Get yourself together. My mother wouldn't have approved of you going to anyone's funeral like this, much less hers," Cheyenne said. With that, she started into the limousine.

Kelsi reached out and grabbed Cheyenne's arm and tugged her roughly to prevent her from getting in the car. Cheyenne sucked in her breath and reluctantly stopped moving to face her friend.

"Don't judge me. Of all fucking people, Chey, don't you start judging me too." Kelsi was familiar with the horrified look Cheyenne wore on her face. Kelsi had seen that look so many times when they were kids—like the time Cheyenne found out what Took had done to Kelsi. She'd looked at Kelsi with a mixture of horror, sympathy, and a tad bit of disgust. It was how she was looking at her now. Kelsi couldn't stand it. She couldn't stomach any of it. Didn't they understand that she was grieving too?

"Get yourself together, Kelsi," Cheyenne replied, tugging her arm away and getting into the limo.

"Go home and sober up like she said. Take care of yourself. You're slipping," Big K growled at her before he joined Cheyenne in the limousine.

Kelsi shifted her weight from one foot to the other, her hands moving aimlessly at her sides. She watched as the limo pulled out, leaving her there alone. She immediately felt the effects of being intoxicated. Kelsi felt warm with anger inside. At that moment, she wished she'd never met the Turners. She closed her eyes, and the memories came flooding back again.

By the time Kelsi and Carlene finished with Carlene's face to face meeting with a welfare case worker, Carlene had been given a stack of what the lady called "emergency food stamps." She said Carlene could expect an increase of one hundred seventy-five dollars plus back money in two weeks.

When they left the office, Kelsi was moving slow. She was so hungry she felt like she would faint. Carlene finally stopped at a street vendor and bought Kelsi one hot dog, a grape soda, and a bag of Bon Ton plain potato chips. It was the first thing she'd eaten since they snatched her from Nana's house. Kelsi gobbled it down so fast she couldn't even taste the food.

When they returned to Carlene's building, Kelsi noticed the same pretty little girl. This time, the little girl was doing the Hula-Hoop instead of playing double Dutch. Kelsi could tell someone cared about the little girl. Her skin was shiny and clear. Her hair was parted in zig-zag parts, and she had pretty heart-shaped baubles and barrettes adorning at least eight long ponytails. She wore a red top with sparkly silver hearts all over it and a red mini skirt. Her socks were folded down with red hearts all over them. She had on pristine white low-top Reebok track sneakers.

The little girl stopped Hula-Hooping when she noticed Kelsi looking at her. She smiled again and waved. Kelsi smiled back and waved, too.

Carlene had stopped to speak to a guy, so she didn't have time to see Kelsi and the little girl waving and smiling at one another. The little girl motioned for Kelsi to come to her, but Kelsi was too scared that moving would get Carlene's attention, so she shook her head no.

The little girl tilted her head in confusion. Her shoulders slumped like she was disappointed, but then she stepped out of her Hula-Hoop. She hung it on the black metal gate that surrounded the small patch of grass in front of the building and walked over to Kelsi.

As soon as the little girl got close enough, Kelsi could smell the fresh scent of baby powder on her. She still had some showing on her neck, too. Kelsi immediately noticed the arm full of plastic bracelets the little girl wore. Kelsi wanted them.

"Why was you scared to come over there?" the little girl boldly asked Kelsi.

Kelsi was in awe. The little girl was even prettier up close. Kelsi immediately grew embarrassed and felt inferior to the pretty little girl.

"I don't know," Kelsi replied softly, looking away to make sure Carlene was still talking. Kelsi saw that Carlene had that stack of food stamps out and was in deep conversation with a guy who looked like he was dismissing her. Carlene looked like she was begging him for something.

"Is Peaches your mother?" the little girl asked, noticing Kelsi stealing glances at Carlene.

Kelsi looked down at her feet. She wished she could cover her dirty "play sneakers" so the little girl couldn't see them. Kelsi also wished that she could blink and make Carlene just disappear.

"What's your name?" Kelsi finally asked the little girl, totally ignoring her question. She didn't want the little girl to know that Carlene was her mother.

"Cheyenne," the little girl answered cheerfully. "I don't live in this building, but I come over here sometimes *because it's a lot of my friends over here. I live in the real houses down Sea Gate."*

Kelsi had no idea what the little girl meant by "real houses," but she knew it was better than Carlene's building, or else why would she point it out so fast?

"My name is Kelsi. I live in the Bronx with my nana, but I had to come here for a little while. I don't live in this building either," Kelsi replied, feeling right away like she had to compete with the pretty little girl.

"I hope you stay a long time. I like you," Cheyenne told her.

Kelsi crinkled her face, thinking, She doesn't even know me. How could she say she likes me? What about me does she like?

Kelsi still had on her "play clothes," so they looked too small, and they didn't match. Her hair needed combing and brushing. Her face was dirty, and to top it all off, she had spilled grape soda down the front of her shirt, trying to drink it so fast. In her own assessment, Kelsi looked dirty as hell, certainly not like someone the dainty, well-dressed, clean, sweet-faced girl would like.

"I like you too," Kelsi lied. Secretly, she instantly hated Cheyenne with her clean clothes, her nicely done hair, and her pretty face. Kelsi imagined how clean Cheyenne's "real house" was.

"Can you stay outside for a little while?" Cheyenne asked.

Don't leave out this house without my permission or if me or Took take you out. You can't go outside unless I say you can go. *Carlene's words resounded in Kelsi's ears.*

"I think I might be going back to the Bronx today, so prolly not," Kelsi answered, lying again.

"Dag. I wish you could stay outside. I want some new friends. The girls around here be my friend for a little while, but then they start getting jealous and talking

about me and stuff, and then we don't be friends no more. I'm bored out here by myself," Cheyenne complained.

Kelsi wanted to tell her to stop complaining, that at least she had nice clothes, nice hair, and a clean "real house."

Kelsi looked over at Carlene again, finally exchanging something with the guy she had been talking to. A car horn sounded and caused Kelsi to look away. Cheyenne turned around too.

"C'mon, baby girl. We going to the rides," a man called from a big, shiny black jeep-looking car.

From where Kelsi stood, she could see that the man had a neck full of thick gold chains and a crisp white shirt on. She couldn't really see his face.

Cheyenne sucked her teeth and turned back toward Kelsi.

"I got to go, Kelsi. That's my father. He don't like me to stay out here that long, so he always makes up excuses to make me want to leave," Cheyenne said, sounding disappointed.

"What's the rides?" Kelsi asked.

Cheyenne looked at Kelsi with furrowed eyebrows. "You never seen all those rides just blocks from here? Coney Island . . . duh. You never went there?" Cheyenne asked like the rides were something or someplace everyone in the entire world knew about.

"I told you I was from the Bronx!" Kelsi snapped, her jaw immediately rocking back and forth. She wanted to punch her new friend. The fireball in Kelsi's chest started sizzling again. It just hadn't gotten as hot as it had for Carlene.

"Even people from the Bronx come to Coney Island. On Easter, on Memorial Day and stuff like that. People get all dressed fresh and come to the rides. We are lucky to live right by the rides, and we go all the time. Ask

*that lady you with if you can go. My father won't care,"
Cheyenne told Kelsi.*

*Was she crazy? Carlene would flip if Kelsi asked her
to go someplace other than wherever she told her to go.*

*"That's okay. I'm just going to stay here. I might be
going back to the Bronx later anyway," Kelsi said, lying
with a straight face. That was wishful thinking.*

*Cheyenne's father blew the horn again. She sucked
her teeth and started walking off, but she didn't walk in
the direction of her father's car.*

*Kelsi thought Cheyenne was going to get her Hula-
Hoop off the fence, but instead, Cheyenne marched right
up to Carlene and the guy. Kelsi's heart began to hammer against her ribs. She crinkled her face in confusion.*

*Cheyenne started saying something to Carlene, then
pointed to Kelsi and looked back at Carlene.*

*Kelsi thought she would faint. Her body got hot all
over, and her heart knocked into the skinny bone in the
center of her chest even harder. Carlene shot Kelsi a
dirty look from where she stood.*

*Cheyenne then marched to her father's car. Her father
had blown the horn again. Kelsi looked over to the car.
Cheyenne's father leaned down and looked in the direction Carlene was standing with the guy.*

*"Yo, Peaches!" Cheyenne's father yelled and blew his
horn again.*

*Kelsi froze in place. What was happening? She
couldn't stop the sweat beads from running a race down
her back. Her underarms itched, and so did her scalp.*

*Carlene turned toward the jeep-car with a fake smile
and waved. "What's up, Big K?" she answered with a
fake song in her tone.*

*The man she'd called Big K waved her over. "Let me
rap with you for a taste," he hollered out.*

Carlene rolled her eyes at Kelsi. "I'll be right back. Stay right there," she grumbled to Kelsi evilly. She sashayed over to where Big K, who sat parked in his big, beautiful, shiny jeep-car.

Kelsi watched nervously. Carlene was all smiles and giggles, like she was talking to her schoolgirl crush. She leaned over and spoke through the window to Big K. Cheyenne put her pointer and middle fingers up and crossed them over each other behind her back. Kelsi didn't know what that meant. Carlene finally looked up from where she'd been leaning down.

"B—Um, Kelsi! C'mere, baby! Hurry up!" Carlene called out, waving Kelsi over like the matter was urgent. It was the first time Carlene had called Kelsi by her name, which sounded more like an owner calling a pet than a mother calling her only child.

Kelsi looked at Carlene strangely. She would not move.

"C'mere and stop acting crazy, girl," Carlene demanded and laughed nervously.

Cheyenne smiled and bounced excitedly. Kelsi couldn't understand none of what was going on. Whatever made Carlene refer to Kelsi as "baby" surely had to be something or someone big. Kelsi finally made it over to the car.

"Kelsi, this Big K . . . Took's boss. His daughter wants you to go with her to the rides. I told Big K I was gonna ask you first. You wanna go?" Carlene said all in one breath. She looked at Kelsi with a knowing, squinty-eyed glance.

Kelsi darted her eyes to Cheyenne, who was shaking her head up and down, motioning for Kelsi to say yes.

"You don't have to go if you don't want to," Carlene said like she was telling Kelsi to say no on the low.

Kelsi felt the chest-fire thingy again. She pictured it growing a little bigger inside of her every time Carlene opened her mouth.

"It's going to be fun," Big K said and flashed a smile.

That was the first time Kelsi looked at him. His eyes were kind and relaxed. They were dark, but not scary like Carlene's. His skin was the color of the walnuts Nana loved so much, and it was smooth and hairless. He had two shiny gold teeth in the front of his mouth that gleamed and sparkled when he smiled, and his watch had a huge face with rows of shiny diamonds going round and round in circles all over it.

"I ain't got no money to give," Carlene started with a bit of urgency lacing her words.

Big K put a halting hand up in Carlene's face. *"Don't insult me, Peaches. Ain't nobody asking you for no paper. I said I was taking shorty to the rides. Slow your roll. What I look like asking you for money?"* he chastised, putting the emphasis on the difference between him and her.

Big K looked at Kelsi and softened his chiseled, handsome face. *"What's it going to be, little lady?"* he asked in more of a cheery tone than he'd used with Carlene.

Carlene moved her jaw furiously.

"I want to go," Kelsi said softly, parting a nervous smile, not daring to look at Carlene. Kelsi didn't know if it was to make Carlene mad as hell, or if it was to be closer to the kind eyes of Big K, but she said it again, louder the second time. *"I want to go to the rides."*

"Yes!" Cheyenne cheered and pumped her fist.

Big K laughed. *"Calm down back there, cheerleader,"* he quipped.

Carlene was sizzling mad; Kelsi knew it. Carlene's eyes had gone low, and her nostrils moved in and out rapidly. She stepped back from the car like it was a big, black monster about to attack her.

"And there you have it," Carlene mumbled while keeping a fake smile on her face. *"Well then, I guess it's fine*

*with me. I ain't going to go against the hand that feeds
me, right?" Carlene said, nodding at Big K and letting
out a half phony snicker.*

*"Get in, little lady. This little one back here been wait-
ing for you," Big K instructed Kelsi.*

*Cheyenne already had the back door open. Kelsi had
to hold on to climb up into the jeep-car. She had never
been in one before. She and Nana had always walked
or took the bus all over the Bronx when they had to go
somewhere.*

*Cheyenne hugged Kelsi's neck like they had been
friends for years.*

*"I'm so happy you can come with us!" Cheyenne
whispered excitedly.*

*It was strange to Kelsi, but she went with it. In Kelsi's
mind, if Cheyenne liked her, Cheyenne's father would
like her too. Kelsi had already decided that she loved
him.*

*"What time y'all coming back?" Carlene asked with
attitude.*

*"It ain't gonna be that long. Just enough time for them
to ride, play some games, and grab some grub. I got to
stop home and get Desi and Lil Kev first. We do things
as a family. You feel me?" Big K replied like he'd been
trying to send a message to Carlene.*

*There were no more words exchanged. Big K pulled
off.*

*Kelsi watched from the back window as Carlene
stared after the jeep-car. Kelsi silently prayed that
going to the rides would be worth whatever Carlene
was going to do when she got back.*

"Ms. Jones," Detective Simpson called from behind
Kelsi, interrupting her thoughts and memories and

bringing her mind back to the present. Kelsi had to blink a few times to snap herself out of the little trance she'd fallen in. She chuckled nervously.

"Detective Simpson?" she replied, getting her mind back to normal. Suddenly, she was completely annoyed that he was there, lurking around like a creep.

"Y'all go to funerals to try to catch people out there now?" Kelsi replied angrily, trying to hide how unnerved she was by the detective's presence. No matter how nice he tried to be, Kelsi hated cops and didn't trust them. Period. She especially hated Detective Simpson because he was always around. He was always asking questions, and inevitably, he would be the one to catch the killer.

"Is that a trick question?" Detective Simpson replied, smiling at Kelsi sarcastically.

She knew full well he wasn't smiling to be nice. Kelsi had seen Detective Simpson go in and out of the building to talk to Cheyenne and Big K several times since the day after the crime. Kelsi had also watched Detective Simpson speak to Cheyenne in the lobby of the funeral home right before the funeral. She was incensed, because in her opinion, Cheyenne was always the goody-goody. The detective didn't seem to be suspicious of her at all, but every time Kelsi encountered him, he spoke to her like she was public enemy number one.

Kelsi had been upset by all the research he'd done about her and everything he'd found out about Carlene. He'd revealed to Kelsi that he knew all about Carlene's drug problem and her stints in and out of jail. Kelsi felt like she had been stripped naked and exposed to the world. It wasn't the first time she felt raw, exposed, and unprotected like that.

"No, I'll leave the trick questions up to you. Is there a reason you're here talking to me and not out searching for a killer?" Kelsi answered, rolling her eyes. Kelsi felt heat sparking up inside of her. It was always the thing that happened when her back was against the wall. Kelsi's cheeks burned. She needed to get away. She needed to go.

"What happened, Kelsi? You didn't want to go see Ms. Desi laid to rest in her final resting place?" Detective Simpson asked, eyeing Kelsi up and down with suspicion glinting in his eyes.

"I'll leave all of that up to her real family. They didn't look like they needed any company or help," Kelsi answered. "I'm the outsider. Always have been and always will," she said flatly.

Detective Simpson made a grunting noise. "Well, can I ask you a question?"

Kelsi noticed that he kept eyeing her clothes, but especially her Timberland boots. She felt uncomfortable under his gaze. If eyes could tell the story, his would've said he thought she was guilty of something.

"There is nothing more you need to know from me. I've told you everything that I know, literally," Kelsi replied.

"Sometimes, with these cases, you think you've heard everything until you speak to people a few times. So, let me ask you a question."

She stared at him silently, so he continued.

"Lil Kev. I've heard you were the one who might've witnessed his dust-up with Scorpio," Detective Simpson said, getting right to the point.

Kelsi swallowed hard. The incident was one she'd wanted to put out of her mind and never relive. A cold chill shot down her back. She closed her eyes for a few seconds, remembering that horrible day.

"Nigga, is you loyal to me or your washed-up-ass pappy?"

Kelsi heard Scorpio bark the question loudly. She was upstairs in Scorpio's bedroom with pain pulsing between her ears like someone had hit a gong right upside her head.

"Mmmm," Kelsi groaned in response to the yelling. She was so hung over she thought she was dreaming.

"Huh? Answer me, li'l nigga! I ain't got time for games! I'm hearing in the streets that your washed-up-ass daddy been trying to step on a nigga toes out there, and your soft ass just playing the passive role!" Scorpio yelled some more.

"Nah, man. You heard wrong." Lil Kev's voice quivered.

Kelsi knew then that she wasn't dreaming. She jumped up so fast that her pounding head threatened to send her right back down on the bed. Kelsi stopped for a minute to gather herself.

"Ugh," she grumbled, feeling like vomit was about to creep up her esophagus. She took a deep breath and powered through the throbbing pain in her head and gut-wrenching nausea in her belly. She grabbed one of Scorpio's T-shirts to cover her naked body.

"I think this li'l nigga ain't got the heart to take care of his pops. This nigga stunting like he want to be the next Big K out here, yet he letting his old-ass pops fuck up the business!" Scorpio said to the crowd of dudes that sat around watching what he was doing. "I think this li'l nigga might deserve to take this L in the name of his father!"

When Kelsi got to the steps, she had a full view. Scorpio had a gun to Lil Kev's head, while Lil Kev sat cowering and crying in one of Scorpio's white leather chairs.

Kelsi didn't know what came over her, but her legs started moving on their own. All she had on was a T-shirt and a thong, but she rushed down those steps like a bat out of hell. Kelsi didn't give two shits about

*her own safety. All she knew at that moment was that
a member of her family was being threatened, and she
wasn't having it.*

*"What the fuck are you doing?" Kelsi boomed as she
plowed straight for Scorpio. Even Scorpio had to look
twice like Kelsi had lost her mind.*

*"Take that fucking gun out of his face! You know he is
like my fucking little brother!" Kelsi growled, her head
still thrumming with pain from her hangover.*

*Scorpio turned his six-foot-three slender frame to-
ward Kelsi. When he swept his long, dark brown, knotty
dreads out of his face, Kelsi saw that his charcoal black
face and big, soup-cooler lips had crumpled into a snarl.*

"Who the fuck is you talking to, bitch?" Scorpio barked.

*When he called Kelsi the name Carlene had been call-
ing her since she was eight years old, Kelsi lost it. She
jumped on Scorpio and dug her nails deep into his skin.*

*"Leave him alone! He's a fucking little kid! Leave him
alone!" she screamed as she bit down into Scorpio's
shoulder.*

"Ahh! Get this crazy bitch off of me!" Scorpio belted out.

*Suddenly, Kelsi felt her body being hoisted in the air.
She felt a few of her ribs crack as she hit a wall.*

*"This dumb bitch must have lost her rabbit-ass mind
today!" Scorpio lifted his Timberland boot and brought
it down on Kelsi's chest.*

*Pain rippled through her body like waves on the
ocean at high tide.*

*"You trying to disrespect me in front of all my niggas?
Huh, bitch?"*

*Another kick from his boot landed square between
Kelsi's legs. She felt vomit come up out of her mouth like
a volcano.*

*"You staying up in they camp, too. I'm feeding your
fiend, nasty ass. You probably fucking this nigga right*

here!" Scorpio barked. This time, he grabbed a handful of Kelsi's hair.

Even with her body wracked with pain, Kelsi wasn't going out like a punk bitch. She spit and kicked. A fire raged inside of her chest bigger than those uncontrollable wildfires that happen in California.

"Get the fuck off me," Kelsi gasped, slob and vomit spewing from her lips. She swiped at Scorpio again, this time taking five fingernails full of skin off his neck.

"Ahhh! This bitch cut me!"

Kelsi heard him wail. She saw the blood on his neck right before he used his gun to hit her across her face. Kelsi's lights went out. Blackness was all she remembered after that.

She woke up the next day in Cheyenne's room in the worst pain she'd felt in a long while. Kelsi's head felt like somebody had been sitting on top of it, hitting it with a hammer. Her body felt like a two-thousand-pound person had sat on her.

When her eyes fluttered open, she immediately snapped them shut. It hurt so badly. Kelsi's right eye wouldn't even open all the way, but she felt tears draining out of the side of it. Kelsi tried to take a deep breath, and even that hurt like hell.

"Hmmm," she moaned. The small vibration from her moan sent pain through her throat and neck.

"Hey, Kels. I'm glad to see you awake." Ms. Desiree's soothing voice came from somewhere to Kelsi's right, but she wasn't able to see her. "I have something you can take for the pain, but it's going to knock you right back out," Ms. Desiree said.

Kelsi swallowed hard. That hurt too. She slowly shook her head up and down. She needed the pills right away. She didn't care if that shit knocked her out for sixty days. Kelsi could not take the pain all over her body.

"Okay. Let me go grab you some water," Ms. Desiree said.

Kelsi closed her eyes back for a few minutes before she felt the presence of someone else in the room. She forced her one good eye open. Pulsating stabs of pain shot through her forehead again. She winced.

"Don't try to open your eyes for me. I'm here." Big K's voice filtered into Kelsi's ears.

She let out a painful sigh and shut her good eye. She got hot with embarrassment for him to see her like this.

"Who did this to you, Kelsi?" he asked.

Kelsi thought the question was strange. Didn't he know? Hadn't Lil Kev been the one to bring her home after the fight with Scorpio? Who had finally saved her from Scorpio's wrath? How many days had passed? Kelsi's mind raced, which intensified her headache.

"They just left you for dead in front of the door. Desi found you on her way out to work . . . in this condition. You could've died out there like that. You're pretty banged up. I want to know who did this shit to you," Big K whispered harshly.

Kelsi could tell without looking at him that he was flexing his strong jaw.

"Where's Lil Kev? Is he ok?" Kelsi mumbled through her swollen jaw, the smell of her own breath making her want to gag.

"We haven't seen him. Rumor in the building is he knows who did this shit. They saying Lil Kev might have been there when this happened to you and ain't do shit to protect you. I'm looking for that little punk too. Now, I'ma ask you again. Who did this shit to you?" Big K responded firmly.

"I don't remember much about it," Kelsi replied, blinking away the horrible memory of what had happened to her.

Detective Simpson looked like he didn't believe her, but she didn't care.

"I just want to help," he said as if that would get Kelsi to tell him anything more than what she'd already told him—which, in her opinion, had been more than enough to get him off her back.

"Whatever. You're probably just like everyone else in my life. Everything will be my fault in the end anyways," Kelsi replied. "If there is nothing else you need to say to me right now, I'll politely excuse myself from this bullshit conversation," Kelsi snapped.

"Take care, Ms. Jones. You don't look so good right now," Detective Simpson said, seemingly unfazed by her attitude.

Kelsi frowned. She and Detective Simpson locked eyes for a few long seconds.

"I don't feel so good either, detective. I just lost the only woman that ever treated me like a daughter. My best friend doesn't have time for me. Her father is totally ignoring me. And her brother almost got me killed. I think I have good reason not to feel good," Kelsi said. With that, she turned and rushed away.

Kelsi's nostrils flared, and her eyes hooded as she sped down the Brooklyn street with a thousand thoughts trampling through her brain.

Chapter 14

Kelsi

When Kelsi got back to the Turners' apartment, all sorts of things ran through her mind. She decided she needed to leave. She looked around the bedroom she'd been sharing with Cheyenne, and a sob bubbled up to her lips. Kelsi's legs went weak. She flopped down on her bed and stared across the room at Cheyenne's empty bed. Kelsi grabbed her pillow, buried her face in it, and screamed as loud as she could. She felt so much guilt as her mind reeled back through everything.

Cheyenne was correct. Her house was a "real house." Big K even used a little card to get into the big black gates. The gates led to a hidden neighborhood with rows and rows of houses. The houses all stood alone, not connected like the buildings Kelsi was used to living in. There were grassy lawns out front with little brick structures around them. There were flowerbeds with yellow, red, pink, and purple flowers in them.

Big K turned the car into a driveway in front of a big, pale brick house. There were tall green curved, spiral, and round bushes in front. Flowers surrounded the front walkway, too.

"C'mon, Kelsi!" Cheyenne said excitedly. "This is my house!"

Kelsi followed Cheyenne out of the car in wide-eyed amazement. Cheyenne ran up the tan, brick steps that led to the beautiful beveled glass front door. She twisted the gold doorknob and bounded inside.

"Let's go to my room until they get ready!" Cheyenne instructed, waving Kelsi on to follow her.

Kelsi moved slowly, taking it all in. Cheyenne walked Kelsi through a grand foyer adorned with beautiful gold-framed pictures of Big K, Cheyenne, a little boy, and a real pretty lady. The house smelled like Kelsi imagined a home to smell in her fantasies—like rose petals and sweet candy.

"Cheyenne!"

Kelsi heard a woman's voice. The voice snapped Kelsi out of her reverie. Cheyenne had already made her way to the steps heading to her room. She turned around and sucked her teeth.

"You took too long," Cheyenne whispered to Kelsi. "C'mon. Now we have to go see my mother before we go to my room," she huffed, grabbing Kelsi's hand and dragging her farther into the beautiful house.

"How are you going to try to go upstairs without introducing me to your company? How rude." The woman's voice filtered down the long hallway Kelsi and Cheyenne were walking through.

Kelsi was busy looking up at the crystal chandeliers that lined the hallway while Cheyenne led her like a blind person through the maze that was her house.

"Mommy, this is my new friend, Kelsi," Cheyenne announced.

Kelsi felt her mouth hanging open, but she couldn't close it.

The woman walked toward Kelsi with a bright, gleaming white smile.

"Oh, you're very pretty, Kelsi. It's nice to meet you. I'm Ms. Desiree," the woman said, sticking out a beautifully manicured hand.

Kelsi smiled and shook her hand. Ms. Desiree was the color of the Disney cartoon character Pocahontas. She was beautiful like a Native American too, with slanted eyes, but not so slanted you would mistake her for Asian. Her hair was long and dark and lay on her left shoulder in soft, coiled tendrils. She had the most perfect mouth. Her lips weren't big and greasy like Carlene's; instead, Ms. Desiree had a small, heart-shaped mouth with a light tint of lip gloss on them. She wore a white tennis dress. Her long, slender legs looked like she really played tennis for a living. Cheyenne looked like the spitting image of Ms. Desiree.

Kelsi's heart raced as she touched Ms. Desiree's hand. She wished that the beautiful woman was her mother instead of Carlene.

"That's Peaches' daughter." Big K's voice boomed from behind them all.

Kelsi turned around and took him in entirely. Big K was tall with strong arms. His shoulders were square, but not too big. Kelsi couldn't stop staring at his eyes. She had never seen a man with kinder eyes than his. He looked at his wife with such love. Kelsi's heart raced, and she felt like she would throw up.

"Peaches. Mm-hmmm," Ms. Desiree said, looking back at Kelsi.

It seemed like they were speaking some secret language about Carlene, and Kelsi could tell from their silent signals that it wasn't good. She wanted to run away and tell Ms. Desiree that she wasn't Carlene's daughter; that she belonged to Nana.

"Either way, she's a cutie pie, and you-know-who is all sold on this one," Ms. Desiree said and tilted her head toward Cheyenne.

"Cheyenne, we're about to go, so why don't you and Kelsi go take a quick shower and change. You have new stuff you can give her to wear. Maybe matching but in different colors," Ms. Desiree said in an overly cheery voice. Again, she seemed to be sending some sort of silent language signal to her daughter.

"I already took a shower today." Cheyenne pouted with her eyebrows crunched up. Her mother smiled and tilted her head again. Kelsi caught it the second time. Obviously, Cheyenne had caught it too. Cheyenne immediately changed her facial expression.

"O-kaay," Cheyenne droned. "C'mon, Kelsi. I want to show you my room. Plus, we have to wash up and change before we get to go to the rides," Cheyenne told Kelsi.

Kelsi understood what was going on now. There was no way the Turner family was going to take her out with them looking the way she did in her dirty play clothes. They had standards to uphold.

Cheyenne's bedroom was every little girl's dream. She had Pepto Bismol pink walls with white trimmings. She had a queen-sized bed with four white posts and a pink canopy. She had a plush Barbie bedspread. Her curtains were Barbie, and so was the throw rug on the floor. There was a tall dresser with crystal knobs and a grand full-length mirror with beautiful white trimming. It was like something from a queen's castle.

"Let's find matching outfits like my mother said," Cheyenne said, stepping over to her double-door closet.

Kelsi couldn't even speak. She was too busy feeling the tornado swirl of emotions surging in her head. Kelsi felt jealous, inferior, happy to be there, and sad to be there all at once. She wished she was back with Nana, but that she could still be friends with Cheyenne. It was so much to think about for a little girl. All Kelsi wanted to do at that point was lie down on that pink carpet and ball up into a knot.

When Cheyenne pulled back the doors on her closet, a lump the size of a handball formed in Kelsi's throat. She had never seen anything like it, except on TV. Cheyenne had rows and rows of clothes—dresses, jeans, skirts, shorts, blouses, and T-shirts, all coordinated and hanging by color and style. She had stacks of shoe and sneaker boxes. There was a long hanging thingy with plastic shelves containing colorful headbands, pocketbooks, and bracelets. It didn't even seem to faze Cheyenne. Having so much seemed to be blah, blah, blah to her.

"Okay, my mother said to find stuff with tags. So, here is four outfits. If you like them, you can have them. I don't even want them. I never wore none of it, so they are yours to keep," Cheyenne said with ease, tossing the color-coordinated outfits onto the bed.

Kelsi blinked rapidly. It was like Cheyenne's closet was a store and Kelsi was on a free shopping spree. Even when she'd been with Nana, Kelsi never had it like that. There were so many skirts, dresses, and jeans in a rainbow of colors.

Outside of the closet was the same. Cheyenne had two huge Barbie dream houses in either corner of her room. She had shelves on her walls with rows and rows of Barbie dolls all dressed in beautiful dresses. She had so many stuffed animals it was like a jungle and a zoo in her room. She had a shelf filled with every board game you could imagine, and a bookshelf filled with all types of books.

Her dresser had a glass tray on it that held at least ten pretty crystal bottles of perfume. Kelsi walked over to it. Cheyenne had gold rings, chains, and earrings all laid nicely on her dresser as well.

Kelsi's heart raced, and she didn't even know why. She picked up a thick, shiny necklace with XOXO made of gold.

"You like that? It's called an X and O link. My daddy gave it to me for my birthday. You know what Xs and Os mean?" Cheyenne asked all in one breath.

Kelsi quickly put the chain back down on the dresser and shook her head.

"For real? You don't know that Xs and Os means hugs and kisses? When Daddy gave me that chain, he said he was the first man to ever shower me with hugs and kisses," Cheyenne recalled dreamily.

Kelsi suddenly became aware that her lips were hanging open. This little girl had the world. Kelsi had nothing. Kelsi silently wondered who would be the first man to shower her with hugs and kisses.

She scanned Cheyenne's room one more time to take it all in.

"Is your family rich or something?" Kelsi finally asked, her throat so dry the words hurt coming out.

Cheyenne stopped moving in and out of her closet and turned her full attention toward Kelsi. She smiled the same pretty, carefree smile she always put on her face. It was so effortless for Cheyenne to smile. Kelsi remembered feeling effortlessly happy like that when she was with Nana. What a difference a few days had made.

"No, silly. My daddy works. He said we ain't rich because rich people don't have to work. One day, he is going to get rich, and then me and my brother won't have to work when we grow up," Cheyenne explained to Kelsi as she continued to toss pretty items of clothing onto the bed.

What she said made sense to Kelsi—rich people didn't work. But her family still seemed rich to Kelsi.

Cheyenne and Kelsi both put on a pair of brand-new jean shorts. Cheyenne's were acid washed, and Kelsi's were dark blue. Cheyenne put on a purple T-shirt with a puffy rainbow on the front, and Kelsi wore a pink one with a puffy heart on the front. Ms. Desiree fixed their hair to match, in six ponytails each, with pretty baubles and barrettes. Cheyenne gave Kelsi a brand-new pair of high-top Reeboks, and although they hurt her feet a little bit, Kelsi didn't dare say anything because she wanted the sneakers so badly.

They all went to the rides at Coney Island that day. Big K spared no expense. He carried a knot of money in his pocket, which he also had no problem peeling from. Cheyenne and Kelsi rode every ride twice. They played every game and had arms full of stuffed animals. They had cotton candy, Nathan's franks, shrimp, soda, and huge swirly-colored lollipops.

Ms. Desiree and Big K danced in front of the Himalaya ride while Cheyenne and Kelsi rode it forward and backward. Kelsi couldn't stop watching them. It was her first time witnessing love between a man and a woman. Big K held Ms. Desiree by the waist and hugged her from the back. He kissed her gently on her neck and acted like she was the only person there, even though there were hundreds of people around. They picked Lil Kevin up out of the stroller and held him between them, showering him with kisses. It was like Kelsi was watching a show on TV. The Turners were the perfect family.

When Cheyenne and Kelsi were done riding, they both ran to Cheyenne's parents.

"Y'all enjoyed that?" Big K asked with his warm smile.

Both girls chimed, "Yes!" in unison.

As they walked around the rides, Big K held Kelsi's hand on one side and Cheyenne's on the other side. He called them his girls the entire night. Each time he did,

Kelsi got a funny feeling inside. She immediately felt like she loved them all. Each one of the Turners touched her in a different way. Kelsi got so lost in being a part of their family that she altogether forgot that she had to return to the hellhole where she now lived.

When Big K pulled his Range Rover up to Carlene's building, Kelsi's stomach immediately knotted up.

"You want to go with me to walk her upstairs, Chey?" Big K asked Cheyenne.

Cheyenne looked like she would cry. Kelsi bit her jaw inside to keep her own tears from falling. Cheyenne and Kelsi moved as slow as molasses through a straw getting out of that car that night.

"Don't forget your clothes," Cheyenne said sadly. She grabbed a big bag of clothes and shoes she had picked out of her closet for Kelsi.

Kelsi held onto the biggest stuffed animal that Big K had won for her.

"Stop acting all sad. There's always tomorrow and the next day. It ain't the end of the world," Big K told them as he took an armful of Kelsi's stuff from the rides to carry.

As soon as they all exited the elevator, Kelsi felt flush with shame. The hallway stank like burning hair and cat shit. Of course, there was a pile of garbage on the floor in front of the incinerator chute.

Big K walked strong and confidently as if the stench and dirt didn't faze him. Kelsi didn't have to lead him to Carlene's apartment. He knew exactly where it was. Big K used the knocker and banged on the door like he was the police.

God, please don't let Carlene answer. God, please don't let Took answer. God, please let them be gone so I have to go home with Big K. *Kelsi chanted prayers inside of her head.*

Big K banged again. Then he screamed out, "Peaches! Took!"

Finally, the door opened a crack. The odor of rotting garbage mixed with bad fish wafted out of the apartment and shot straight up Kelsi's nose. She knew Cheyenne and Big K smelled it if she could. Kelsi looked at Cheyenne, but Cheyenne kept her eyes down toward the floor.

"Yo, Peaches, open the damn door all the way," Big K demanded.

Carlene opened the door a little bit wider.

"I'm bringing your shorty back," Big K said, peering inside.

Carlene had turned off the lights so Big K couldn't see inside.

"Thanks for taking her," Carlene said dryly.

Big K looked at Kelsi pitifully, as if he were taking a stray dog to an animal shelter to be put to sleep.

"I'm going to come see you tomorrow," Cheyenne piped up sadly.

Kelsi nodded and stepped toward Carlene.

Big K handed Carlene the bags and all of Kelsi's goodies. With her stomach in knots, Kelsi stepped inside of her reality and moved around in the darkness.

"Yo, Peaches. Clean up this fucking place. You got a real good kid right there. She don't deserve to live like this. What you do as an adult is your business, but a kid don't ask to be here. I'ma be checking on that little one, so you better do the right thing by her. Clean up this rat trap before I do something about it," Big K lectured and warned at the same time.

Carlene shifted her weight from one foot to the next like she had to pee.

Kelsi felt that funny feeling inside again. It couldn't be anything other than her immediate love for Big K growing. Kelsi didn't know which grew faster, her love for Big K or her hatred for Carlene.

Big K kept the promise he made that day. Over the next year, he checked up on Kelsi daily. He kept Carlene in line, which made life a little bit easier for Kelsi. Between Big K and the welfare caseworker, Carlene had no choice but to put Kelsi in school that September. Kelsi had turned nine years old the month before school started.

Cheyenne and Kelsi were definitely best friends by then. They never wanted to be separated. They shared everything. Cheyenne didn't judge Kelsi based on Carlene, and Kelsi stopped feeling jealous of Cheyenne's life and settled for being happy to be a part of it.

During the school year, Cheyenne and Kelsi got to see each other every day, even though Cheyenne went to private school and Kelsi went to public school. Kelsi spent a lot of time with the Turners on the weekends because Carlene and Took were too scared of Big K to protest.

The living conditions at Carlene's only changed for a few weeks after Big K threatened Carlene, but Kelsi did what she could around the house to make herself feel better about living there. Big K also bought Kelsi a daybed with a clean, comfortable mattress and a pretty Barbie comforter set with matching pillows. Kelsi grew to love him more and more each day. She would secretly write him love letters, but then she'd use Carlene's lighters to burn the letters before anyone read them.

It was June of 1996 when everything in everyone's lives went haywire. It was the first day of summer break from school. An unusual heat wave swept through Brooklyn. The weatherman said the heat index made it feel like 102 degrees outside. He warned old people and children to stay indoors. It was so hot the old oscillating fan Carlene had in the living room did nothing but blow hot air. Kelsi wasn't allowed in Carlene's room where the air conditioner was.

The heat kept Kelsi from sleeping. She got up for the fifth time that night to stick her head in the cool breeze of the freezer door. It was the only little bit of relief she could get.

As Kelsi dragged her feet and sweaty body back to her bed, she was startled by something moving in the dark. Kelsi jumped so hard a little bit of pee came out into her panties.

Took was sitting on the end of her bed. His pale, naked chest seemed to glow almost neon in the little bit of light that was coming in the window from the streetlight outside. Kelsi let out a long sigh.

"What are you doing on my bed?" she grumbled sassily. She hated Took, and he hated her. They'd never had a good word to say to one another over the year Kelsi had been there. He always let Kelsi know that she was a mouth to feed and a burden on him since Carlene didn't do shit around the house.

Kelsi used to pray every day for Took to leave the house. Most days he did, unless he was in the kitchen cooking something that required baking soda, Boric acid, and sometimes he'd spray something real stink on his concoctions.

"Get off my bed. I'm sleepy, and I want to lay back down," Kelsi snapped.

Took patted the bed next to where he sat with his nasty white hand.

Kelsi squinted her eyes in the darkness. He can't be talking to me! she screamed in her head.

"Come over here and don't make no noise," he whispered, sounding like a snake hissing.

His command sounded like a foreign language to Kelsi. She folded her face into a frown and folded her arms indignantly. Was he out of his mind?

"What? You stupid? You better get off my bed right now! I'm not coming on the bed until you get out!" Kelsi said, raising her voice.

Took jumped to his feet. Kelsi jumped too, because his sudden motion scared the shit out of her. Before Kelsi could move, run, put her hands up in defense, or anything, Took barreled into her like a bulldozer. Kelsi fell backward. Her ass hit the tiled floor so hard her butt cheeks ached.

"I said to come here, bitch," he growled almost inaudibly. He grabbed Kelsi roughly by her arm, and that was when she saw that he had a gun in his other hand.

A lot of pee escaped her bladder, enough to wet her panties all the way through. Kelsi's chest moved up and down like she'd just run a relay race. She couldn't catch her breath as she remembered that gun from the day Took had hit Nana with it.

"Whatchu doing?" Kelsi huffed, trying in vain to loosen his painful grip on her arm.

Took threw her on the bed roughly. He'd gotten naked except for a pair of boxers. He got so close to Kelsi that she could see that the nappy, coiled hairs on his chest were the same ugly shade of brassy blond as the hair on his head. His nipples were pink, and they stuck straight out like devil's eyes.

"Shut the fuck up," Took whispered harshly in her face. His mouth reeked of whatever he had been drinking. His entire body stank like liquor, sweat, and the stuff inside of firecrackers.

"Ahh!" Kelsi started to scream, but it was short lived. She felt a sharp pain across her face that sent the scream tumbling right back down her throat. Her eyes

shut involuntarily, and little streaks of silver lights swirled around on the inside of her eyelids.

Took slapped Kelsi again, this time on the other side of her face. Something popped at the back of Kelsi's neck, and a sharp, stabbing pain shot down her spine. Her arms and legs felt weak, and her chest ignited with fire.

I'm gonna kill you! I'm gonna kill you! a voice inside Kelsi's head screamed over and over. No words came to her mouth. She felt buried alive because her brain was saying run, fight, scream, but her body would not listen.

Suddenly, Kelsi couldn't breathe. The smell of Took's sweaty hand filled her nostrils as he clamped it down roughly over her nose and mouth. Kelsi finally tried to kick her legs, but his weight was too much. She was pinned down. Pain swirled through her head so badly that she could barely open her eyes.

"If you fight, it's gon' hurt. Relax and it won't hurt much."

Kelsi heard Took's muffled words hot against her ear. He used one of his muscular legs to force hers apart, and then he fumbled under her. Kelsi suddenly felt his rough hand moving over her private parts. She squeezed her eyes shut. Nana had told her to never let anyone touch her there.

Kelsi couldn't fight Took. She couldn't move. She couldn't breathe. She heard Took spit, and then she felt his wet hand moving over her body down there. She tried to moan in preparation for a scream.

"I got this gun right next to your head. If you make noise, I'ma use it," Took panted into her ear.

Kelsi felt dribble coming out of the sides of her mouth under his smothering hand. There was more movement. Next, she felt something slimy up against her left thigh.

Took grunted hard and started shaking like his nerves were bad. Kelsi could tell the slimy thing had moved to his hand. He let out a sigh. After that, he pushed against her. His chest hairs stabbed Kelsi in the face, like how the Brillo stabbed her hands when she washed dirty pots.

Took let out a long sigh. Then, more animal grunts.

The sudden pain that filled Kelsi's torso, abdomen, butt, and legs was almost indescribable. It felt like someone had stuck a thick, fire-lit tree branch up her ass and twisted it over and over. The grunts that came from Took were like a horse after it had run a race or a bull seeing red before it attacked.

Kelsi knew then that what was happening would change her life forever. She also knew that she would never allow it to happen again. She wished for Took to die. The last thing Kelsi remembered was praying for God to strike him down.

Kelsi passed out from the pain. The next thing she remembered was waking up to Carlene's usual rant.

"Listen, bitch, if you think you going to sleep and play with Cheyenne all day this summer, that shit ain't fucking happening. Get your lazy ass up and clean that kitchen and make something to eat," Carlene was ranting.

It hurt for Kelsi to even open her eyes. Her stomach felt like someone had cut her open and gutted her from the inside out. The heat was so thick in the room that her body fluids had her sheets completely soaked.

When Kelsi finally opened her eyes, Carlene's naked ass came into focus. Kelsi was used to that by then.

Carlene had no motherly boundaries at all. Sometimes, she didn't even close her door, and Kelsi could hear her moan and groaning with Took. Cheyenne had told Kelsi that those noises were from sex. She'd learned that from a fast girl on her block named Nasty Neecy.

"What the fuck happened to you? You sick or something?" Carlene rasped.

Kelsi saw the terror etched on Carlene's face.

"Where is you bleeding from?" Carlene screeched. She yanked the sheet all the way off the bed.

There was blood on Kelsi's nightgown. She couldn't unfold her legs. She couldn't blink. She couldn't swallow. She couldn't lift her head. Everything Kelsi attempted to do sent butcher-knife stabs of pain through her entire body.

"Get up and go to the bathroom!" Carlene screamed, grabbing Kelsi's arm roughly. She dragged Kelsi off the bed until her feet hit the floor. Kelsi's knees buckled, and she went down. She hit her chin on the cold tile floor. More pain swirled at the backs of her eyes.

"I know what you did now! I can see it and smell it on you! You fucked around with my fucking man, didn't you? Oh, bitch! I told you I wasn't tolerating that shit! Get the fuck in the bathroom and clean yourself up! Now!" Carlene boomed.

Tears spilled out of Kelsi's eyes. Carlene's accusatory words hurt worse than Took forcing his dick into her virginal opening. With each step toward the bathroom, a fire raged under Kelsi's navel.

"Wash every bit of him off of you! I knew you was going to do this shit! I knew it! I guess your nana ain't teach you no different than she taught me!" Carlene screamed some more. Her voice cracked like she was about to cry.

Kelsi finally made it into the bathroom, and with what little strength she had left, she slammed the door. She plopped down on the toilet, but that made the fire between her legs rage even worse.

Kelsi turned on the water in the tub. When she sat down in the warm water, she knew she might pass out again from the pain. Kelsi used all her might to fight through it.

"Aggggghhhhh!" she screamed over and over again. That fireball of anger in her chest had grown so big it exploded out of her mouth. She had finally reached her breaking point.

Cheyenne figured out right away something was wrong after she knocked on Kelsi's door and Kelsi said she didn't want to go outside to play with her. Kelsi had never and would have never turned down an opportunity to see her best friend in the whole, wide world. Cheyenne and Kelsi had been waiting the entire school year for summertime so that they could spend every hour of every day together until they had to go to bed at night.

"I don't want to go outside. I don't want to go to your house either. Just leave me alone," Kelsi snapped at Cheyenne.

Cheyenne walked away that day, shoulders slumped, on the brink of tears. Kelsi had been so mean to her.

Kelsi felt horrible, but she couldn't take a chance with Cheyenne finding out. Carlene had threatened Kelsi in every which way that if she ever told anyone what Took had done to her, she would be dead. Carlene said she would take Kelsi away from Carey Gardens for good, and she would never see the Turners again. The thought of not seeing Cheyenne, Big K, Ms. Desiree, and Lil Kev made Kelsi change her mind about going to the police on Took.

Kelsi knew that a grown man fucking a nine-year-old was against the law. For two days after what Took had done to her, Kelsi didn't eat. She didn't drink. She didn't sleep. She didn't talk. She didn't cry. She didn't feel. She just felt numb. Kelsi hardly moved from her bed. Whenever she peed, it hurt so badly that Kelsi would hold it until she couldn't take it any longer.

Carlene would come into the front room where Kelsi slept and look at Kelsi like she was the lowest scum of the earth. Carlene would curse, mumble, and then crawl her ass back into her room. She didn't go outside either. Kelsi swore that Carlene had aged ten years in those two days. Her face started looking sunken in, and the skin on her neck looked loose like a turkey's neck. Her body didn't look as filled out as it had. In fact, Carlene's former reindeer ass was barely like a squirrel ass. Her beautifully painted nails became chipped, broken, and brittle looking. Even Carlene's hair didn't look thick and shiny like it had been.

Kelsi hadn't noticed Carlene losing all of her weight over the year that Kelsi had been there, because she was too busy spending time with the Turners. But during those two days, Kelsi stayed in the house and saw Carlene so much that she noticed a drastic change. Carlene had gotten boney, drawn up, and looked older than Ms. Lula now.

Took came and went like he usually did. Whenever Kelsi heard him put his keys into the door to come in, she would snap her eyes shut and pretend to be asleep. He didn't speak to Kelsi. He didn't use the kitchen to cook his stuff either. When Kelsi's eyes were closed, she'd envision sixty different ways she could torture Took while he was awake.

On the fifth day of Kelsi's isolation, Carlene finally left the house. With not so much as a word to Kelsi, Carlene click-clacked her heels down the hallway and out of the apartment.

Kelsi knew Carlene had gotten all dressed up in her saggy dress with no place to go. Carlene hadn't even asked Kelsi if she was hungry or needed anything before she slammed out of the apartment. Kelsi had gotten used to Carlene's neglect.

An hour after Carlene had left, the door rattled from someone knocking on it.

"Kelsi, I know you in there!" Cheyenne screamed from the other side of the door. She wasn't taking no for an answer. She had come to the door with her father.

When Kelsi pulled back the door, her heart felt like it jumped up into her throat.

"Aye, little lady, what's going on with you?" Big K asked, his infectious smile gleaming as usual. Cheyenne stood behind her father with her arms folded, dressed nicely, looking color coordinated, clean, neat, and beautiful as ever. "Why you been giving my princess the cold shoulder and not coming outside or to the house? Did she do something to you?"

"I'm sick," Kelsi lied, dropping her eyes to the floor. She hated lying to Big K. She was not prepared to tell anyone the truth about what had happened to her. How would she have even formulated the words at the time? What would she have said to Big K? It wasn't like she could tell him what Took had done to her and that she was now bleeding and could hardly walk.

"Oh, yeah? What kind of sick? Let me take you to the doctor if you're sick," Big K said as he looked beyond Kelsi and into the apartment.

Kelsi knew he must've been wondering where Peaches was. Kelsi wasn't exactly of age to be home alone.

"No. Um . . . I don't need no doctor. I have medicine and stuff here," Kelsi lied again, a little more frantically.

There was no way Kelsi could let Big K take her to a doctor. She knew by the way she had to pee and make number two that there was something definitely wrong down there, and a doctor would tell right away. She figured the doctor would ask her what happened, and she would have to tell on Took. Kelsi believed if she did that, Carlene would take her away from Cheyenne and Big K forever.

"*Let me come inside and see what kind of medicine you got,*" *Big K said. It wasn't a question or a real hard demand, but Kelsi knew he wasn't going to take no for an answer, especially from her.*

Kelsi stepped aside, and Big K and Cheyenne stepped inside. He looked around curiously. His usually kind eyes grew serious, dark, and scanning. Kelsi could tell Big K knew something was not right.

"*Listen, little lady, why don't you throw on some clothes? I'll take you to the house, and you can get dressed over there. We're going to your favorite place today,*" *Big K said in the most comforting voice he could muster while trying to hide his obvious anger.*

Kelsi was young, but she was old enough in her mind to know that Big K was fighting against his true feelings, because she noticed that his fists were balled so tight the tops of his hands had turned white, and he bit down hard on his bottom lip.

There was no sense in saying no to Big K's request. Kelsi knew by the way Big K started pacing up and down that he was not going to leave her there. Kelsi looked at the tears rimming Cheyenne's eyes as she limped around, trying to get dressed. Even Cheyenne could tell that Kelsi would never be the same.

Chapter 15

Brice

Brice made it to the cemetery just in time to see the Turner family and friends exit the long line of cars filled with people there to see Desiree Turner laid in her final resting place. He was particularly interested in Lil Kev and his crew, who'd boldly come to the services in their gang colors. Some of the biggest drug dealers in Scorpio's crew were in attendance. Through his research of the crew, Brice recognized at least six.

Brice watched from a distance as Desiree Turner was given last prayers and the sendoffs that she deserved. He had been determined to attend the funeral, although his bosses told him it might come across as an invasion of the family's privacy. He refused to miss the funeral. Whoever had killed Desiree Turner might show up, and he wanted to be there in case something might give him a clue about who would want to kill her.

He still wasn't one hundred percent convinced that Desiree's murder was unrelated to Lil Kev and his street beef. Brice had been trying to play Lil Kev close in the days leading up to the funeral, only leaving his surveillance of the boy for short periods at a time so he could conduct his business.

Brice stood back between two huge, ancient-looking slate gray mausoleums and watched the crowd standing around the casket. He watched from his hiding spot as the dudes with Lil Kev kept their heads on a swivel. They looked like they were up to no good. He got a stabbing feeling in his gut. It was never wrong, either.

Suddenly, his cell phone vibrated in his pocket. "Shit," he huffed, taking it out. He got ready to shut it off but saw his lieutenant's phone number flashing on the screen. Brice crinkled his brow, and again, his gut felt like someone had stabbed him in it, so he answered.

"Simpson, it's me. I know you went to that funeral, but I need you to leave right now. We just got a threat here. Someone called it in," the lieutenant said, rushing his words out.

"What? What's going on?" Brice huffed into the phone, his eyes checking his surroundings like the threat was nearby.

"Just leave now. Get the fuck out of there, Simp," the lieutenant yelled into the phone. "Leave now for your own good. I got units on the way, but they might not get there in time."

From his hiding spot, Brice watched as the burial service started breaking up. His heart rate sped up because nothing had happened. He was relieved as he watched the funeral attendees, including Cheyenne, shuffle toward their cars.

Brice moved downhill in the cemetery and headed for his car as well. Brice watched as Lil Kev and three of his crew members climbed into the silver Suburban. There was another SUV full of dudes from Scorpio's crew.

"Shit!" Brice cursed. "Why don't y'all get the fuck out of here," he whispered. He didn't know if the threat called in was credible, but he'd rather be safe than sorry. He kept a safe distance until he saw Cheyenne running back to the spot where her mother's casket was being lowered into the ground.

"Fuck. I'm going to have to go tell her," Brice cursed, getting set to move out of his hiding spot. But he wasn't fast enough.

Boom! The blast sent Brice reeling backward, and a cloud of dust that resembled a huge tornado rose into the sky.

Screams erupted everywhere. The force of the blast sent Cheyenne face first into the dirt, and several other people were knocked down. Cemetery headstones were torn from the ground and went flying into the air. The entire place erupted into massive chaos with people running and screaming.

Brice got up and raced down the hill toward Cheyenne. His ears were ringing, and his head pounded from the sound of the blast, but his mind was clear about what he needed to do.

"Gun! He's got a gun!" someone screamed out. The blast had only been a distraction.

"Oh, shit!" Brice's eyes went round as he raced toward Cheyenne. Frantically, he ran like he was heading for the finish line in an Olympic race. Brice wanted to place his hand inside of his jacket where his weapon was secured in his shoulder rig, but he didn't want to risk slowing himself down.

Before he reached Cheyenne, the sound of rapid-fire explosions cut through the air again. Brice continued to run at full speed down the hill. Dirt and grass flew in his wake as more shots rattled off.

Two of Lil Kev's crew members were picked off, falling to the grass like bowling pins. Screams pierced the air from every direction.

Brice finally reached Cheyenne. She was on her knees in the dirt, covering her ears and screaming at an ear-shattering pitch. Brice grabbed her.

"Come on! Come with me!" he barked.

She seemed to be too shocked to move.

"Come on!" Brice screamed at her even louder this time.

They both looked over just in time to see Big K's body jerk from the impact of the bullets. His arms flew up, bent at the elbow and flailing like he was a puppet on a string.

"Daddy!" Cheyenne screeched as she and Brice watched Big K's body crumple like a rag doll and fall into an awkward heap on the ground.

Brice finally got Cheyenne to her feet, but she stood frozen, her feet seemingly rooted into the earth around her.

"Daddy! No! No!" Cheyenne shrieked, finally finding her voice.

"We gotta go!" Brice yelled.

The sounds of tires screeching and more loud booms exploded around them. Cheyenne coughed as the grainy, metallic grit of gunpowder settled at the back of her throat. She inched in the dirt to where her father lay. The smell of bloody raw meat wafted up her nose. The earth around him pooled into a deep burgundy lake of his blood.

"Daddy!" she screamed, her throat burning with acid. Cheyenne grabbed her father's shoulders and shook them, hoping for a response.

"They got me," Big K croaked out.

"Help! He's alive! Help him!" Cheyenne belted out.

Brice looked up just as the units he'd expected flooded onto the chaotic scene.

Chapter 16

Brice

Brice splashed water on his face, took a deep breath, and looked up at himself in the small, dull mirror that hung in the men's bathroom inside the precinct. He noticed the bags that were starting to form under his eyes, but he knew those came with the territory. Fighting with his sister, helping his mother, and trying to solve a murder case with a victim who had no known enemies wasn't easy. Brice had barely been sleeping.

Shaking off his jitters, he stared at himself and agreed that as soon as this was all over, he would treat himself to a vacation. He would go someplace far away from New York City for sure.

"You got this. This is going to be what you need for this case," Brice spoke to himself as he checked his gear—gun in holster, bulletproof vest on tight, handcuffs loaded for fast application. Everything was set. He would be out there with the Emergency Service Unit. They'd be the ones to knock, announce, and then ram the door, but he still had to make sure he was putting his safety first.

Brice shrugged into his raid jacket. It was five o'clock in the morning, and he had to get into the right state of mind for the task at hand. Walking back out into the squad room, he put his game face on.

"I hope everybody is ready to rock and fucking roll. These young dudes ain't got shit to live for. I've been over there, and they're loose cannons. They shot up a funeral, for Christ's sake. Fucking heartless. Only thing on our side is they'll be 'sleep . . . caught off guard for sure," Brice announced to the officers waiting for the early morning search warrant.

All the ESU officers and a few of Brice's squad detectives stood at attention and started gathering their battle gear as well.

"Yo, Simp. You want to carry this, or should I?" Officer Coolidge asked, picking up the new MP-5 they had just acquired.

"I'll leave that up to you tough guys, but judging from how these little motherfuckers operate, we'll need it," Brice replied, chuckling as they all began to file out the door.

Brice sometimes felt like shit conducting raids in areas he'd grown up in, but not this time. He remembered being a kid, watching the police destroy people's apartments just to get one wayward family member. Brice remembered the devastation some mothers felt after the cops had not only taken away their sons but had also totally destroyed the tiny collection of nice things they'd worked hard as hell to acquire. Living and working in the roughest part of Brooklyn, Brice had seen it all. He had also put in work, moving up from a car-chasing, ticket-giving patrol officer to a homicide detective.

Brice had done his homework on Scorpio and his little crew now. He knew all about the so-called Banger Boys and their notorious leader. Everyone in Brooklyn knew about Scorpio and his powerful drug ring. Apparently, Scorpio had been reigning terror on the streets for years now. He was considered the craziest drug kingpin to hit the streets of Brooklyn since the 1980s. Rumor had it that on his climb to the top, Scorpio had taken out some undercover police officers and a Fed. But with no proof and witnesses that always turned up dead or missing, it had been an almost impossible undertaking for the NYPD to touch him. Brice found out from his friend Pop that Scorpio had bought his way out of being under Pop's tutelage, and once he'd done that, he became a wrecking ball in a china shop. He'd tried to kill Big K at his own wife's burial. That meant he had not one moral fiber in his entire body.

All that Brice had heard wasn't going to stop him from conducting this search warrant on Scorpio's stash spot. Brice was not only interested in bringing down whoever was responsible for shooting up the funeral, but he still wanted to get his hands on Lil Kev's boots. He had a strong suspicion that the boots were going to match the print left at the crime scene. He just hoped his strong suspicion was going to be right.

As Brice rode in the black van with the other officers, he thought about what he knew about the streets himself. There were some dangerous people living amongst the everyday citizens of New York City.

As Brice and the ESU unit arrived at their destination in the worst hood in Brooklyn, Brice shook his head and got ready.

"Here we fucking go," he mumbled under his breath, his heart beating so fast it threatened to jump out of his chest.

Yanking his gun out of his hip holster, Brice barely swung the van door open and jumped out. He waved his hands over his head, placed his fingers up to his lips, and made a fist, signaling his unit to get into their rehearsed raid positions. They all silently exited. They filed into the building and up the stairs in a stack. Once they arrived at the targeted door, they fell in line one behind the other and stacked on the door. Brice was first in the stack—he would knock and announce. The ram holder stood on the opposite side of the door, and the rest of the unit knew their roles in bringing up the back of the stack.

Brice raised his right hand and silently counted down. *One, two, three.* At that, the ram holder sent the heavy-duty metal crashing into the door. The door took several hits before it finally flew off the hinges. Inside, bodies began scrambling in all directions.

"Police! Police! Police with a search warrant! Put your fucking hands where I can see them! Don't move!" Brice screamed, waving his weapon back and forth, pointing it at all of Scorpio's scrambling workers for emphasis.

All the officers trampled inside, grabbing who they could and tossing them to the floor for safety reasons. Brice continued into the house with his gun drawn and keeping his back close to the walls. He had his eye on the prize, and he wasn't going to stop until he had it in custody.

Brice came to a closed door at the back of the apartment. With his gun trained on the door, he kicked it open.

"Damn, man. Put the gun down. You ain't got to go all hard like a fucking cocksucker," Lil Kev snarled as he put his pants on calmly.

Brice was confused by how calm the kid was acting. It was like Lil Kev had been expecting this. He didn't even flinch when the door came crashing in around him.

"Put your fucking hands up, you little bastard!" Brice screamed, pointing his gun right at Lil Kev's chest.

"A'ight, a'ight. Calm down," Lil Kev said, smirking.

Brice was growing more incensed by the minute. He knew the kid was trying to make him look silly, while Lil Kev was looking cool, calm, and collected.

"They pay you to rough niggas up for no reason?" Lil Kev asked, smiling.

"They pay you to get your whole family killed?" Brice shot back. "Let's go! Stand the fuck up!"

"I got one better for you. I will put my hands out so you can cuff me, even though you ain't got one fucking reason to be arresting me," Lil Kev said. "I know my rights, and when my lawyer gets finished with the NYPD, I'll be feeding you crackers out of my hand for the rest of your miserable fucking life." Then he laughed like he'd heard a joke.

Lil Kev turned around and assumed the handcuffing position. He'd pissed Brice off, and the old Brice was at the surface, threatening to come out. Little did Lil Kev know, the old Brice would've kicked his ass, blacked his eyes, and broke a few teeth. Then, he would've turned around and blamed it on Lil Kev resisting arrest. Brice shook his head, thinking Lil Kev was lucky. Real lucky.

"Cuff this little son of a bitch!" Brice spat as one of the officers moved in swiftly to lock the cuffs on Lil Kev.

"Son of a bitch? Oh, now my moms is a bitch," Lil Kev replied, still laughing.

Brice grabbed the cuffs roughly, making sure he gripped them extra tight to cause the metal to cut into Lil Kev's skin. Brice led him out of the apartment and down and out of the building. And, just like he had planned, the media trucks and cameras were right on time to get coverage of the raid.

Brice had to counteract the cemetery shootout with action. He couldn't risk the NYPD looking weak on these crimes. Now, all he had to do was match those boots he'd seized to the ones the killer wore.

Chapter 17

Cheyenne

Cheyenne popped up out of her sleep at the sound of her father's moans. She uncurled her body from the uncomfortable hospital chair, grimacing from the knots in her muscles.

"Daddy?" she called, her voice still heavy with sleep.

Cheyenne swiped her hands over her face, getting rid of the sleep from her eyes and crust from the side of her mouth. Her father stirred again and made another mousy noise. This time, Cheyenne stood up. She stretched the kinks out of her neck and rushed to his bedside.

"Daddy, are you okay?" She touched his hand, being careful not to tug on the intravenous tubes that were taped on top. "I'm here. I'm right here."

Her father's eyes fluttered open. He turned his head to the right and looked up at Cheyenne. She wore a warm smile as she stroked his hand.

"You okay?" he rasped, the oxygen cannula in his nose making his words sound more like puffs of air. "What . . . what happened. Where's Kelsi?" he grumbled.

Cheyenne balked, feeling her insides twist. Her father had just awoken after being shot and almost killed, and he was asking for Kelsi?

"She's not here yet. I couldn't get in contact with her, but I'm sure once she hears about what happened, she's going to come. I am here, though. What do you need?"

Cheyenne said, although she was fighting with her emotions. As usual, she was trying to please her father no matter how she felt inside.

"Call her again," her father said. "If I'm going to die, I want to see her."

Cheyenne bunched her toes up in her shoes and bit the inside of her cheek. Her fingers drummed against her thigh. She was trying to stay patient and play her position as a good daughter, but the feelings she'd been having over the past couple of weeks couldn't be ignored. Still, she put them aside. Watching her father lie there in this condition had scared the shit out of Cheyenne. If he died, she would've become an orphan all in the matter of a month.

"How are you feeling? Are you hungry? Here, let me fluff your pillows," she prattled, although she had a hard knot in the back of her throat and tears burned at the backs of her eyes.

Her father had fallen back off to sleep, side effects of the pain medications. Cheyenne shut her eyes and took a shaky breath.

Cheyenne replayed things in her mind, trying to place what she might have missed with everyone. She thought back on the day she'd spoken to Kelsi seriously about Lil Kev's street ties.

"I'm real proud of you, Cheyenne. I can't front. You always been smart, beautiful, and driven. You ain't let shit stop you from getting that piece of paper. Especially no niggas. I always looked up to you. You way stronger than me. Shit, I ain't even get that li'l high school paper. You got the big dog paper . . . degrees and shit. I'm amazed by your strength. Even when shit got fucked up at home, you still fought through it. I love you for that

power. That power I wish I had," Kelsi said, interrupting the quiet that had settled around them.

Cheyenne lowered her eyes to the floor. Something inside of her felt funny. She was happy Kelsi had said those things, but sad for her. Kelsi's words threatened to make Cheyenne cry. Cheyenne knew Kelsi had been speaking from the heart. Cheyenne also knew Kelsi wished she had listened to Cheyenne all the times she preached to her about finishing high school and going to college.

"Aw, c'mon, chica. Don't be getting all sentimental on me," Cheyenne joked, sniffling back the snot about to run out of her nose. "Real talk, Kel, I look up to you, too. Not many people can deal with what you had to deal with and still be in one piece. I mean, I had my mother there by my side this whole time. You had to fend for yourself, and I really don't think I could ever be that strong. Pat yourself on the back too. You're a damn survivor, girlie," Cheyenne said, changing her tone to serious.

Kelsi rolled up on the bed and sat Indian style. "Well, thank you, Chey. That means a lot coming from you, boo. Now, enough of the sappy shit," Kelsi replied, clapping her hands. "What's the plan now? Ms. Desi said you got into some med school all the way in Texas?" Kelsi continued, hiding her emotions like she always tried to do.

Cheyenne bit into her jaw. She wished her mother didn't have such a big mouth. Cheyenne wanted to be the one to break the news to Kelsi. Cheyenne knew the thought of her leaving Brooklyn wasn't going to be so easy for Kelsi to handle. At that moment, Cheyenne had no choice but to be honest.

"Yeah, I did get into the University of Texas at Austin medical program. It's real hard to get in, so I'm kind of proud I made the cut. But I don't know what I'm going

to do yet. I'm scared to leave my mother. Especially with Lil Kev running the streets now," Cheyenne said solemnly.

Lil Kev was just going into his teenage years and was already trying to build a reputation in their neighborhood. Everybody knew Lil Kev was following in their father's footsteps, like it or not. Some people on the street gave him respect because he was Big K's son, but other people wanted to see him suffer because of it.

Kelsi lowered her head when Cheyenne spoke about Lil Kev. Kelsi knew how serious shit had gotten with him.

"Yeah, I know. I was going to talk to you about that. I was with Scorpio the other night, and Lil Kev came to the crib talking about he was there to re-up. I said to him, 'I know you ain't calling yourself selling for Scorpio.' Girl, he like to damn near cuss me out. Chey, I wanted to take a belt and beat his little ass. You know he's my baby brother too. I mean, shit, I been around since the nigga was knee-high to a fly. Broke my fuckin' heart seeing him waste his life away when Ms. Desiree tried to keep y'all clear of the street bullshit. These fucking streets are mean, Cheyenne. They will swallow his little ass up," Kelsi lamented.

Cheyenne shook her head in disgust. She knew Kelsi was right about Lil Kev, but what about her?

"Neither one of y'all should be fucking with Scorpio," Cheyenne replied quickly. She wasn't going to hide her feelings on that topic. "Scorpio is a fucking snake in the grass, Kelsi. He worked for my father back in the day, and everybody around here says he was a part of the setup that took shit down. He was a part of the crew that got my father knocked. It was just crazy how fast he took over things. And even as young as he was then, do you know how many times he tried to get at my mother after my father was gone?" Cheyenne said to Kelsi

seriously. She wanted Kelsi to know the kind of low-life she was dealing with.

Kelsi rolled her eyes and let out a long sigh. "Cheyenne, I've heard it all before. I mean, I fuck with Scorpio as a means to an end. That's it. Nothing more, nothing less. You think I don't know his history? I'm not trying to marry the nigga. He got fifty-eleven women out here in C.I. But right now, this nigga is keeping clothes on my black-ass back. I ain't got nobody doing shit for me. I mean, look, I'm damn near living with y'all because Peaches' fucked-up ass ain't never did shit for me. Scorpio gives up the loot. I give up the ass, and we got an understanding," Kelsi told Cheyenne with feeling.

Cheyenne guessed that was as honest as Kelsi could be about the situation. Kelsi had already become known around their neighborhood for being a gold-digger and a user.

That was the day Cheyenne realized that she and Kelsi were complete opposites when it came to most things. Cheyenne Turner wasn't depending on a man for shit. She saw where that got her mother.

"Well, why don't you do me a favor? Tell Scorpio to leave my baby brother alone. Tell him don't let Lil Kev work for him or fuck with that business at all. I don't think my mother can take my brother getting knocked. She already suffered twelve years of heartbreak with my father," Cheyenne said seriously, her voice trailing off.

It had already been long, hard years since her father's arrest. Life had surely not played out the way Cheyenne thought it would back when she was nine years old.

"You think I haven't already tried that? Lil Kev is far gone in that shit, Cheyenne. Believe me, my ear is to the street. He got his own thing going on, and ain't nobody going to stop that. Scorpio acting like Lil Kev daddy

now, teaching him the ropes, protecting him, and most
of all influencing him," Kelsi said solemnly.

Hearing that broke Cheyenne's heart. They had a
father. Absent or not, Lil Kev didn't need a two-bit drug
dealer acting as his father. An ominous feeling came
over Cheyenne. Nothing good was going to come of her
brother being in the game. Nothing good at all.

Her father finally got his wish. Kelsi came rushing into
the hospital room, tears flooding down her face.

"Chey! I just heard! What the fuck happened?" Kelsi
cried out loudly. "Oh my God!"

Cheyenne jumped to her feet and grabbed Kelsi, trying
to calm her down. It was too late. Her father's eyes
fluttered open, a clear sign that he was not dead or going
to die. No, he was very much alive.

He kicked his right foot and lifted his left hand to grab
for Kelsi. The heart monitor next to his bed sounded off
with a high-pitched scream. Two nurses rushed into the
room to his bedside.

"What's happening?" Kelsi huffed, panicked, moving
toward the bed within seconds.

The nurses ushered Kelsi and Cheyenne to the side of
the room, away from the patient.

"Unh-uh! I want to know what's happening!" Kelsi
demanded, balling up her fists, ready to charge.

"Please, stay back. We need to treat the patient!" a
nurse chastised from Big K's bedside.

Kelsi kept her hands curled into fists. "Bitch, don't
push me again!"

Cheyenne grabbed Kelsi.

"No, Chey! That's your fucking father lying there. And
he's the only man that ever loved me. They can't just turn
us away like that. I want to know what's happening to him."

The nurse drew one side of the curtain around the bed, shutting Cheyenne and Kelsi out for a few minutes. Cheyenne noticed how emotional Kelsi was and took a mental note that Kelsi hadn't even cried that much when her mother was murdered.

"Mr. Turner, it's going to be okay. You have to remain calm. Don't pull on the tubes or try to get up. You'll injure yourself," a short, stocky nurse with calm eyes and coffee bean–colored skin consoled.

"We're going to have to ask you both to step out," the taller nurse instructed Cheyenne and Kelsi as she peeked out from behind the curtain.

"I'm not going nowhere!" Kelsi boomed.

Cheyenne tightened her grasp and tugged Kelsi toward the doorway. "C'mon, Kels. We've been through enough drama. I don't want to get kicked out of here. Then we won't know shit about what's going on with him. We have to play by the rules for a few minutes, and it'll be okay after that," Cheyenne said as she pulled Kelsi from the room.

Cheyenne forced Kelsi down into a hospital waiting room chair and stared at her best friend for a few minutes. Kelsi was complicated. Cheyenne remembered the day she'd finally figured it out.

"So, how does it feel to be turning twenty-one and graduating from college all at the same damn time?" Kelsi asked excitedly as she flopped down on the other bed in Cheyenne's room, which, over the years, had become Kelsi's bed.

Cheyenne tilted her head to the side and smiled at Kelsi as she worked to remove the last big bobby pin from her doobie.

"It feels like I can finally go legally get drunk after all my fucking hard work," Cheyenne answered, giggling as she shook her long, newly straightened locks of hair out.

They both laughed.

"Shit, I know that's right. But fuck that. I turned twenty-one in August, and I been waiting to get drunk with your ass. I need a fucking drink like nobody's business," Kelsi said, following up with a long sigh. She was staring up at the ceiling.

Cheyenne knew Kelsi was telling the truth about needing a drink. She had a lot to deal with. Kelsi was beautiful, but she didn't think so. She was a little chubby around her stomach, but she had big hips and a big butt. Her face was pretty to Cheyenne, but Kelsi had always hated the acne that left dark marks on her cheeks. Kelsi kept her hair in micro-braids so that she could pretend she had long hair. No matter what flaws Kelsi had pointed out on herself over the years, Cheyenne always thought Kelsi was beautiful.

Kelsi let dudes treat her any kind of way. She'd had many black eyes, broken ribs, and trips to the hospital over the years from dudes putting their hands on her. They'd taken advantage of the fact that Kelsi didn't have a father around. Cheyenne knew Kelsi had been looking for love and acceptance from a man, but Kelsi was the one that didn't think so. She thought she played the "game" so well and that she was always "playing niggas." From Cheyenne's vantage point, Kelsi had always been the one who suffered in the end. All Cheyenne could do was love Kelsi through the rough times as her best friend, so that's exactly what she did.

Chapter 18

Kelsi

Kelsi flopped into the chair in the hospital waiting room, seething. She hated hospitals. Period. Cheyenne was talking, but all Kelsi could see was her mouth moving. Kelsi's mind reeled back to her experience with the hospital.

After Took raped her, Kelsi ended up at Coney Island Hospital. As much as she screamed and begged them not to take her to the emergency room, Ms. Desiree and Big K had taken her anyway. The end result was that Kelsi had to have her perineum stitched. That, as she learned at barely nine years old, was the area between a girl's vagina and rectum. Kelsi stayed overnight at the hospital with Ms. Desiree right by her side.

Cheyenne wasn't really able to understand what was going on. Her mother told her that Kelsi had gotten sick and needed to get better.

Ms. Desiree cried and cried for Kelsi. "She's just a baby. What kind of monster would do that to a baby?" Ms. Desiree whispered to Big K through tears.

"Trust, it ain't gonna be left at this. Any motherfucker that would do this to a kid don't deserve to live," Big K said with feeling.

They thought Kelsi was asleep. Listening to them talk, Kelsi knew then that they really loved her.

Big K picked them up from the hospital the next day with Cheyenne and Lil Kevin. None of them spoke on the way to the Turner house. Kelsi felt too ashamed to speak. Ms. Desiree cried every time she tried to open her mouth to speak. Big K huffed, puffed, and cussed, so he couldn't even speak. Cheyenne sensed that there was something terribly wrong, so she just didn't speak. Lil Kevin was only a baby, so he could barely speak.

When they arrived at the Turner house, Cheyenne and Kelsi went up to Cheyenne's room.

"Surprise!" she yelled as she pushed open the door.

Kelsi's eyes lit up. The room was filled with balloons, teddy bears, and flowers.

"Daddy got all of these for you." Cheyenne beamed.

Kelsi inched into the room slowly, the stitches still making her walk funny. The doctor had said they would dissolve on their own. Kelsi stood in the middle of the floor like a lost child. Hot tears ran a race down her cheeks.

"You don't like them?" Cheyenne asked, moving toward Kelsi

"No, I love them. I love them a lot. I love all of y'all a lot," Kelsi cried, unable to control the floodgate of tears that had opened up.

Cheyenne hugged her tight. "We love you too, Kelsi, and we ain't never going to let nothing bad happen to you again," Cheyenne promised.

For the first time in Kelsi's life, she believed someone's promise. Even Nana hadn't kept her promise to keep her in the Bronx with her. But with the Turners, something in Kelsi's heart told her the promise was real.

Cheyenne was the one who told Kelsi about what happened to Took. He was beaten so badly, she said, that his entire face had become unrecognizable. All his fingers were broken, and every tooth in his mouth was knocked out. Cheyenne told Kelsi she also heard that whoever beat up on Took had also shoved three broomsticks taped together up his butt hole. Cheyenne was been the first one to start laughing when she said " up his butt hole," and then Kelsi burst out laughing right behind her.

Kelsi laughed so hard at the end she was crying. She didn't feel sorry for Took, not one bit. But for the weeks that she stayed at the Turner's, Kelsi often wondered about Carlene. Took was always the one who made sure Carlene had stuff, like food, the medicine she took to keep from being sick every morning, and just basic things like soap to wash her ass. Kelsi could only imagine what Carlene was doing to stay afloat while Took was gone.

After a few days of worrying about Carlene, Kelsi stopped thinking about her entirely. Out of sight, out of mind.

It was almost the end of summer before Kelsi's body fully healed. She finally got well enough to go back out-side with Cheyenne. Although Kelsi thought about what had happened to her every day, she put on a happy face and tried to be a normal nine-year-old.

Cheyenne and Kelsi were sisters in every sense of the word. Ms. Desiree treated them as equals, even when they got in trouble for giggling all night when they were supposed to be asleep. They would ride with Big K over to the projects every day. While he "worked," they played double-dutch, hopscotch, hula-hoops, red light green light, steal the bacon, and skelly.

Cheyenne and Kelsi were called the Bobsie twins. They dressed alike. They acted alike. They liked the same foods. The Turners had essentially adopted Kelsi.

Most days, when Big K finished up his work at the building, he would take Cheyenne and Kelsi to the rides.

Sometimes, he got finished early and would pick up Ms. Desiree and Lil Kev, and they'd all go to the movies and dinner in Sheepshead Bay. Those nights became Kelsi's favorites because she got to watch how Big K loved all over Ms. Desiree. How he opened doors for her, held her hand, kissed her, and smiled at her like she was the only woman alive. Kelsi would pretend she was Ms. Desiree and Big K was her husband instead.

Kelsi would never forget the day when life as they all knew it came to a screeching halt. It was a blazing hot August day in 1996. Kelsi had just turned ten the week before. Cheyenne and Kelsi were about to jump out of Big K's Range Rover with their matching Guess jean skirt outfits, hula-hoops, and two bags filled with candy.

"Stay right in front, little ladies. I'm not staying that long today," Big K said as he parked the Range Rover.

"Okay, Daddy," Cheyenne said as she and Kelsi giggled out of the door.

"Okay, Daddy," Kelsi whispered after her.

They started laughing harder. Big K parked and got out. Kelsi watched him walk with his distinct bop toward the building. She always watched him go in and come out with his money.

That day, as he walked closer to the door, something seemed different to Kelsi. There weren't half as many people outside as usual. Lula was even missing from her bench.

Cheyenne was gabbing to Kelsi about something because she was nowhere near as observant or street smart as Kelsi was. Being raped had done away with the little carefree kid in Kelsi. She noticed everything, and she was always watching people.

"Where is everybody?" Cheyenne finally asked, stopping for a minute.

Kelsi swung her head from left to right. Her face grew serious as her eyes scanned. She opened her mouth to respond but never got the chance. She had her eye on Big K's back, and then BOOM!

It all happened in slow motion. Big K yanked on the door handle of the building, and as soon as he pulled it back, Kelsi and Cheyenne heard it. It was like thunder and lightning had struck. The rumble of feet came from everywhere like a herd of wild elephants were trampling through the block.

"Police! Police! Don't move! Put your fucking hands on your head!"

Cheyenne whipped her head around and saw what Kelsi had already been watching.

"Daddy!" Cheyenne screeched at the top of her lungs.

Kelsi grabbed her and pulled her down to the ground. Loud flash bangs erupted around them. Kelsi felt her heart hammering against her chest.

"Daddy!" Cheyenne screamed again.

Kelsi held onto Cheyenne with all her might to keep her from running toward Big K and the danger. Police with long guns, short guns, helmets, and black bullet-proof vests had surrounded Big K. Kelsi and Cheyenne watched in horror as they threw Big K to the ground face first.

Kelsi saw blood explode from Big K's face and nose. That was when she started screaming too.

"Big K! No! You can't take him! He didn't do nothing wrong!" Kelsi let out a guttural scream. "Don't hurt him!" She got to her feet and raced toward Big K with Cheyenne hot on her heels.

Within seconds, Kelsi was scooped off her feet like a little ragdoll.

"Hey! Get out of here, little girl, before you get hurt!" a police officer chastised.

Cheyenne was right next to Kelsi, flailing wildly as another officer held her. She sobbed uncontrollably.

"Let her go. Let her go," Kelsi screeched.

Cheyenne was thrown right down next to Kelsi. They hugged each other tightly up against a fence and watched as Big K was hoisted up off the ground in handcuffs.

"It's going to be all right, little ladies," was the last thing Big K said to them before he was thrown into the back of a waiting black van.

Sixteen other guys that they knew from Kelsi's building were also arrested and carted off like animals.

Cheyenne and Kelsi cried for two days straight after. Ms. Desiree cried for months, maybe years after. The final word about Big K's arrest was that Took had snitched on Big K and taken down his entire empire just like that. It was all because of Kelsi and the beating Took had been given by Big K and his workers. Big K had risked everything—all because he was protecting Kelsi.

Chapter 19

Brice

"Fuck!" Brice growled as he slammed the phone at his desk down. He got to his feet and paced, the vein at his temple throbbing.

"What's going on, Simp?" the lieutenant asked, coming out of his office in response to the noise.

"The fucking boots we got at the search warrant don't match," Brice replied, pinching the bridge of his nose, trying to ease the pressure cooker in his brain that was about to blow its top.

"Did you test any others?" the lieutenant asked.

"No," Brice grumbled. "I thought for sure these would match. I had a lot of reason to believe this kid might've been there when it happened. All fingers pointed to him or his enemies," Brice huffed, shaking his head in disgust.

"What about the husband?" the lieutenant asked. "We always have to check the husbands."

"He's laid up in the hospital after thugs shot up his wife's funeral trying to get revenge on his son," Brice said.

"How do you know those same thugs weren't trying to kill the man they shot?"

Brice sat back in his chair and rubbed his chin. He'd been so laser focused on Lil Kev that he might've missed a lot. He picked up his phone and dialed Cheyenne's number. He was going to need to see her

***

Cheyenne had been waiting for Brice. As soon as he knocked, the door swung open.

"I heard you had to let my brother go," Cheyenne said as soon as Brice crossed the threshold.

Brice's cheeks flamed over. "Yeah, his boots didn't match the print left at the scene."

"Well, I've been thinking a lot and seeing a lot around here. So, here. I bagged these up for testing," Cheyenne said, pushing a bag of boots toward Brice.

"Damn. How many pairs are here?" he asked.

"Everybody in the house owns more than one pair. Kelsi had hers packed up. I found out she was leaving town before she found out my father got shot. Now she can't leave his bedside. Just so weird," Cheyenne confessed.

"Tell me a little bit about that. Is there anything I should know about those two?" Brice asked.

"All I can say for sure is that Kelsi is definitely in love with my father. It is not the same as when we were kids and she thought of him as a father figure. Kelsi Jones is in full-out love with my father. It's no longer a gut feeling. It's the truth," Cheyenne said with feeling.

Brice sucked in his breath. He had to get to the lab quick before Kelsi had a chance to leave town. He had an entirely new outlook on Desiree Turner's case.

Within a week, Brice had a match to the print. He'd also found blood on one of the shoes that matched his victim and his suspect.

Chapter 20

Kelsi

Kelsi knew when she heard the police radios that they'd come to the apartment for her. She stood up beside the bed and slipped on a shirt and some sweats. Cheyenne had stayed out the night before, so Kelsi was smart enough to understand that her best friend knew exactly what was going to happen to her. Big K was still in the hospital, so he couldn't help her.

Kelsi put her hands up before Detective Simpson could instruct her to do it. She didn't cry. She didn't fight. She didn't curse. She was actually relieved, and her relaxed stance said as much. The guilt of what she'd done and how it had all gone had been killing her inside. The only thing Kelsi regretted at that moment was that she hadn't killed herself.

The police carted her out of the building in handcuffs to the shock of everyone in the neighborhood. Her head was pushed down into the police car, and she looked out of the window at the building. She looked out at all the faces. She stared into space, thinking about how she'd gone from the friend to a foe. Kelsi thought back on how she'd gotten to this place.

The day Cheyenne left for medical school, she left Kelsi with a huge void, a hole in Kelsi's life so big that

*nothing or no one could ever fill it. Kelsi moped around
the apartment for hours alone. Being alone forced her
to look back on her life. She was twenty-one years old,
the daughter of a crack whore, a high school dropout,
and the sex toy of the local drug dealer, who treated her
like a piece of shit under his Prada shoes. Kelsi would
do anything for a quick buck, including suck dick, fuck
in public places, and let herself be passed around for
enjoyment. Kelsi had the stereotypical hood chick's
story, even with the good influence of the Turners.*

*Kelsi was in Cheyenne's room on her bed when she
heard the apartment door slam. She figured it was
Ms. Desiree coming back from the airport from taking
Cheyenne. Kelsi had so many questions for Ms. Desi
about whether Cheyenne finally broke down at the airport or if Cheyenne had sent her any parting messages.
Kelsi wrapped herself in her robe and went toward the
front of the apartment.*

*"Oh, shit!" She had bumped straight into Big K. "You
scared the shit out of me," Kelsi wolfed as she stumbled
backward.*

*"You ran into me, so how I scared you? There you go
again, walking with that head down," he joked.*

Kelsi smiled.

*"Pretty girls are not supposed to walk with their heads
down. I told you that before," Big K chastised playfully.*

Kelsi blushed.

*He changed his course, and they both headed into the
living room/kitchen area. That was the first time in a
long while that Kelsi felt that old tingly feeling again.
She felt an overwhelming closeness and tingling inside
for Big K that she used to feel when she first was around
him as a kid.*

*"So, how did things go with Cheyenne at the airport?"
Kelsi asked, grabbing some orange juice from the
refrigerator.*

Big K frowned so hard his eyebrows dipped between his eyes.

"I didn't go with them. I thought you knew that. Cheyenne probably didn't want me there anyway. She's her mother's child. I can't compete there," Big K said sadly. "I thought for sure you would go," he followed up, more like a question than a statement.

Kelsi stopped pouring the juice and gave him an equally strange frown. "I couldn't even take helping her pack without crying all over the place. No way I was going to make it in the airport. I would've been a damn blubbering fool out there," she answered.

"Yeah, same here," he said solemnly. "I didn't want to crowd her mother either. You know? I already feel like the outsider around here. I wanted to give them their space and time before she got on that plane."

Kelsi heard the hurt in his voice. Something flashed red inside of her. How dare they leave him out of such an important event! They are both selfish bitches for that! *She ranted in her head. That was the first time she was angry at Cheyenne and Ms. Desi in defense of Big K. It wouldn't be the last.*

"So, tell me about you. I have been so caught up in getting my family to want me here that I haven't even had time to find out how you're really doing . . . I mean, with Peaches all fucked up and—" Big K started.

Kelsi twisted her lips. He noticed and stopped talking.

"Damn. I never realize how awkward it is when someone asks me how I'm doing. I'm so used to people not really giving a fuck, or either they just know what's up," Kelsi replied, pushing the glass away as she'd suddenly lost her desire to drink the juice.

"I always cared, though. Since Cheyenne met you, I've always cared about you . . . a lot," Big K replied.

Kelsi smiled. She noticed that he never said he cared for Kelsi like a daughter. Kelsi thought maybe he felt the same tingly, man-and-woman love for her that she'd felt for him all of these years. At least that was how she took his statement.

"I know you did. I always felt that you cared. I never stopped feeling that even when you were away," Kelsi said, her voice going low. She wasn't able to look him in the eyes. She felt so vulnerable at that moment.

Big K reached over and used his hand to lift Kelsi's chin. "I already told you . . . pretty girls don't walk around with their heads down. No matter what the situation is, you hold your head up high. Always," Big K said, letting the kind smile she remembered from back in the day spread across his face.

Kelsi hadn't seen that smile since he'd been home. She felt powerful that the first time she saw it come back was while he was speaking to her and not to Ms. Desiree.

Big K and Kelsi talked for hours that first day Cheyenne was gone. Kelsi bared her soul and told him everything. She held nothing back about her past relationships— who she had fucked in the neighborhood, how many times she had been pregnant and had abortions. Kelsi told him all about her abusive relationship with Scorpio. And, most revealing of all, Kelsi disclosed to Big K all the trouble she still had with sex after what Took had done to her. She talked to Big K that day like he was a licensed professional therapist. Never once did she feel like Big K was judging her. In fact, the way he listened so intently made Kelsi feel a deeper love and respect for him. It wasn't like a father/daughter love and respect, either. It was that mutual respect that two adults have for one another when both have nothing else to hide.

Big K and Kelsi also joked and recalled their little run-in one time in the house. They spoke about how between

Big K and Ms. Desiree, Kelsi had gotten back on her feet in a month after the beating she'd taken from Scorpio. Ms. Desiree had wrapped Kelsi's ribs so that they could heal, and Big K had sat guard-dog by Kelsi's side every day when Ms. Desiree had to work. Kelsi heard Carlene had come by once, but it wasn't to see how Kelsi was doing. She had wanted to borrow some money, as usual. Big K told Kelsi he had run Carlene off with some of his old-school threats. Kelsi and Big K had a good laugh behind that.

The first full shower Kelsi took took after Scorpio's assault felt so good. Even the initial painful pinpricks all over her skin from the hot water hurt so good. Kelsi spent more than an hour letting the water beat over her tender body. When she finally turned the water off, she pulled back the shower curtain and—

"Ahh!" she screamed. She was so startled that she almost slipped and busted her ass in the wet tub.

"Oh, shit! Kelsi! I thought that was Desiree in there," Big K yelled in response, startled himself.

Kelsi was butt naked right in front of him. She couldn't even reach her towel. It was too far away. Kelsi was too shocked to think to cover her nakedness with the shower curtain. Her heart hammered in her chest. It seemed like everything was going in slow motion.

Big K stood there, seemingly stuck on stupid. Staring at Kelsi, he didn't turn and run away.

Kelsi was also stuck on stupid, letting him take in an eyeful of her body. It seemed like an eternity before either one of them did anything to fix it.

"Shit! I'm really sorry about this. I'm so sorry," Big K said over and over as he backed out of the bathroom and slammed the door.

Kelsi stepped out of the tub on wobbly legs. Maybe I need to just take my ass to Carlene's and stop staying here. Especially because Cheyenne ain't here and Ms. Desiree is always at work, *Kelsi thought. Her brain felt scrambled. She wrapped herself in a thick, plush towel, but she still felt like it wasn't big enough to cover her.*

Kelsi stood in the bathroom an extra twenty minutes, gathering her thoughts. She looked at herself in the mirror that hung over the bathroom sink and touched the remnants of the scars that remained on her forehead and above her lip.

"You need to get your life together, Kelsi," she whispered to herself. Kelsi didn't even know where to start when it came to getting her shit together, but she knew the way she had been living was destructive for sure.

Kelsi opened the bathroom door slowly, peeked her head out real quick, and dipped back into the bathroom. Her chest was rising and falling rapidly. She peeked out one more time, then darted for Cheyenne's room. Kelsi made it into the room without running into Big K again. Once she was in the room, she flopped down on the bed, and oddly enough, Kelsi smiled. Big K had seen her naked. She smiled at the thought. As sick as it sounded, Kelsi smiled and smiled some more.

Two nights after the bathroom incident with Big K, Kelsi awoke to another one of Big K and Ms. Desiree's arguments. They had been arguing way more often since Cheyenne and Lil Kev were gone from the house. Sometimes Kelsi thought her being there when their own kids had left might be awkward for them. Kelsi thought maybe she should just go home and deal with her crackhead mother. Good, bad, or indifferent, Carlene was what God had given her.

After a few minutes of Big K and Ms. Desiree screaming back and forth, Kelsi heard the apartment door slam shut. Either Big K or Ms. Desiree had left.

Kelsi lay there for a little while, wondering who had stayed and who had gone. She looked at the clock. It was 4:42 a.m. Her curiosity finally got the best of her, and she got up and walked to the kitchen, faking like she wanted something to drink.

The entire apartment was dark. Kelsi flipped on the kitchen light. That was when she saw who had stayed.

"Damn, I was trying to be quiet and not wake you up. Could you tell by all of the yelling how hard I tried?" Big K joked, smiling even though Kelsi knew he was really stressed.

She smiled at his little joke. He was at the table, in the dark, with his head down. Kelsi pulled up a chair, set her glass of juice on the table, and joined him.

"I could barely hear anything," she lied jokingly. They both laughed.

Big K shook his head from side to side like the weight of the world was set on his broad shoulders. He looked at Kelsi and let out a windstorm of breath.

"You know it's fucked up when a man comes home after what felt like a hundred long years of being locked up with motherfuckers that act like animals every day and feel like he wants to be back in the lockup. All those long-ass years of fighting, clawing, praying, politicking, fighting some more, just to stay in one piece so he could come home to his woman and kids. But when he gets home, he can't even fit in with his own family. Everybody is a stranger in his own home. He can't fit in nowhere in their lives at all. You know how fucked up I am behind this? Nah, you wouldn't know. Nobody knows what it's like to have your manhood tested by your own flesh and blood," Big K preached sadly.

Kelsi felt a twinge in her stomach. She felt the pain in his words. She couldn't even imagine what it must have been like for Big K inside that prison, dying to get home, only to come home to an ungrateful-ass family.

"It might take them some time to adjust. They got so used to living on their own," Kelsi comforted softly, choosing her words carefully. The truth was, in Kelsi's opinion, his family members were all resentful that they had to fend for themselves after Big K got locked up. The selfish-ass Turners had been used to being spoiled by the lifestyle they lived when Big K was on the outside. They had no use for him after he came home.

Not Kelsi. She didn't see things the way Ms. Desiree, Cheyenne, and Lil Kev saw them. In Kelsi's eyes, Big K was still the man. He had come home, and to her, he was the same motherfucker that used to feed the hood on Thanksgiving. He was the same nigga that would take other people's kids to get school clothes.

Kelsi was able to hold on to the good deeds Big K had done for her before he got locked up. She was able to hold onto them so tight that she ended up being the only one who really treated him with the respect that the man of the house deserved. Kelsi held tight to every last good deed he'd done for her. She understood that Big K had really risked everything to get revenge on Took for her. With those memories fresh in Kelsi's mind, she was able to stay loving Big K even after years of missing him.

"Time to adjust! They had years to think about shit. I mean, how is my teenage son so deep in the streets that I can't say a word to him? How is my daughter so far removed from me that when she calls from Texas, she forgets to ask to speak to me? And my wife . . . man, listen. Truth be told, she doesn't even want me to touch her. You know what that's like for a man? A man like me who always lived and breathed for his family? Every risk I took back then on the come-up was to make shit better for all of them. Not for me, for them!" Big K lamented, hitting his chest with his hands to emphasize his pain.

He spoke so powerfully Kelsi was moved to tears. She touched his arm gently. "If it makes you feel any better, I always have and always will appreciate you. You are the only man who has ever shown me any love," Kelsi said sincerely.

Afterward, she'd lowered her head and stared down at the table. That was the damn truth as raw as she could've ever delivered it. It was the first time Kelsi told Big K how she'd always felt about him.

Big K grabbed Kelsi's hand. The warmth of his skin against hers sent stabs of heated sparks up her arm and down her spine. Something jumped inside of her. Right at the core of her being, his touch let her know there was something between them. There had always been something between them. He was old enough to be her father, but the connection could not be denied. It was immediate, magnetic, and undeniable right from that moment.

There was an awkward, silent pause. Kelsi couldn't say for sure who made the first move after that, but one of them certainly did. The next thing she knew, Big K's tongue parted her lips. Kelsi gladly opened her mouth to welcome his tongue inside. It was warm and tasted like Big Red cinnamon gum.

Their tongues did a wicked dance with one another. Heat engulfed Kelsi's entire body. Her sore ribs ached, but Big K's touch hurt so good. The achy feeling that throbbed through Kelsi's torso intensified her desire for Big K.

His hands moved all over her so fast she wasn't able to tell what he was touching at any given moment. Kelsi didn't feel like herself. She felt ravenous. Wild. Freaky.

Kelsi reached down and grabbed a handful of his manhood. He's your best friend's father. The thought flitted through her mind, but she ignored it. He was the man Kelsi had loved from the time she could feel the emotion.

She clamped down on his swollen member. Big K let out a gasp. Kelsi moved her mouth to his bottom lip and sucked on it as she massaged his throbbing bulge.

"Oh, shit!" he gasped. "What are we doing?" he whispered as he pulled Kelsi's T-shirt over her head, exposing her bouncy C-cup breasts.

Big K hoisted Kelsi onto the table. The glass of juice she had poured earlier shattered to the floor. Neither one of them cared. Kelsi eased back, her entire body trembling. Big K leaned in and took a mouthful of her left areola.

"Oh God!" Kelsi huffed out, panting. Her breasts had always been her weak spot.

Big K suckled both of her breasts until she was ready to explode. Kelsi's head fell back as he moved his mouth down to her navel. Her body quaked all over, and her pussy got soaking wet. As Big K removed Kelsi's panties, she felt her own juices leaking down her butt crack.

"You okay?" he whispered as he continued his journey downward.

They were really doing this! Kelsi was more than okay with it.

"Oh God! Yes! Yes!" Kelsi wolfed, barely able to get her words out. Her mind had gone blank. Nothing registered, except that pure feeling of ecstasy that had come over her.

Next, Big K put his warm mouth over her clit. Kelsi let her thighs fall open and invited him to taste her, lick her, and suck her. Big K flicked his tongue over her dripping hot box rapidly. Then, in and out. In and out.

"Ahh! Ahh!" Kelsi panted. She had never been handled like that.

"Please! I want you! I want you so bad!" Kelsi groaned out, her words labored like she'd been running on a treadmill.

Big K lifted his head from between Kelsi's legs. She heard the elastic on his boxers snap and knew what it meant. Kelsi shut her eyes tighter, waiting. Big K grabbed her with his strong, muscular arms and pulled her toward him. She wrapped her legs around him.

"Agghh!" Kelsi belted out.

Big K entered her, and his dick immediately filled her up. She felt a little bit of pain shoot through her pussy, but it quickly subsided into pleasure.

"Huh! Huh! Huh!" Big K wheezed as he rammed his body into her pelvis with the vigor of a jackhammer. Big K moved so fast Kelsi started slipping off the table. She tightened her legs around him, which forced him deeper into her. Kelsi could've sworn his dick was touching her cervix.

"Oh God!" she gasped as he grinded into her. Kelsi bit into his neck. She didn't mean to, but she couldn't help it.

Big K hoisted her up and moved her over to the couch without taking his dick out of her. He moved carefully with his boxers around his ankles.

"Your shit it so good! So good!" he wolfed through labored breaths.

They made it to the couch without falling. He laid Kelsi down on the couch and kneeled in front of her. He pulled her closer, which caused her to feel his thickness way up inside.

Big K moved his hips in circular motions as he held onto Kelsi's hips. He wanted to make sure she felt every bit of him.

Kelsi also wanted to make sure she pleased him. In her crazed state, Kelsi told herself she wanted to do what Ms. Desiree couldn't do. Kelsi wanted to be the best woman. After all, the best woman wins, right?

"Yes, grind it. Grind this pussy! It's your pussy! I'm not giving it to nobody else ever again. It's all yours," Kelsi huffed. She didn't know what had come over her. She felt like she'd been possessed by the deep love she had for Big K. She couldn't help it. He'd taken over her mind and body.

"Oh, fuck me! I'm right there! I'm right there!" Kelsi panted. She felt a few drops of dribble escaping the sides of her mouth. Big K had her mouth literally watering. Kelsi had never felt like this. None of the punk-ass dudes she had fucked had ever hit the right spot. The overwhelming feeling invading her was like what she imagined a sunburst must feel like. She felt as if spurts or flashes of sunlight were exploding inside of her groin.

Then it happened. It all burst.

"Ahhhhh! Yes! Ahhh!!!" Kelsi screamed over and over. She had just experienced her very first orgasm, and she knew it as soon as she felt it.

"Arrrgggh!" Big K followed right after. His body completely relaxed. He moved out of Kelsi, still hard. Then he collapsed onto the floor while she was still on the couch.

Neither of them said a word after. They both realized that they had crossed a boundary that they could never take back. Kelsi never wanted to take it back, either.

Chapter 21

Brice

Brice sat across from Kelsi Jones, waiting to hear her statement. He'd been shocked to find out that it was her boot that matched the footprint at the crime scene. She'd let him arrest her without incident, almost like she'd been waiting for it.

Brice had learned a lot about the entire family during the investigation, but he certainly wanted to hear from Kelsi now. He wanted to know why she'd done what she did.

"Well, Kelsi. I feel like we know each other well enough," Brice said.

"Yup. I'm not going to make this shit hard for nobody. I'm just going to tell you exactly what the fuck happened," Kelsi came back, full of attitude.

Brice put his hands up. "Whenever you're ready," he said, clicking on the recorder that sat on the table between them.

"After that first time we fucked, Big K and I fucked every chance we got. As soon as Ms. Desi left for work. Right before we knew she'd be home. Sometimes, we had quickies while she showered. It was foul. It was risky. It was exciting. At first, it was a game to me, but it quickly became obvious that I was in love with this man. If he had asked me to jump off the Verrazano Bridge to prove my love, I would've asked what time and from what point.

Anyone who couldn't understand where I was coming from after going unloved almost my entire life could kiss my ass," Kelsi started off.

Brice swallowed the lump that had formed in his throat, and without realizing it, his hand went up to his temple. He got an immediate headache listening to Kelsi.

"Two months after our love affair started, I got up one morning and found Big K at the kitchen table with a stack of papers in front of him. I smiled at him, but he didn't smile back at me. 'Good morning to you too,' I said to him. Like, shit—I knew we hadn't had a disagreement or nothing.

"'Check this shit out,' he told me, and then he slid the stack toward me.

"I read the headline: NATIONAL BENEFiT LIFE INSURANCE COMPANY and looked at him like, *yeah and*?

"'Desiree took out a one-point-five-million-dollar policy on me. She also made me the beneficiary of her two-million-dollar policy. She gives me these fucking papers and tells me to sign them. She don't discuss them with me or nothing,' he told me, kind of angry. He seemed stressed, like he thought there was some sinister reason for her taking the insurance out on him.

"'So, what's wrong with that?' I asked him. I wasn't tracking with him. A lot of husbands and wives had insurance on each other.

"He looked at me seriously. 'She also gave me these,' he said, sliding some more papers toward me. I read them over, and my heart began racing wildly in my chest. She's buying them a house? In Long Island? What about me? How will I see Big K? My mind raced like crazy, but I never actually said the questions to Big K that day.

"'She's trying to get us up out of these projects. The only place I've ever know is Coney Island,' Big K complained. He never said anything about not being able to see me anymore. I mean, I was grown now. The chances of Ms. Desi inviting me to move into their new house with them would probably be slim. I was quiet," Kelsi said, her voice cracking.

Brice was hanging on Kelsi's every word. He was thinking this shit was like a movie or something. "Okay, so she wanted to move and had taken insurance out on him," Brice said, moving Kelsi along in her story.

"Yeah, so Big K was like immediately plotting or something. 'You know what two million could do for us right now? Me and you? We could get rid of everybody. We could really be together for good. I would have enough to be a real factor in the game out there. I could put my investment up and triple that shit in no time. I could take you with me to another country where we could live like a fucking king and queen off that, baby girl,' he told me. It was like he was selling me a dream. Those were the words I'd been dying to hear my whole entire life. Big K speaking about us having a future together. As insane as it might've seemed at the time, I was longing for that.

"'You hear me, baby girl? That money could free us,' he told me as he pulled me onto his lap. He wrapped his arms around me and massaged my breasts. I closed my eyes and smiled. I could actually picture us living together happily ever after. I was quiet while I dreamt of what it would actually be like to have our love on public display instead of all of the sneaking around we were doing. He knew I was desperate for love. He wanted to play on that.

"'Too bad Desiree would be in the way of our dream. I mean, she would have to die before I got that shit,' Big K said to me all sad-like. It was the furthest thing from my mind. Honestly, I always loved Ms. Desi.

"'Yeah, we might as well forget it. She's the picture of health. She won't be dying no time soon,' I told him, totally dismissing the idea that she might die. I stood up

from his lap. I was uncomfortable all of a sudden. We
were getting a little too bold for our own good.

"'Even people who are the picture of health die. They
could die in accidents. They could die in a robbery gone
wrong. I mean, good health ain't got shit to do with
it. Especially when you live in the projects. Especially
when your husband and son was in the game and made
enemies. You feel me?' Big K told me.

"I remember screwing up my face as I listened to him. I
was confused. What the fuck was he trying to say? I asked
myself.

"He didn't keep his intentions a secret for long at all.
Right after that, Big K fucked me in the shower. He
fucked me so good I got nauseous and threw up after-
wards," Kelsi said, her voice cracking with emotion. She
looked up at Brice to gauge his reaction.

His eyes were wide, but he quickly put on his poker
face. He was completely flabbergasted by what he was
hearing, but he knew, in order to keep her talking, he'd
have to play it cool.

"He . . . he was kind of proud that I had gotten sick.
'Damn, I fucked the shit out you, huh?' he asked me as I
threw up in the toilet. 'Either that or your ass is pregnant
with my seed.'

"I hadn't even considered that possibility. A cold feeling
shot down my spine when he said that. In all the time
we'd been having sex, I hadn't even realized that my
period was missing.

"*Kelsi! What the fuck is wrong with you? What are you
doing?* I screamed in my head. Big K didn't care. He just
grabbed me from the back and fucked me some more.

"When Ms. Desi came home that night, I faked like I
was asleep. I heard her come to the room and tiptoe back
out when she saw that I was asleep. I listened as she took
her shower. Then, I heard it. I was frozen. Paralyzed by

anger. That fire had sparked up in my chest again, and I could hardly control my breathing.

"I lay there listening as Big K had sex with Ms. Desi. I immediately hated her. I hated her for being his real wife. I hated her for being able to fuck him while someone else was in the apartment. I hated her for having what I thought was mine. That night, I put myself against Ms. Desi. It was a crazy way to think, but in my crazy-ass mind, she had become my enemy.

"Every day for three weeks, Big K worked his magic on me. He fucked me. He fed me lies. He pumped me up, and he made a plan. We would be together forever. He would love me forever—if I did this one thing to make sure," Kelsi said, and then paused like she couldn't bring herself to go any further.

Brice needed her to say it. He needed to know what exactly happened. "Kelsi, you've been brave and courageous talking to me up to this point. I know you loved Ms. Desi. I know you love Cheyenne. I know you know that they both deserve closure. Tell me what happened . . . your side of the story. The only thing you have left is your side of the story," Brice said, urging Kelsi to tell him everything.

Kelsi was sobbing until her body rocked, but she talked. "The night Big K gave me the nine-millimeter Glock, he handed it to me and said, 'This is what is going to make things for us official. We won't have anybody to worry about, and we will have the money we need.' I took the gun, stuffed it into my bag, and left the apartment. I had had five shots of Patron that served as my liquid courage that night.

"I tried to clear my muddled mind. I couldn't allow myself to think about Nana, who I had missed dearly. I couldn't think about my friendship with Cheyenne. I couldn't think about my past. I couldn't think about my piece-of-shit mother. I couldn't think of anything except being with the man I had always loved. Finally getting love from somebody was motivation enough for me.

"I started to fantasize about the future Big K and me would have. Being able to walk down the street holding his hand. Being able to marry him in a church. Most of all, being able to give birth to the baby I was carrying and celebrate with Big K like parents of a newborn should. Those fantasies propelled me to do what I did. I can't remember much from that night because I have purposely put it out of my mind. But just like Amy Fisher, I know that I pulled the trigger to do away with the wife of the man I loved. I was finally going to have someone of my own. At least that's what I had convinced myself. As crazy as it may seem now, I actually felt like I'd done the right thing for everyone involved."

Kelsi and Brice sat in silence for what seemed like an eternity. Brice was stuck. He had seen and heard a lot of things, but this . . . this was something else. This girl had been practically raised as Big K's other daughter. She had been more than a friend in the Turner family, and suddenly, she'd turned into a foe. Brice realized then that there was a thin line between love and hate.

Chapter 22

Kelsi

Kelsi remembered exactly what happened and how it happened. She could and would never forget.

Big K timed it all out for Kelsi. He had been watching Ms. Desiree at work for months because he thought she was cheating on him with some doctor. He was the one who told Kelsi which stairwell to hide in near the elevator Ms. Desiree would take to the man's BMW.

Ms. Desiree had her bag flung over her arm, and she was humming a tune when she got off the elevator. At that moment, Kelsi wondered what the fuck she could be so happy about. She was planning on buying a house and trying to leave Kelsi behind! That's what Kelsi told herself.

Kelsi took her last swig of Patron from the flask Big K had given her. She winced as it burned her chest going down. It eased her nerves a lot. Kelsi fingered the Glock in her hoodie jacket pocket. It's now or never, she told herself.

She stepped out of the darkness. "Waiting for someone?" Kelsi asked in an eerily low voice.

Ms. Desiree jumped so hard she almost tripped and fell. "Ah! Oh my God! Kelsi, why would you scare me like that?" Ms. Desiree huffed, holding her chest in a clutch-

the-pearls manner. "What in the world are you doing here? And how did you . . . ?" she rambled, her voice still trembling from the scare.

"Don't talk. Just stop talking," Kelsi demanded. She felt the alcohol taking over her speech. Her heart hammered so hard she felt short of breath.

Ms. Desiree's eyes went wide. She saw the gun before Kelsi had intended for her to see it. "Kelsi! What are you do—"

"Shut up! Shhhh! Don't talk, I told you! If you talk, it will make this harder!" Kelsi growled at her, looking around to make sure no one was coming.

Big K had told Kelsi to keep her back to the left where the camera was. With the black hoodie on, she'd look like a robber.

"Okay. I won't," Ms. Desiree whispered. "But think about—"

"I'm done talking. I said shut up!" Kelsi hissed. This time she pushed the gun toward Ms. Desiree's chest.

Ms. Desiree started blinking rapidly in response. She was too shocked to speak. Tears started falling from her eyes. "Why?" she mouthed.

Even in the haze of her intoxication, Kelsi felt something in her heart burst. She felt herself about to give in to emotion and run away. But she had come too far for that. Now that Ms. Desiree had seen her with the gun, she would report Kelsi to the police if she left things as they were.

"You could've walked away and left him with me! Why didn't you just do that? You tried to move to a house and leave me!" Kelsi said through her own tears now.

Ms. Desiree was shaking her head from side to side. "Please, Kelsi. What is the matter? Are you on something?" Ms. Desiree whispered.

"Why did you have to always control everything? Get in the way all the fucking time?"

Desiree blinked rapidly, her heart ramming into her chest like a wrecking ball taking down a skyscraper. She was too shocked to speak and couldn't help her knees from knocking against one another. The harsh question resonated through her brain like loud clanging.

"Huh? Answer me! You always have to act so perfect, right? You easily forgot where you came from!"

The booming, shrill voice made Desiree shiver. Her lips moved apart, but no sound came out. She would've answered the question, but given the circumstances, an answer would probably have made things worse. Was this what they meant when they said the cat got your tongue? Desiree's mind turned into mush. She saw the faces of her children flash by her. Something in her gut told her it might be the last time she saw those faces.

"Oh, you ain't got shit to say now, Ms. Goody Goody?"

Desiree flinched as her tormentor waved a gun around, haphazardly dangling it in front of her. This had to be a nightmare. There was no way she could be seeing this correctly. Desiree was too afraid to move her hands to even pinch herself to check. Any sudden movements could be deadly, she reasoned—if reasoning was a thing with the kind of fear she was experiencing at the moment.

"Please." Desiree finally managed a shaky whisper. Her lips trembled so fiercely she couldn't even pro-nounce the L in please. "Can't we talk about this? I . . . I can . . ." she murmured, tears racing down her cheeks in fast streaks.

The shock of seeing the familiar face made the situa-tion even worse for Desiree. She couldn't think back to what she'd done to deserve this. In fact, she had never harmed a hair on anyone's head or ever muttered a

malicious word about another person. Desiree had
practically given up her entire life for everyone around
her. It was her nature to take care of others. All she
could think of was, why me?

"No! Don't you understand there is nothing to discuss?
This has to be done! Especially now! You think I'm that
stupid now that you've seen my fuckin' face?"

The crazed but familiar eyes were scarier for Desiree
than the fact that she was staring down the end of a
wavering silver handgun. She'd seen guns before, but
never had she had one pointed at her.

Desiree started to pray silently. She should've seen
this coming. But how? Why? A million thoughts played
in her head, rewinding, staticky like an old VHS movie.
Desiree quickly scolded herself. She had ignored the
writing on the wall, all the signs.

"After all I've—" she whispered, closing her eyes. Her
words were cut short.

Kelsi heard a noise on the other side of the parking
garage. She jumped. Ms. Desiree went to open her
mouth. Maybe she was going to scream. That's when
Kelsi panicked. She had gone over the time allotted that
Big K had given her to get the job done.

"Oh, shit!" she huffed.

Kelsi pulled the trigger. The sound of the gun exploded
in her ears. She hadn't anticipated it being so loud. She
immediately felt nauseous, and she'd gone deaf in both
ears. Kelsi couldn't concentrate on the pain throbbing at
the center of her eardrums.

She took off running as fast she could go. As she ran,
the hood flew back off her head. Kelsi knew then that one
of those surveillance cameras in that parking garage
was going to get her. She ran and ran until her body
finally gave out.

Chapter 23

Cheyenne

Cheyenne screamed so loud and for so long that Detective Simpson had to almost carry her to the couch. What he told her couldn't possibly be true. Not Kelsi. Not her father. There was no way the two of them had had an affair and then plotted and killed her mother. There was just no way that was possible. That was what Detective Simpson had told her. It was the worst thing she'd ever heard in her entire life.

Six months after Cheyenne got that bad news, she slipped into one of her mother's nice Anne Klein suits and took a look at herself in the long mirror in her mother's bedroom.

"I'm going to court today to hear the sentence, Mommy. It has been a long road, but justice will be served. Everyone involved will get what they deserve." Cheyenne spoke out loud, believing that her mother was always with her and would hear her.

"Chey! You ready?" Lil Kev called out from the other side of the door. He'd been sticking with her since they both found out the truth.

Lil Kev had been locked up for a while until all the gun and drug charges from the raid were settled. He never snitched on the cemetery shooters, but he found they were actually some Mexicans Big K had got in over his head with. They were shooting for the person they ended up hitting.

"Yeah, I'm coming," Cheyenne called back. She exhaled loudly and opened the door and stepped out.

"Damn. You look just like Mommy in that suit," Lil Kev commented.

Cheyenne smiled. If she could ever be half the woman that her mother was, her mother's life wouldn't have been lived in vain.

"You clean up pretty nicely yourself," she said to her brother. She grabbed his arm, and they headed out to the court together.

Chapter 24

Kelsi, Cheyenne, Brice

The incessant drone of two tall metal fans situated at the back corners of the stuffy, hot courtroom felt like small flies buzzing in Kelsi's ears— the annoying kind of flies that buzz around shit and then come land on your skin. The ones you keep swatting away but can never seem to get rid of.

The hottest day of the year and Kelsi was on the hot seat. Her legs swung in and out. It felt good to move them apart and then back together without the restraint of the leg irons she had worn to court from Riker's Island. Kelsi ignored the hum of the crowd in the courtroom. It wasn't lost on her that everyone there was talking about her. Some probably came because they wanted a piece of her too—hood vigilantes who wanted justice for the wrong. Yeah, right. They wanted to be nosey.

Kelsi's lawyer kept telling her, "Not since the Long Island Lolita has New York seen a case like this. The difference is Mary Jo Buttafuoco lived."

Kelsi knew that she was probably the most hated twenty-three-year-old in all of New York City. That was all good with her. Shit, she had hated herself since she was about eight or nine anyway. Her mother hated her. Her father must've hated her because he never tried to find her. Girls in school had hated her. Teachers hated her. Adults she'd met hated her. Right now, her best friend in the whole world definitely hated her, so what the fuck did Kelsi care if all these strangers hated her? Kelsi knew the one person who had ever really loved her was in the back of that courtroom talking about her too.

Kelsi kept seeing Cheyenne's face behind her eyelids like she was watching still photos on a projector screen. Kelsi could picture Cheyenne in all of the stages of their lives—little kids playing double-dutch, pre-teens taking up for each other on the battlefield they called a neighborhood, teenagers sneaking out to parties, and now, as women both in pain and distress. Cheyenne wasn't ever going to forgive Kelsi for what she'd done. Never. Kelsi didn't deserve to be forgiven, either.

The court officer's booming baritone interrupted Kelsi's thoughts.

"All rise! The Honorable Rowena Graves presiding."

The rustle of suits and dresses as the crowd inside the packed courtroom rose to their feet was so pronounced it was like someone was scratching sandpaper next to Kelsi's ears. It sent an uneasy feeling through her empty stomach. Trying to eat breakfast had been useless. Who could eat when the fate of their life was in the hands of some white bitch judge with the last name Graves? Graves, as in a place where people are buried. Grave, as in something that signaled danger or harm. Those were the definitions Kelsi had read in the jail library. Yeah, shit was grave for her, all right. She had put herself in the fucked-up situation all because she was looking for love.

Kelsi's legs felt like two strands of cooked pasta as she stood up. The muscles burned in every part of her body like she'd worked out for ten hours without stopping, the result of the all-night pacing she'd done back on her cellblock.

Kelsi's lawyer stood next to her, clutching Kelsi's right elbow as if he could sense that she was about to take a spill onto the courtroom floor. Kelsi's lips curled from the wave of nausea that crept up from the pit of her stomach to her esophagus.

Judge Graves took her seat. There was nothing attractive about the judge, and Kelsi wasn't just thinking that because she was about to decide the fate of her life. The judge was small and hunched over like she was about to look for something on the floor. Kelsi could tell that the lump that had settled between the judge's shoulders as easily as a camel's grew was just what was meant to happen to her as she got older. Judge Graves reminded Kelsi of a witch she had seen in the book Hansel and Gretel when she was back with Nana, when Kelsi was still allowed to attend school. If she remembered it right, the witch in the book ate kids or something like that. Judge Graves did too.

To Kelsi, the judge looked like she smoked ten packs of cigarettes a day. Kelsi knew a smoker when she saw one. That drawn-up, ashen, purplish-toned skin. Those square, grey, stained teeth. Those burnt-tipped fingers and greenish-gray fingernails. Kelsi had lived with smokers all her life. Judge Graves probably hid her pack-a-day habit from her family and friends. Of course, they'd be too bourgie to recognize the signs of a chain smoker. Kelsi pictured Graves spraying something minty into her mouth and using that stink-ass White Diamonds perfume that old ladies wore just because Elizabeth Taylor made it. That was a fleeting thought—Kelsi wondering if Judge Graves had family who cared about her.

The judge waved her wrinkled hand and motioned for everyone to be seated. "Except for the defendant and her counsel," Graves growled, that distinct smoker's rattle bubbling in her throat.

Kelsi's lawyer gave her elbow a quick squeeze. Kelsi ignored him.

"Counsel, I am going to address your client directly. No sense in prolonging this. Your client has been convicted by a jury of her peers, and I am prepared to sentence her today. Is that understood?" Judge Graves announced.

Her attorney said, "Yes, Your Honor," and let go of Kelsi's arm like it was a venomous snake.

Kelsi stared straight at the judge. Her thoughts raced like the cars at the Daytona 500. Jury of her peers? Kelsi hardly thought that five old white ladies, two white men, two Hispanic ladies, one Chinese guy, one black dude who slept the entire trial, and one old black lady who kept crying whenever somebody mentioned the victim, counted as a fucking jury of her peers. There wasn't one black girl on there that had been through the shit Kelsi had been through. Not one chick that could believe how that could have happened to Kelsi. Jury of her peers, her ass.

Kelsi's legs were moving, but she wasn't making them move. She also couldn't make them stop moving.

"Miss Jones, the crime you have committed is abominable, to say the least. In my opinion, you don't ever need to walk the streets again. You crossed not only legal boundaries, but you trampled all moral and civil boundaries. Trust is something that you earn, and in light of the situation, no one on God's green earth should ever trust you again.

"Under New York State sentencing guidelines, this court is prepared to sentence you to life in prison without the possibility of parole. However, it is your due process of the law that we give you an opportunity to tell me, and this court, why I should not render the most punitive sentence available to me under the guidelines. You can tell me why, in your own words, I might have leniency on you and maybe sentence you to twenty-five years to life with the possibility of parole. What that means is maybe one day some parole board will have mercy on your soul and let you back onto the streets.

"Before I render a final sentence, you will also have the opportunity to present members of society who can speak on your behalf, to tell me why they think I should have leniency on you during this sentencing.

"Miss Jones, I must tell you, that just as it is your right to bring forth others who can speak for you, it is also the victim's family's opportunity to tell me why I should put you away for the rest of your natural born life. Under this process, it is their right as well. Do you have any questions?" Graves grumbled, looking over the edge of her thick oyster-shell frames. Her words resounded loudly off the hollow oak-covered courtroom walls.

The gravity of what she was saying felt like a thousand-pound anchor around Kelsi's neck. She realized that the small dashes of light fluttering at the backs of her eyes were just her starting to get dizzy. A few sighs could be heard from the back of the room. Kelsi swore she could feel the heat from all the eyes boring holes into the back of her head.

She could only imagine what Cheyenne must've been thinking when she heard "the victim's family." Probably crying and biting her lip. Kelsi knew her so well. She had seen Cheyenne when Kelsi was first led into the courtroom. Still pretty. Still way more conservative than Kelsi had ever been. She never took her eyes off of Kelsi. Aside from the first quick glance, Kelsi couldn't look at Cheyenne directly, so she lowered her eyes.

"Miss Jones, after I hear you out, I have the discretion to formulate a sentence as I see fit according to the sentencing guidelines. Whatever sentence is imposed, you will be remanded to the State of New York for the duration of your sentence. We are prepared to hear your statement. So, I ask, do you have anything you would like to say to the court or the family members of the victim who are present in the courtroom today?" Judge Graves continued.

Kelsi licked her dry, cracked lips. She was prepared to recite the long apology she had rehearsed over and over again with her lawyer. She had let some of the girls on her jail tier hear it. They said they would've given her a break if they were the judge. Picture that, any of them ever being a judge. They all lived in a fantasy a lot in jail.

Kelsi opened her mouth several times to speak. Finally, when the words were about to come, she heard that familiar, raspy voice exploding in her ears.

"Hmmm, I told you, bitch. I told you you wouldn't amount to shit! You was never shit. You came from shit, and ain't never going to be shit either!"

It was Carlene, the sorry sack of shit that gave birth to Kelsi. A birth canal was what Carlene was to her. Carlene surely had never been a mother. Kelsi felt like somebody had hit her in the chest with one of those big, metal sledgehammers they use at carnivals to hit the small ball into the bell at the top of a tall pole. The stronger the person, the more effective the hit.

Kelsi couldn't breathe. A flame ignited on her skin, and her cheeks burned. A ball of fire that had been growing inside of her since she was a little girl finally exploded. Kelsi didn't turn around. She was afraid of what she might do if she did. Her entire body shook. She couldn't stop her teeth from chattering. Kelsi willed herself to stay still, although in her mind's eye, she could see herself jumping over the wooden divider and wilding out. Anything she did now would just make sentencing worse on her.

The court officers rushed over to Carlene to make sure she was put out. The judge banged her gavel and screamed, "Order!"

Kelsi bit into the side of her cheek until she drew the sweet and metallic taste of her own blood. Her chest heaved in and out, and she swayed on her feet. The nerve of that bitch! Kelsi's fists involuntarily curled so tight her bones felt like they'd bust through her knuckles. Tears burned at the backs of her eyes, but she refused to let them fall. Carlene had gotten enough tears out of her.

Enough! Kelsi screamed over and over in her head. The chaotic scene made the spot directly above her right ear throb with pain.

"Order!" Judge Graves yelled again as the crowd in the courtroom murmured about the outburst. "Order!" the judge yelled again, quieting the room once more.

"Miss Jones?" Judge Graves continued, giving Kelsi the nod to speak her last words.

Kelsi was ready. She was motivated by the ball of fire sizzling in her chest.

"Yes, Your Honor, I have something to say," Kelsi said, crumpling the paper in front of her. She could feel her fresh-out-of-law-school attorney shifting next to her.

"What are you doing?" he whispered harshly in Kelsi's ear. He knew then that she was not going to read the remorse speech he had prepared for her. He lifted his hand up to interrupt her. "Ah, judge, my client—" the attorney started.

"Sit the fuck down! I have something to say," Kelsi boomed. She was not letting anyone else in the world speak for her. She had done that all her life.

The judge seemed a little thrown off her game by the power of Kelsi's voice.

"Mr. Broughton, please. Sit down. Go ahead, Miss Jones," Graves ordered, her voice showing a hint of respect for Kelsi.

"Ahem. I am Kelsi Jones, and I regret what I did so much, but I want everyone to know that I am a victim myself. Please allow me to tell my story," Kelsi said, choking back tears, although she knew none would come. She had been all cried out. It was so quiet in the courtroom you could probably hear a mouse pissing on a cotton ball. Kelsi had everyone's full attention now.

Life without the possibility of parole. Life without the possibility of parole.

The words kept replaying over and over in Kelsi's mind. Loud gasps rolled through the crowded courtroom.

Reporters burst out of the courtroom doors so they'd be the first to report the story.

Kelsi didn't even react. She didn't cry. She didn't get weak at the knees. She stood there while Judge Graves read her the riot act for what seemed like the one hundredth time. Kelsi kept her head up high. After all, pretty girls didn't go around with their heads down.

She deserved it. After reliving everything, Kelsi realized just how much she deserved it. All her life, she had blamed others for any mistakes she'd made, but it was her. Kelsi was the one who had pulled that trigger. She was the one who had slept with another woman's husband after that same woman had been more than a mother to her. She had tried to steal her life. Kelsi was finally able to take responsibility for her actions. She'd done it, and she deserved to rot in prison for the rest of her life.

Kelsi didn't turn around after the sentence was handed down. The court officers flanked her on either side. They'd come to take her away. She didn't have the courage to turn around and look at the faces of the ones she had hurt. She never wanted her son to see her face. Although he was only a few months old, she knew it best that he never had to grow up ashamed of his biological mother like Kelsi had.

She was sure that Cheyenne was going to give him a good life. Cheyenne had loved Kelsi at some point in their lives. She was just like Ms. Desiree, selfless and like a saint. Kelsi's son was Cheyenne's baby brother, and after Kelsi had given birth to him, in her heart, she had named Cheyenne the godmother, just like they'd planned it as kids.

Kelsi kept her head up all the way back to the courthouse holding cells. Her attorney was the last person she saw that day. He handed Kelsi a sealed envelope and told her to open it when she was alone. Kelsi stuffed it down her panties since she knew that once she got to the jail, they'd take it away.

When Kelsi was finally alone with no guards breathing down her back, she opened the envelope. There was a card inside. Kelsi opened it. She immediately recognized the handwriting.

> *Kelsi,*
> *You are not like my daughter; you are my other daughter.*
> *Here is your set of keys to our new home. I told you that I would always be here for you. Well, I meant it. Now, get to packing!*
> *Love always,*
> *Ms. Desiree*

That was it. Kelsi fell to the floor. She had nothing left. She curled her body into a ball and closed her eyes. She finally relived what she'd done. Her eyelids were like a movie projector as she watched it unfold again and again and again.

Right before Kelsi was sentenced and after everyone had heard her life story, the judge spoke. "The court has heard from the defendant. It is now time for the court to hear from the victim's family," Judge Graves rasped. She had taken off her glasses and was pinching the bridge of her nose as she spoke.

Cheyenne couldn't tell if the judge wanted to cry or what. Kelsi's story had touched the judge in some way. Cheyenne hadn't thought about the years before her father got locked up in so long that she found herself hanging on Kelsi's every word. Those were the best days of Cheyenne's life. She found herself tearing up as she recalled how much she loved Kelsi back then. Kelsi was truly like Cheyenne's sister then.

Cheyenne shook her head left to right, trying to get her focus back. She had a very important job to do. A very important story to tell.

Cheyenne tapped Lil Kev on his shoulder. "Kev, it's our turn to talk," she said to him.

His fists were balled tightly, his mouth was pursed, and he rocked his legs furiously. Cheyenne knew what that meant, but she still wanted to give him the chance to say something if he wanted.

"C'mon," she whispered, touching his shoulder.

He wouldn't move.

Cheyenne looked up at the judge with a simple, nervous grin on her face. It was all on her to speak on behalf of their family. As Cheyenne inched out of the row where she and Lil Kev sat, she suddenly felt the acids in her stomach burning. Her mother's suit suddenly seemed too tight, and sweat lined up like ready soldiers at her hairline.

It seemed like it took Cheyenne forever to walk up to the little wooden podium where the microphone stood. The courtroom was eerily quiet, although it was packed. She filled her cheeks with air, an attempt at staving off the wave of nausea that swept over her.

Cheyenne felt Kelsi staring at her, but she couldn't bring herself to look at her. She'd taught Cheyenne a huge life lesson—there was nothing deeper than love turned to hate. Cheyenne had loved Kelsi. She had loved Kelsi so deeply that now she hated her enough to kill her with her bare hands.

"Ms. Turner, are you all right?" Judge Graves asked, her eyes going low at the sides.

Cheyenne cleared her dry throat, closed her eyes, pictured her mother's face, and shook her head up and down. She took a quick glance over at Kelsi then. Kelsi quickly averted her eyes. Cheyenne knew Kelsi would never be able to hold eye contact with her. Kelsi was a coward in Cheyenne's book.

"Yes, judge. I . . . I'm fine." Cheyenne spoke softly. She realized she needed to adjust the microphone, so she attempted to move it. It made an ear-piercing screech. Cheyenne jumped back.

The court officer raced over and fixed it. He put the microphone directly in front of Cheyenne's mouth. She used the back of her hand to wipe sweat from her forehead.

"Okay, Ms. Turner. When you're ready to speak, you can address the defendant and this court. Take your time," Judge Graves told her.

Cheyenne nodded and closed her eyes. "My name is Cheyenne Turner. The person everyone keeps referring to as the victim is my mother. Her name is Desiree Turner, and she didn't deserve to die. She didn't deserve to be slaughtered for nothing.

"There are very few people in the world like my mother. I want to tell you all about the years leading up to her senseless murder, because Kelsi told you hers, but we also have a story," Cheyenne said, hearing her voice echoing off the courtroom walls. She was sure everyone was holding their breath, waiting for her next sentence.

There were so many news reporters outside of the courthouse after the sentencing. Lil Kev and Cheyenne had all types of microphones and recording devices being shoved into their faces. They didn't have anything to say. They stood behind the prosecutor while he took the opportunity to speak about how justice had been served.

Through the crowd, Cheyenne saw his face. He was fighting his way toward them. Finally, he started up the courthouse steps. He had a serious look on his face. Cheyenne's heart skipped a beat. She balled up her toes inside her shoes.

"Congratulations," he said, grabbing Cheyenne's hand and giving it a squeeze.

She was fighting back her tears. "Thank you for keeping your promise," Cheyenne whispered to Detective Brice Simpson.

He squeezed her hand again. "Thank you for letting me," he replied. "I've got to get out of here. Seeing my mother and sister off to another country today. Bittersweet, but the only compromise that would work," Brice said.

"Good luck to them. Remember to cherish them both," Cheyenne replied.

She felt an inner peace come over her. *Everything for a reason*, she thought to herself. *Everything for a reason.*

Big K was murdered six months after his conviction for the conspiracy to murder his wife. Cheyenne and Lil Kev didn't attend his funeral. Cheyenne received a package a month after with a stack of letters he'd written to her and Lil Kev. They sat together and burned the letters in the back yard of the home their mother had bought before her death. They burned the letters without ever reading them. A month after that, Cheyenne received a check for $1.5 million from National Benefit Life Insurance Company. Cheyenne was the beneficiary of her father's insurance policy. Cheyenne smiled as she stared at the check. Her mother was still looking out for them . . . even in death.